THE RETURN
OF JUAN MIGUEL

ANNA K. SARGENT

Publisher's Note

This is a work of fiction. Names, characters, places, and incidents are either the product of the author's imagination or are used fictitiously. Any resemblance to actual persons, living or dead, business establishments, events, or locales is entirely coincidental.

Cover and interior design by Kathryn Sargent

Marketing by Enchanted Indie Press

Printed and published in the United States of America

ISBN: 978-1-938749-31-5
978-1-938749-32-2

ANNA K. SARGENT

THE RETURN
OF JUAN MIGUEL

THE THIRD BOOK
IN THE JUAN MIGUEL SERIES

BOOKS BY ANNA K. SARGENT:

THE JUAN MIGUEL SERIES

THE LEGEND OF JUAN MIGUEL

THE PASSION OF JUAN MIGUEL

THE RETURN OF JUAN MIGUEL

PROLOGUE

He watched his guide, Panchito, descending the trail, getting smaller and smaller as he receded into the distance and then completely disappeared around a bend. His last connection with the civilized world was gone. He was on his own.

He unburdened himself from the backpack and sat down against a rock. He pulled out one of the last few cigarettes in his shirt pocket and lit it. After a few drags, he began to wheeze. Panchito was right. The high altitude and tobacco were not compatible, so he put it out.

It was mid-afternoon and the sun shone but the day was still cold, especially in the shade. Above his head, the sky was deep blue, the color of a lapis stone, against the rugged snow-covered peaks. And the clouds, they drifted, so close he could almost reach up and touch them. Below, the trail wound around the side of the steep mountainside, weaving itself downward to the tree line where he'd seen parrots the size of chickens and tropical flowers growing in bushes as tall as trees.

He put his head back to think. It was the first chance he'd had in many days of traveling and asking questions and giving out bribes for information. In all his years, this was the deepest hole he'd been in. A deep hole high up in the Sierra Madres. He smiled at the irony of it all and slumped against the sheer rock cliff behind him.

Not his months in a Monterrey prison. Not the death of his beloved Marguerite. Not the beating that left his face disfigured and scarred for more than a year. Nothing had ever left him feeling as alone as he did at this moment. And the reason was simple. This time, he didn't know who his enemy was. It was a nameless, faceless, amorphous antagonist. A system of greed and power and cravenness, a web of corruption so far-reaching, so pervasive that perhaps only a revolution could cure it. And if that's what was required, he was prepared to accept that, too.

The world he left—his world—seemed far away. Even Jícama had been left behind, stabled in a rudimentary fenced pasture on the outskirts of San Bernardo. God knows if he would still be there when he returned—*if* he returned. His life seemed as precarious as the narrow, steep trails he'd been made to walk along, and still he could not find his footing. His search for answers had taken him deep into Mexico, as far from home and defenseless as he'd ever been. A mountain hideaway of *bandidos* and *insurrectos* in the remote upper reaches of the Sierra Madres was his last chance to find out who was out to kill him and why. He'd better make it count.

He would play it safe this time. He would not try to fool anyone. He would be himself. But he was also carrying a pistol strapped across his chest and plenty of ammunition. In his lifetime, he had been many people, but never a fool.

THE RETURN OF JUAN MIGUEL

PART I

CHAPTER ONE

The day Annabelle arrived in El Paso by train was the day her eyes were opened, never to close again. It rained all the way from San Antonio. Crossing the desert in a rainstorm was like a bad dream. Water rushed through the shallow arroyos and fell in sheets down the embankments. On high ledges, it seemed that the wheels, no longer visible beneath the mudslides, might leave the tracks. In the gullies, the water billowed out like waterfalls on both sides of the engine as it sliced its way through high water.

Out the train window, she saw a land and sky awash in gray. Inside, her fellow travelers looked tired and depressed, disillusioned with the journey as it neared its destination, a city renowned for a sunny, warm climate and a carefree life. They were seriously lacking either at the moment.

She covered her yawn and stretched her arms up above her head about the same time the conductor pushed open the outside door and dripped and slushed his way into the coach car.

"El Paso," he said, his voice sounding croaky. "Prepare to disembark."

Disembark? What made him use the word disembark? Would they have to swim to shore when they arrived?

Annabelle pulled a pad of paper out of her bag and jotted down the word, disembark, to look up later. She hated when people misused words. Words were her passion.

The train jerked, then jerked again. Annabelle lurched forward and caught herself on the seat in front of her. The huge man next to her—her father's most trusted *compadre*, Pedro—belched a foul smell and huffed and took out his handkerchief. Annabelle felt the train's brakes pulling on the wheels and she heard them squealing. The conductor leaned over to look out the window and so did the passengers.

"What's going on?" they yelled at him. "Why're we stopping out here?"

"I don't know. Settle down, keep your seats. I'll go see."

The train had jerked to a stop with no signs of civilization in sight. The rain had slacked off to a shower. The sun popped out.

A contingent of soldiers wearing blue coats and large

conical hats and carrying long rifles galloped past the coach heading to the front of the train.

"It's the *rurales*," Pedro said. "They're not supposed to come north of the border ... but they do."

"Who're they after?" Annabelle asked him.

"*Insurrectos*," he said.

"They're Diaz's soldiers?"

"Shhh," he warned her. "Don't say that so loud."

She stood, put her bag on the seat, and went to the window for a better look. Annabelle Palmer had an instinct to follow the action. She always liked to know what was going on. More than anything, she wanted to be a newspaper writer and she hoped to accomplish that goal in El Paso while she visited her father, who was there for the summer. She had heard that El Paso was a hotbed of journalism, especially political tabloid journalism.

"They have beautiful horses," she said gazing out the window at the soldiers, now gathered in a group and listening to their officer. Each of them rode a fine chestnut steed with dark manes and white hooves and heads. They were larger and more muscular than any horse she'd seen in San Antonio.

"Stay back from the windows," said Pedro. He grabbed her arm, pulled her back to her seat, and gently pushed her down into it. "Let's stay low and be quiet."

Annabelle craned her neck to see as the soldiers dismounted and stepped into the door of the coach up ahead. After a few minutes, they dragged several men who looked like Mexican peasants out to the ditch running alongside the tracks and pushed them face down into the standing water. The soldiers stood over them and shot all of them at once. The volley of rifle rounds rang out across the valley and echoed against the flat mesas.

Annabelle couldn't believe what she just saw. It seemed like a dream, not anything real. She looked at Pedro. He looked back at her with a stern expression, so she sat still.

The soldiers regrouped and turned their attention to Annabelle's coach. She heard them outside the door, laughing and talking, then the door opened and they rushed in. An officer in a pressed green jacket and a black broad-brimmed hat stood out front surveying the passengers, his rifle ready but pointed down. She could feel the fear all around her but there was dead silence. When he reached Annabelle, his eyes met hers and she saw the eyes of a man who kills for a living. They were hard and unyielding like steel but veiled with alcohol, perhaps, or just hatred. His eyes lingered for a second or two and she looked away first, sensing it would be foolhardy to challenge him to a stare-down. Then he saw Pedro next to her and he looked more than a bit intimidated.

"¡Vámonos!," the officer said in a nasty tone. He turned and left and the others followed. Once they were gone, she saw Pedro's rifle had been pointed at them the whole time, just out of sight below the seat backs.

The passengers watched the *rurales* mount their

horses and ride off in the direction they came from and then everyone in the coach started talking at once. They rushed to the windows to see whether anyone was still alive but there were no signs of life. Four bodies lay face down in the ditch water, which had turned into a scarlet pool of blood, and that's where they would leave them. The train pitched forward and went on its way.

"Aren't we going to take their bodies?" Annabelle screeched above the noise of the engine chugging to get under way. On his way out the door, the conductor, who didn't bother to turn around, yelled, "It's not the responsibility of the Southern Pacific Railroad ..." And his sentence trailed off as he closed the door and disappeared.

Annabelle felt a rush of excitement in spite of her disgust at the horrible sight of the murdered men and she was shocked to realize a person could be taken off a train and killed without anyone caring. No wonder El Paso was a hotbed of rebels fomenting a Mexican revolution. The Mexican *federales* seemed brutal and lawless and had no regard for human life.

She settled down into her seat and picked up her bag. It should be only a few more minutes until they pulled into the El Paso station and she would greet her father. He would be furious if he knew she had just witnessed an execution. He would undoubtedly demand that she never travel without him again. She only hoped that she could write about it someday.

She had thought of the Mexican *insurrectos* as foreign

and strange, people who had radical political views they wanted to foist on the nation south of the American border. She had heard they congregated in El Paso and met in their secret dark rooms cooking up plans to overthrow the legitimate government of Mexico simply because it was led by an aging old patriarch who everyone knew would die soon. Most of her views came from her favorite teacher, a prominent newspaper publisher himself once who had written editorials condemning the fledgling revolutionary movement. It was going to be interesting to hear what her father thought about it. He was her bellwether, the person she most trusted to be fair in all circumstances. Except, of course, when he thought she was in danger. Then he could be downright unreasonable.

A few low buildings, scattered here and there along the tracks came into sight. The buildings got bigger and grander and the streets busier with traffic and pedestrians and suddenly the train slowed and the station appeared.

The ubiquitous south Texas weather had righted itself and the sun reflected off of every wet, shiny surface of the newly shriven desert town. But Annabelle saw only her father standing on the platform, his hat in hand, waiting for her when she stepped down from the coach. His brown curls shone like polished brass, his smile was wide, and his blue suit impeccable. As usual, her father's presence reassured her. Everywhere he went, he carried his own atmosphere of calm.

She ran to him and stepped into his embrace, clinging to him, reluctant to let him go. It was not until she felt the safety of his arms that she realized how frightened she'd been. Tears came into her eyes and rolled down her pale cheeks on to his jacket.

"Annabelle, *mi amor*, what is it?" he asked, holding her close and rocking her as he used to when she was a child.

She pulled back and looked up into his eyes. "The *rurales* ... they stopped the train and murdered some people," she gasped.

"It is over now, *mi amor*, it is over ... you are safe."

He looked at Pedro who said nothing. He didn't have to. Juan Lopez knew that Pedro would have given his life for Annabelle if that were necessary.

Juan put on his hat, put his arm around her, and prepared to show her to the trolley, but their way was suddenly blocked by a crush of people. The train platform that was almost empty only a few minutes before began to feel crowded.

People swarmed at them, encircling them as if they were celebrities. But it was not Annabelle and her father they came to see. It was a short dark-haired woman wearing an angelic white dress in the midst of them.

"Who is that?" Annabelle asked.

"The woman known as Saint Teresa," he said. He took her by the arm and led her to a place of safety by the station's clapboard wall.

Saint Teresa proceeded at a slow pace, surrounded by a phalanx of armed men. Women in the crowd beseeched her. As they reached out to touch her or her garments, she smiled a serene expression under her heavy brow. Some went so far as to kiss her hands or press their lips to her shawl. They followed her all the way to the train, and then after she was seated, reached their children up to be kissed through the coach window.

Annabelle looked at her father. He leaned down to whisper in her ear because of the commotion. "She is a heroine of the *insurrectos* ... their spiritual leader," he said.

"A woman, *Papá*?"

"*Sí* ... women can be leaders, too."

"I know ... but why is she leaving them?"

"She is being driven out of town by the powerful. They fear her influence." He pulled her along beside him away from the station. "The crowd is thinning. Let us go home, *mi amor*."

About a month earlier, Annabelle received a letter from her father telling her he was leaving their south Texas rancho and moving to El Paso for a while, at the suggestion of his doctor. He'd suffered from excruciating headaches since the day six years ago when he was beaten almost to death by the hired toughs of the Galveston shippers whose corruption he sought to expose. Although the

El Paso climate wasn't much warmer or dryer than the south Texas ranchlands, he would be near health sanitariums that were practicing some advanced medical techniques.

She had been in the Catholic school for girls in San Antonio since she was ten and although she missed her father more than anything, it had opened her mind and heart to many things. In her six years there, she'd grown into an intellectually curious student favored by the nuns and instructors. And she'd grown into a beauty who had her father's magnetic charm.

"*Papá* ... where is home?" she said, once they were settled in the trolley.

"We will be staying at the St. Charles Hotel," he said. "You will like it. It reminds me of Claridge's in London."

"I don't really like hotels, you know."

"I know but it's only for the summer." He grinned and leaned down toward her. "Do you think you can tolerate it for three months, little one?"

The scars from the terrible beating were almost vanished from his face and only some faint white ridges remained. He was as handsome as he once was, and though he looked older, the sweet expression was still there—still beguiling the women and confusing the men. She reached up and kissed his scarred cheek.

The town of El Paso was small compared to San Antonio but it had a similar feel, the same sampling of Anglos, *mestizos, Tejanos*, Germans, Irish, and every other sort, but the culture and pace of life were decidedly *Hispanic*. Just across the Rio Grande bridge was the equally flourishing city of Juarez. Together, they formed the largest border settlement between Mexico and the United States. The area was the seat of political intrigue aimed at overturning the heavy-handed Diaz government in Mexico City.

On this June day, though, the town was quiet. Few people were out in the midday heat. The streets were almost deserted except for some poor *mestizos* lining the road to the hotel with their belongings piled on carts. Annabelle was used to seeing the poor but they were greater in number than she had ever seen.

"*Papá*, who are those people?" she asked.

He put his hand on hers. "They are families from Smeltertown who were displaced by the May flood. The whole south section of town next to the river flooded and almost everyone lost their homes."

"Can nothing be done for them?"

"Many have given money ... I have given money. But the workers are exploited by a system that is far beyond my reach, a system with tentacles in this country and deep into Mexico."

"What is Smeltertown?"

"It is just the workers' small adobes and wooden shanties that grew up around the ore smelting plant. Ores from the rich mines of Mexico come here by rail for smelting ... silver, copper ... many other metals."

Annabelle watched the low adobe buildings and the new tall brick ones going by and wondered whether she would be bored.

"What shall we do all summer in this place, *Papá*?" she asked.

"I'll enjoy the company of my beautiful daughter and ... let's see, perhaps eat some fine food, read some good books, see a play or two. What would you like to do?"

"I would like to work at one of the newspapers."

The statement surprised him. He looked at her for a few minutes then said, "That is an idea we will need to discuss ..."

"But *Papá*, I'm old enough ... I want to write ... please, please let me."

"We will discuss it later, *mi amor* ... later. You have hit me with a request I didn't anticipate. It will take some thought."

"There are forty newspapers in this town. Did you know that? "

"No ... I did not know it."

"I witnessed a murder, *Papá*. I could write about it if someone would just give me an opportunity. There is so much here to write about ... so many causes."

He smiled at her. "Let's not take the world on our shoulders just yet. Not until we've had dinner."

Feeling a bit guilty for depriving Annabelle of her carefree summer at the rancho, Juan had gone overboard in decorating the rented rooms at the St. Charles. For some reason, he couldn't face another summer mourning the loss of Annabelle's mother who died there years ago at about this time of year. So he decided to stay for the summer and make the best of it by having a few pieces of their furniture packed up and transported to El Paso.

Annabelle grinned when her father opened the door and looked at her face for some sign of approval. The rooms did look like Claridge's, only better. Along the wall, the mahogany sideboard he bought in Normandy last summer and above it a gold-framed mirror topped with the familiar Louis XVI *cartouche*. The seating was simple but comfortable, covered in damask and leather.

A row of windows looked out on the Franklin Mountains, the city's backdrop. Stone hard and russet brown, the mountains formed a backbone extending south through the desert and pointing at the city, which lay to their south within a broad curve of the Rio Grande. Compared to the grandeur of the mountains and desert, though, the town of El Paso seemed like nothing more than a small collection of buildings huddled together in the barren expanse. Everything was bare. There wasn't a tree in sight.

Annabelle stood at the windows staring at the harsh desert landscape. Her father, sensing her unease, walked up behind her.

"I know it's not France, Annabelle, but Beatriz and Jose

are here to keep us company. At least the food will be good."

"I can't get the sights out of my head, ... of the bloody men lying face down in the ditch ... of the helpless people along the road. I don't think I will ever like this place."

She wiped at tears in her eyes and he put his arm around her. In the next room, Beatriz was also sniveling, wiping her nose and eyes with a hanky, her head down as she cleaned and fussed with a water pitcher.

"*¿Que paso?*" Juan said. "You too? Is everybody crying today?"

Beatriz put down the pitcher and wiped her eyes. "My cousin, Tomás, was one of those killed today ... my auntie, she is in such grief over it."

"You mean, he was one of those taken off the train by the *rurales*?"

She nodded and more tears came into her eyes.

"Tell me. What happened?"

She sat opposite him on the couch, teetering on the edge of it like someone who feels uncomfortable in the situation she finds herself. Her eyes were red and her pudgy knees trembled. She put the wet hanky to her nose and wiped it. "They say he was one of the Teresitas, that he took part in a raid south of the border several weeks ago."

"The Teresitas? The followers of Saint Teresa?"

"*Si* ... but they were taking revenge, not raiding for stealing, but avenging the deaths of the many *paisanos* who have been killed by Diaz and his men."

"And was he there? Did he take part?"

"I don't think so ... he has never been interested in politics ... but maybe. He was just a poor laborer at the smelter, not an important person."

Juan Lopez really didn't want to know anything further about the murders. He'd been burned before for taking the less fortunate and the mistreated on his shoulders, and he had no desire to do it again.

"Bea, *lo siento*. What can I do?" he said. "Does your aunt need money for the funeral?"

"She wants to know who is responsible for this ... the money does not matter."

"I will ask around, but that is all I can do. I don't want to endanger Annabelle by getting embroiled in the back and forth of the coming revolt. I just cannot risk it."

"*Gracias, Señor*." She stood to go but remained looking down at him. "Señor Juan, very few people except you would understand ..." She began to sob again, holding the handkerchief to her eyes with both hands. "Very few people but you could find out who did this."

He'd been put on the spot, like a man who's been volunteered for something. Feeling uneasy and guilty at the same time, he stood and put his arm around her. "I will do what I can ... I promise," he said.

"*Gracias*, Juan Miguel, I will go now and let you and Annabelle be alone."

The name Juan Miguel startled him. He hadn't been

called that in many years.

"What are we going to do about it?" Annabelle had a plaintive tone in her voice.

"There is nothing I can do for now."

"But you will do something ... won't you, *Papá*?"

"I told Beatriz that I would ask around, find out what I can ... that is all I can do. Not everything in life is so simple. The forces at play are complicated. It's not so easy to pick a side sometimes."

"*Papá* ... they were murdered ... I saw it." Annabelle stood in front of her father looking stricken and, looking up at him, her eyes beseeched him. Rarely, if ever, had he been able to refuse her anything when she looked at him in that way. She reminded him of Marguerite, her mother, the only woman he had ever loved. Like her mother, she believed he could do anything.

He watched as, in turn, peachy orange and lavender and deep steel blue of the late El Paso sunset tipped the mountaintops outside the window until they had reverted to their natural colorless state. At last, he was alone with time to think about the day's events.

For many years now, the guise of Juan Lopez had provided a warm, safe haven for his psyche. He felt comfortable in it. It allowed him to be self-indulgent and generous to those he loved. Juan Lopez was a practical man who had no desire to reform the world. He accepted it the way it was—imperfect yet complex although sometimes beautiful to the senses. Since his beating at the hands of the Galveston shippers, he'd stayed out of other people's affairs and concentrated on his rancho and his family.

Lurking somewhere beneath the surface, though, was Juan Miguel del Valle, his original identity, a man who had cared deeply and righted wrongs with a mixture of craftiness and compassion. Juan Miguel had been on retreat for years now. After he lost his true love, Marguerite, his former identity sank even further beneath his consciousness and he regretted the one time he had allowed it to surface.

Because of those regrets, when Beatriz said his real name, Juan Miguel, it went through him like an ancient, rusty sword, twisting and ripping at old wounds. Every time those wounds were opened, his compassion came pouring out.

On the other hand, this new place brought back his youthful vigor. He felt renewed and, looking out at the flickering lights of El Paso against the mountains in the distance, he had a fresh desire to leap into the fray. The life he'd been living felt stale and flat.

He took a sip of wine and put his boots up on the small iron table before him. Annabelle had reached an age when she no longer needed his full attention. Perhaps a new kind of freedom was in his future.

For years, he'd been constrained by his devotion to Annabelle. Women and adventures had come and gone.

Nothing that aroused his passion above a low hum. That was about to change, he sensed, and he couldn't say why. It was just a feeling.

The reckless behavior of the *rurales* who murdered the Mexican peasants on the train had put his daughter and the other passengers in danger. That was something he could not excuse, and the death of Beatriz's nephew, Tomás, was a loose thread in his brain. He decided to pull it.

He stood, walked to the window, and leaned down to feel the soil of the Bergamot plants he was growing in clay pots, just as his Tia Marina had done when he was growing up. He brought them from Florida on his last trip there. They were almost tall enough to harvest and use in a special tea he liked. That was good. He was almost out of his last batch. Bergamot tea, an herbal remedy he learned from the old *abuelas* on his rancho, had a medicinal effect that eased his headaches.

He picked a few leaves and crushed them between his fingers. They smelled orangey and minty, a scent that always reminded him of his Tia. He remembered her words—love comes seldom, maybe only once. Was that true? Would he truly love a woman only once? Now that Marguerite was gone, would he never find love again? Tomorrow he would find a place to dry the leaves—someplace outside in full sun. The plants were just not thriving, as they should, inside.

CHAPTER TWO

The Copper Hills Ranch house had been in an uproar since the previous day when the ranch's owner found out that three of her workers were snatched from a train and killed by Mexican *rurales*. Charlotte Borden didn't know whether the workers had been guilty of insurrection, as they were accused of doing, or whether her ranch was being singled out for a message or whether the authorities were taking advantage of her for being a woman in a man's job.

Charlotte needed good ranch hands and she hadn't been one to ask them their political views before she hired them. She also hadn't asked them to prove they were American citizens because that would eliminate almost everyone. Most of the best cowboys came from south of the border.

For about a year, she had been in charge of the Copper Hills Ranch. She was living in the south of France, in a place called Provence, when she received a wire telling her that her father died suddenly of a heart attack. It was something she had never imagined would happen to Samuel Borden, a larger than life bull of a man who was one of the pioneers of ranching in the Franklin Mountains and their foothills.

She arrived back in El Paso on the train as a ranching dilettante who knew about the latest in fashion and French poetry and how to cook a fine French sauce but who knew next to nothing about the ranch where she'd grown up. She'd come a long way and learned a lot about ranching in a year. However, she still questioned her own ability to discern the motives of those around her. This was one of those times.

Right after sunup, Charlotte called all the hands together for a meeting outside the ranch house. She stood on the wooden front porch and looked down on the gathering of Mexican workers and the ranch foreman, Lyle Peterson, who stood off to the side with his hat pulled down over his eyes.

"I want to know what you know about the men who were killed yesterday," she said in Spanish, her voice sharp and confident in the cool dry morning air. "Anyone who knows something should step forward and tell me what you know."

The men looked up at her with stoical expressions she couldn't read. She waited and still, no one spoke up.

"I can't do anything about their killing if I don't understand why they were killed," she said. "*Que paso, mis amigos?* ... speak up."

A man in the middle of the crowd said, "They were Teresitas ... they sought to avenge the death of their families and friends ... that is all."

"So they went on the raids south of the border, then?"

"*Si, Señorita*, they did go ... but for a reason ... not just to kill and rob."

Lyle suddenly stepped onto the first step in front of her and said, "Let this be a warning. If any of the rest of you got ideas about raiding. If I find out about it, you're fired and I'll tell the authorities ... by God, I will."

"Lyle, Lyle, none of that please," Charlotte said, pushing him gently on the shoulder. "Step aside, please, this is my meeting ... and my responsibility."

Lyle walked up the steps and stood behind her, his hat once more pulled down over his eyes.

"*Compadres*," she began, "you must spend your time earning your salary here on this ranch and not engaging in raids." They looked at her with little expression on their faces but she could see her words sank in. "Your political ideas are your own, but what you do on my time is my business, *comprende?*"

They nodded then walked away in silence. The ranch foreman followed after them to get them ready for the day's tasks.

Charlotte walked back into the house feeling she had made her point but that perhaps the passion they felt for fighting against injustice was something she couldn't squelch—or maybe shouldn't squelch.

Charlotte Borden had always been an attractive woman. However in the past year she'd spent on the Copper Hills Ranch she'd blossomed. The dry clear air of southern Texas agreed with her, brought a high color to her complexion and a spring to her step. But the responsibility of running the ranch had also heightened her impatience, which manifested itself this morning after the meeting with the hands.

She walked into the kitchen, picked up a pottery colander on a table by the door, and threw it hard against the far wall.

"That stupid foreman ..." she said, her voice quiet but angry. "He'll either figure out who's in charge here or he'll have to leave."

Her housekeeper, Mina, stepped back a few steps and watched the colander shatter against the adobe walls then scatter across the floor. "*Ai, ai, ai ... que paso, Señora?*" she said.

"Sometimes it seems like we're having a revolution right here on this ranch, Mina."

"What did he do this time, *Señora*?"

"He just keeps butting into things, speaking for me when he should keep quiet and back me up."

"Well, he was used to being the one in charge, the head man. *Tu padre*, he left everything to Lyle the last few years, you know."

"I know ... I know."

"He is the best foreman in this area. You should try to get along with him."

Charlotte sighed and bent down to pick up the pottery shards. "He is right about one thing ... I will have to put my foot down ... I know that. If I don't, we'll be in real trouble. If more hands go on raids or join the *insurrectos*, the ranch will suffer."

She raised up and put the broken pieces on the cabinet. "Which hands are *insurrectos*, Mina? Do you know who they are?"

Mina shook her head, put out her hand, and walked away, a familiar gesture that meant Charlotte had overstepped her bounds as an employer. "*No se ... no se*," she said.

Annabelle Palmer's habit of eating sweets at breakfast had become an entrenched one. Her father usually found it funny, and this morning was no exception. He chuckled when he saw her shove her eggs under the napkin and grab another piece of *pan dulce*. Beatriz had offered to make their breakfast but he decided he wanted to show off his daughter a bit at the restaurant downstairs. They sat at a table by the window watching the morning shoppers walking past on Mesa Street.

"Still not eating eggs, I see?" he said to her.

"*Papá*, I'm almost grown. Can I not eat what I please?"

"Whatever you've been doing, it agrees with you. You look more beautiful than ever."

She smiled. Her father's opinion of her beauty meant little to her. He'd been telling her she was beautiful all her life, even through the awkward period when she was twelve and thirteen, when her auburn hair frizzed and her teeth were too big for her face. Things had fallen into place since then. Her face had grown more pretty and she managed to tame her unruly hair with pins and special ointments. Still, she had no idea whether she was really pretty or not.

She turned her gaze to the people outside and just as she did, a woman with dark hair, striding down the street with a purposeful gait, appeared.

"Look at her, *Papá* ... look, *Papá*," she said motioning with her head and shoulder for him to look out the window.

"What, *mi amor*, what is it?"

"That woman, *Papá*. Is she not something?"

Juan Lopez put down his cup and looked up in time to see an attractive young woman for a moment or two. It was only a glimpse but it was enough to stick in his mind. The sable waves and pale skin and dark eyes imprinted on his brain.

"Who is she, *Papá*?"

"I don't know ..."

"We should find out. Come on; let's go for a stroll. Come on, *Papá*. Finish your coffee."

At sunup every morning, Juanita Salazar' Grocery and Supply downtown on the corner of Paisano and San Antonio streets opened its doors, selling everything from homemade tacos to horse bridles to poultices and cures. The front portico was a gathering place in the mornings for area businessmen, ranchers, and anyone who wanted to chat while they stood amongst the barrels of crackers and dried beans and lines of red peppers strung from one end of the overhang to the other.

Every few days, Charlotte went there to catch up on the latest news from the other ranchers in the area. Most of them were older men, seasoned and brusque, but friendly nonetheless. They had accepted her into their midst because she was Samuel Borden's daughter and they did so out of respect. They were honest with her, didn't pull punches or talk down. But in the back of their minds they had doubts about the longevity of her tenure as a ranch owner. In short, they expected her to fail. It was just a matter of when.

Charlotte stood on the portico talking to three of those ranchers, trying to elicit some advice about *insurrectos* among their cowhands. One of them, the oldest and one of the crankiest, put it bluntly, "Why doncha' jes' let Lyle handle that ... won't do for you to get involved. Lyle, he can ride herd on 'em, whereas you cain't."

Charlotte raised her cup of coffee and took a sip. She nodded. She had learned that quarreling with them was futile.

"But have you had this problem?" she asked.

"I wouldn't have it long ..." one of them interjected. "I'd send 'em packin' 'fore sunset."

"So, how do you know ... which ones are sympathetic to the revolt?"

"Ask 'em ... then get rid of 'em."

Charlotte shook her head and smiled. Everything boiled down to its simplest terms for them. No fancy ideas. No fancy talk.

Annabelle and her father took in the sights and sounds of the small city, the mixture of old and new. Lavish hotels and restaurants of the busy railroad hub amidst the saloons and whorehouses and small adobe shops of the rough western town of the past. They spotted Juanita's store and its crowd of customers and gravitated to it.

Juan approached Juanita and asked permission to hang his Bergamot plants on her sunny portico. Juanita clasped her hands in front of her and looked up at the tall man with the handsome face and looked as if she would give him almost anything he asked for. Her eyes sparkled and she smiled in spite of herself. "Come inside and let's talk," Juanita said, ushering him and his young companion through the door.

When he stepped inside the store, he glanced out the window and noticed the group of ranchers, including the dark-haired woman they saw earlier, chattering. The same people who'd watched him and Annabelle in silence and all but rebuffed them. Then the woman left the portico, mounted her horse, and rode north.

Once he had agreed on a small price for space to hang his herbs, Juan sent Annabelle to the back of the store to look at the clothing. He pulled Juanita aside and asked her, "The young woman outside ... who was she?"

Juanita raised her eyebrows. "Her name is Charlotte, old Samuel Borden's daughter. She owns the Copper Hills Ranch, *Señor*. Not one to trifle with ... do you catch my meaning, *Señor*?"

Juan nodded and repeated, "Charlotte Borden."

"*Si* ... what else, *Señor*?"

"The men on the porch, were they unfriendly because I am not *Anglo*?"

"Well, you know, *Señor*, a *mestizo* store owner is one thing but a *mestizo* rancher is another."

Juan raised his eyebrows and nodded in recognition of what she was saying. "Where can I get information about the *rurales* and the men who were killed yesterday?"

"Oh, *Señor* ... you do not want to get involved in that."

"Ah ... but I do. Please, *Señora*, with whom can I consult

on this matter?"

"I refer you to Alberto Salazar, the editor of *La Revuelta*. But be careful, my friend, you wade into choppy waters."

Juanita looked as if she wanted to add something. Finally, after pausing and looking out the front door, she said, "Charlotte ... it was some of her men who were killed."

"Workers on her ranch?"

"*Si* ... but the ranchers, they are on the other side, *Señor*. They do not support the *insurrectos.* In fact, they fight openly against it."

"But the hands at the Copper Hills ... they might well have information about the men who were killed?"

"*Si, Señor*, but I doubt that the ranch foreman would allow you to talk to them. He is not *simpatico,* if you get what I mean. He hates Mexicans."

Juan Lopez was beginning to get the picture of a community split along racial lines when it came to politics. He still had no intention of taking sides. He just wanted to find out who was responsible for his daughter's frightening experience on the train so he could decide whether to confront them or avoid them.

Years ago, they say—perhaps centuries ago—Catholic monks worked a silver mine in the mountains north of the El Paso del Norte. It was a risky business, working a mine in the middle of hostile uncivilized territory, transporting precious cargo out of the area. It might be viewed as stealing, some would say. That is likely how the local native Indian population viewed it and one day they banded together and prepared to mount an assault on the monk miners. The monks got wind of the attack and quickly abandoned the mine, heading south for the protection of the Spanish Crown. But they left one lonely, unlucky monk in charge of guarding the mine. He was killed, of course, and now his ghost roams the mountain passes, locked in a perpetual limbo between heaven and earth. Ranchers and travelers see the ghostly monk with his burro often, traversing the passes, climbing the rocky hills.

Annabelle sat transfixed, listening to the story of the ghostly monk that evening at dinner. Señor Lopez and his daughter had been invited to the home of Consuela and Francisco Diablo, the owners of large vineyards west of the city. On the southern edge sat their hacienda, a spacious adobe dwelling with numerous outbuildings, including the Santa Clara winery and a small mission church, which the Spanish built years ago for the Ysleta Indians. Sprawled along the Rio Grande River, surrounded by a few small trees and fields of staked grape vines, it was an oasis in that vast treeless desert that went on for miles in every direction.

In the center of the hacienda was a courtyard with a garden of violet sage and yellow Lantanas mingling with spiky yuccas. The centerpiece was a fountain of perfectly chiseled sandy limestone, flowing with water pumped up from the Rio Grande. It all reminded Juan and Annabelle of their own patio.

Señor Diablo finished the story of the ghostly monk and took a sip of wine, his pale bearded face flickering in the firelight across the table from Annabelle. A shudder went up her spine. She sat back and looked at her father.

"It is a myth, *mon ami*, only a myth," he said, looking at her with affection. "Like all myths it holds a truth. The poor *Indios* were losing their land and their riches. They fought back against a superior force and for the time being they won a victory, but alas, they were eventually overcome. Their descendants are still attempting to fight back."

"It's not quite that simple," Señor Diablo interjected. "There are outside forces who have arrived from New York and other faraway places to stir up trouble between the local *mestizos* and the admittedly bad government in Mexico."

Señor Diablo picked up the wine bottle and offered to pour another drink for Juan, who shook his head no and sat back in his chair.

"Come now, have another glass of Vin Santo," Diablo said. "It's the best in the area … the vines are from Italy … no?"

"No, one glass is my limit, but tell me more about the coming revolution in Mexico. Would you call it a racial struggle?"

"It is not so much a racial war as it is a class war. President Diaz favors his rich friends, there is no doubt. The poor have suffered under his presidency. But the violence is in danger of spilling over the border into this country. If that happens ..." Señor Diablo raised his hands in a gesture of "who knows?"

"The ranch owners in the area are against the *insurrectos*, I have heard," Juan said. "Would that not be a mistake to align themselves against their own workers? Why not sympathize with their desire to help their families who still live south of the border?"

Señor Diablo nodded and touched his beard. "And you, *amigo*, how do you see the *insurrectos*? It sounds as if you do sympathize with them." He reached over and picked up the bottle and started to pour Juan another drink, but Juan put his hand over it. "No, *Señor*, as I said, I never drink more than one. As for what I think of the idea of revolution ... it is not my business. But whenever my daughter is put in danger, it becomes my business."

"I see your point. There are truths on both sides ... but anyone who sympathizes with the *insurrectos* could be putting himself ... and his family ... in danger."

"Your words are sounding like a threat, *amigo*," Juan said.

"Not a threat, *Señor* ... advice," he said, his teeth in a grin but his eyes narrowed. "Powerful people have powerful passions. Have a cigar ... imported from Cuba ... unless you have changed your mind about another glass of the wine?"

Juan took one of the fat, rolled cigars out of a box. "How does President Diaz and his men ... the *rurales* ... get away with coming north of the border and snatching people from trains and killing them?" Juan asked, lighting his cigar. "Someone must be averting their eyes ... someone like the local authorities."

"Ah ... I'm afraid we are only a few years away from frontier justice here. But yes, the local sheriff turns his head sometimes, perhaps for money ... and then there is the government in Washington as well. Our own president sends his agents down here to stir things up. It remains to be seen what Washington will do ... which side it will come down on."

"And you, my friend? I've known you for years. How can you not sympathize with the plight of the *mestizos* ... their poverty and their treatment at the hands of the powerful?"

"Oh, I do ... I do. But if the revolution were to happen, turn over the government in Mexico, and then move north ... that would be troublesome. It could threaten the stability of the whole area and my vineyards would be in danger. More than anything else, I prize my vineyards and this winery. My family has owned it for over one hundred years and I have no intention of letting it go."

"So you see it from a purely selfish point of view?"

Señor Diablo chuckled. "Of course. But for now shall we walk outside and enjoy the evening since it has cooled down?" He rose and led the way. Inside, he turned and smiled at Annabelle when he reached the double doors to the patio, he said, "I have a little surprise for the *señorita*."

Waiting for them by the fountain was one of the hacienda workers, holding a strange contraption Annabelle had seen many of in Europe. It was a bicycle, one designed especially for women and of the latest *derailleur* style, meaning it had gears and sprockets to facilitate the propelling of the wheels.

"I ordered this for my wife," Señor Diablo said, "but she doesn't fancy it. Would you like to have it?"

"I would love it," Annabelle said, visions of the freedom it would afford her already going through her head. "May I, *Papá*? May I keep it?"

"It is too much," Juan said.

"But I insist," Señor Diablo responded. "A young lady must have freedom as well as protection, no?"

Juan pulled out his watch. "I'm afraid we must decline the gift, *Señor*. It is late. If we don't leave soon, it will be too dark for us to find the way back to town."

Overnight, Señor Diablo had the bicycle loaded onto a donkey-drawn cart, hauled into town, and left at the hotel for Annabelle, which Juan took as a sign of disrespect, an attempt to undermine his influence with his daughter. But once it was there, he found it difficult to deny her. Forgetting how pugnacious she could be about something she wanted, he said, "If you can teach yourself to ride, I will let you keep it."

It was a sweltering day. A humid, tropical wind blew up from the southwest and the temperature soared. Annabelle had stripped down to the bare bones of her attire, only a thin blouse and skirt and stockings. A few hundred feet away Jose watched over her, leaning against the hotel wall with his hat pulled down. He had offered to help but he himself had never ridden a bicycle so he wasn't much help.

She wrestled with how to keep the bicycle upright but it eluded her. Every time she tried to push off and balance herself, it went careening to one side and she ended up either crouched on the dirt street or, once or twice, on her back side with the bicycle on top of her. A few hours into it, she was feeling frustrated but she had no intention of quitting. She'd seen women riding bicycles in France and England and she envied them. They seemed so self-sufficient, so modern. She'd wanted one for a long time.

Once more she hoisted herself up onto the seat and prepared to try again, just as she heard a voice behind her.

"*Esperar ... esperar,*" the disembodied voice said. "You need someone to hold you up while you get the feel."

She looked around and saw a young man reaching out to hold her up. She caught a fleeting glimpse of his pleasant dark face before she faced forward and prepared to ride. She felt his arms holding the bicycle, brushing against her back and her arm. They were strong and steady arms.

He ran alongside her, holding her up. Then in an exhil-arating moment of freedom, she felt him let go. She rode on for maybe thirty feet before she lost confidence and teetered to one side. She stepped down, looked around to thank him, and he rushed up to hold her again.

"*De nuevo*," he said. "Don't stop now."

Once more he held onto her. This time she rode all the way to the next intersection. She stopped, turned, and smiled at him. He came rushing up to her and put out his hand for a handshake.

"I believe, *Señorita*, that you have mastered it. You no longer need me."

She shook his hand and said, "*Gracias*, my name is Annabelle. You are?"

"Ricardo ... my name is Ricardo but people call me Cinco ... I am the fifth son. I work part-time at the news-paper office," he said, pointing to a small, run-down look-ing brick building across from them on the adjoining street. "I do a bit of everything."

"Are you a writer?"

"I aspire to be a writer ... but for now I'm just a lowly errand boy and typesetter. Except on Sundays, I get to write a little bit ... *un poco* ... because the owner stays home with his family."

"Thank you for helping me ... can I repay you with a cool drink at the hotel restaurant?"

"Oh ... *Señorita*, I don't think they want me in there,"

Cinco said with a wry smile. "I am known about town as a friend of Carlito Intrepido, the bullfighter whom many of *the insurrectos* love. So by extension, they think I am one as well."

"But you are not a bullfighter or an *insurrecto*?"

"Heavens, no ... my pen is my sword. You know what they say ... a sharp tongue is mightier than the sword."

Annabelle looked a bit puzzled.

"That is a joke, *Señorita*, an old journalism joke." Backing up across the street with his hand over his heart, he said, "All true ... every bit ... I swear. I'm a journalist. I say nothing that isn't true."

"I, too, am a journalist," she shouted at the disappearing Cinco.

He turned his head and smiled and waved at her before he opened the door and disappeared inside.

Juan Lopez was a man of intelligence and impeccable manners but also a soft heart. In some ways, he knew himself well enough to avoid knowing too much about injustices he couldn't cure. In other ways, he did not. Yes, the voice in his head was warning him to hold back. But he went forward anyway. Because all around him in this city he saw the plight of the poor and powerless. The simple laborers pulled off the train and murdered in plain sight was only the tip of the iceberg. The peasants trickled across the border pulling their carts of meager belongings, looking to get away from Diaz's government-sanc-tioned terrorists. They clung to the image of Saint Teresa, a woman who offered them a ray of hope. He wasn't one of them. He came from a different world—the Spanish world. They were the natives of this country and now, they were barely tolerated.

These things preyed on his mind the morning after dinner at the Diablos. He decided to pay a visit to *La Revuelta* newspaper and hear the side of the argument he hadn't heard yet, the side of the Mexican *paisanos*.

El Paso was a backwater compared to what Señor Lopez was used to. It lacked the amenities he craved. Last year at this time, he was in London listening to the Tsar's Imperial Orchestra play Rimsky Korsakov's *Capriccio Espagnol*, a lively, rhythmic piece so evocative of the culture he loved, the heritage running through his veins, that it brought tears to his eyes. This year, there is almost no music to listen to at all, but someone had mentioned the McGinty Band, a local musical group that played concerts in San Jacinto Plaza, a downtown park. The band would be playing that evening, the concierge reminded him on his way out the door of the hotel.

"*Si* … I will try them out," Juan said.

"They are very good, *Señor*. Everybody loves them," the concierge all but shouted at him.

Juan nodded, put on his hat, and set out to find *La Revuelta*. A passerby directed him to the office behind and opposite the hotel. He peered in the window at two men setting type and another one working a respectable look-ing printing press that appeared to be a drum cylinder press, a type commonly used by newspapers. Nonetheless, a press like that was a big investment for anyone. The owner must be well-funded.

He stepped inside and removed his hat. None of the three even looked up. He cleared his throat. Still no reaction. "May I speak to the owner, please?" he said.

The portly gentleman in the back running the press stepped on a shuttle and stopped the printing. He picked up an oily rag and wiped his hands.

"That would be me, *Señor*. I'm the owner ... Alberto Salazar. What can I do for you? And, make it fast, please ... *pronto, Señor* ... we're on deadline."

"I wish to pick your brain ... so to speak, so maybe another time would be better?"

"*Si ... si.* Another time would be better ... we're rushed for time, *Señor*. The authorities are breathing down our necks. It's very important that I get this paper out before I'm raided."

"Raided?"

"It's coming, *Señor*. The sheriff stopped by this morning to threaten us. But it will be a cold day in hell when Alberto Salazar holds back the truth." He stepped on the shuttle and the big wheel started to turn and move the clapper up and down.

Juan put his hat back on and instinctively pulled it down over his eyes. "I will come back," he said.

That night after dinner, Annabelle lingered at the windows, watching people stream through the streets of El Paso toward the square.

"Can we go to the band concert, *Papá*?" she said, hoping to get an approval.

"Not today, little one. Not today."

She walked over to him and sat down next to him. She put her hand on his hand, which was resting on his thigh.

"What is it, *Papá*? Do you not like it here after all?"

He took her hand and held it. "I do like it ... I am just tired ... very tired."

"You tired? I don't believe you."

"There are different kinds of tired, Annabelle. Why don't you go visit with Beatriz. She could use a friend right now."

Annabelle squeezed his hand and stood to leave. She looked back at him to reassure herself that he was all right before she walked out.

Left alone with his thoughts, Juan allowed the specter of Marguerite that had been lingering all evening to come into his mind full force. She was still there. Not in the way she had been during the first years after her death when she haunted his every waking minute and appeared to him in his dreams. But she was there and he could feel her sometimes as if she'd just left the room. He knew it was Annabelle who prompted these memories. Annabelle was so like her mother that it was uncanny. The hair was slightly darker and the face a bit fuller perhaps. But her voice and mannerisms were the same.

He put his head back on the sofa and closed his eyes. Several years before she died, the three of them were in Paris on business. It was a warm evening much like this one. They strolled down the *Champ D'elyse* hand in hand with Annabelle in the center. Marguerite wore a dark burgundy dress and hat that lit up her flaming red hair. She smiled and laughed at everything and nothing, her happiness radiating outward to those who passed by. The next year, she started to show signs of deteriorating health and two years later, she died.

Tears came into his eyes and he quickly wiped at them with his fingers. How had he let himself give into the grief once more? Why did it feel so fresh at times? He dabbed at his cheeks with his sleeves and cleared his throat.

"Annabelle," he shouted. "Annabelle ... put on your hat and shoes."

She appeared at the door with an expectant look on her face.

"Get ready ... we are going to the concert."

She smiled and disappeared into her room.

He pushed down his sleeves and buttoned them, found his hat, and pulled on his boots.

CHAPTER THREE

A stack of handbills held down by a rock on top of a tree stump on the southwest corner of the plaza had attracted a crowd. People of every description and station in life were gathered around it, waiting for their turn to take one. One by one they lifted the rock and took a handbill then stood off to the side reading it.

"What are they looking at, *Papá*?" Annabelle said.

"A few years ago, there was a tree there called the 'newspaper tree', where all of the town's news was posted. It was cut down when newspapers became popular, but people still use it as a place to leave messages."

"Go get one, *Papá* ... let's see what it says."

He made his way through the crush of people and picked up one of the last handbills. Across the top of it, in extra large type, were the words, "Three El Paso newspapers raided; editors jailed."

Underneath was a short story, only one paragraph, about government raids at three of the newspapers known for their sympathies toward *insurrectos*. Alberto Salazar's paper was among them, it said. The raid must have come soon after he left.

"Who do you think printed these handbills, *Papá*?"

"I don't know ... maybe a disgruntled writer who is now out of work ... maybe an irate wife?"

He looked up across the plaza, and his eyes rested on one person, although he was surrounded by a number of people and almost hidden from view. An imperious looking man with an oily complexion and beady eyes he'd noticed several times before in the evening, walking his three enormous dogs in San Jacinto Plaza. The man always held the leashes with his right hand, with his left hand tucked inside his jacket like the famous dictator Napoleon. He had heard the people of El Paso call him the "dog marcher" because he seemed to walk in precision step around and around the square.

"What is it, *Papá*?" Annabelle asked. "Do you see someone you know?"

"Perhaps ... I don't know. Forget it, *mon ami*, it is nothing." He put his arm around her and smiled. "We are here to have a good time ... not stare at the people." But even as they walked away to find a place to sit for the concert, he stole glances at the man, and every time he did, he tried to convince himself that he'd never seen him before.

The man across the plaza was General Maximiliano Cordova. In the spring of 1897, he and his wife, Mariani, and nephew, Carlos, had traveled from Mexico City to El Paso for an extended stay with his wife's relatives, living a peaceful existence, doting on his three silver gray Great Danes, which he brought with him to El Paso.

The Cordovas were staying in the home of Mariani's sister, who was married to a successful local Anglo landowner and businessman named McMurray. The general retired from military service the previous fall and had been at loose ends ever since. They settled in quickly and enjoyed the mountain air although the heat of the summer approached.

The former Mexican general also consulted with medical experts at the sanitarium about his limp left arm and hand. Although he was a veteran of numerous military campaigns, he suffered the injury years ago from a beating. For almost a year, Cordova was bed-ridden from his injuries, although slowly he recovered enough to resume his career. He applied for, and received, a military commission by the Mexican President Porfirio Diaz and rose to the rank of general based largely on patronage.

Maximiliano Cordova had been a decorated Mexican officer but he also served under a cloud of suspicion and eventually was reprimanded for his behavior. He was known to give favored treatment to certain junior officers he found attractive, summoning them to his quarters late at night for questionable reasons. Finally, after a low-level scandal ensued, he retired and forfeited his commission rather than put his family through the embarrassment of a long, drawn-out court martial. He remained a government minister and was a chief adviser to President Porfirio Diaz. His wife and sons never caught wind of the accusations and the gossip died out after he retired from military service.

The McMurray's sprawling one-story adobe dwelling a few blocks from the square was one of the largest homes in El Paso and was the site of many Friday evening dinner parties. Mariani's sister would pull the dining table into the home's long hallway, extend its size with additional leaves, hire a mariachi band, and serve food from the restaurant next door. Everyone in El Paso society wanted to be invited to these *soirees*, which tended to go on most of the night.

But there were no *soirees* at the McMurray house on Saturday evenings because that is when the McGinty Band played their concerts in the plaza. The three Cordovas and their hosts walked to the square together, speaking to others along the streets. The general had been talked out of taking his dogs along and everyone was in a better mood for it. All except Carlos, the nephew. He had been in a foul mood since he arrived in El Paso, having been forced there against his will. The young man aspired to be a matador, and he considered every minute he spent in El Paso to be a waste of his time.

Carlos Cordova—Carlito—was nothing like his uncle. Nor was he like his father, who died before he was born. Possessed of steely determination and an athletic body, he had had a distinctive character all his life. His family called him "*poco torero*" long before he was old enough to fancy being one.

Carlito trailed behind his family on the way to the concert, reading one of the many local newspapers, *La Revuelta*. Bored to tears by the sleepy little American town, he took to reading the many newspapers and pamphlets produced there every day. They opened his eyes to the brewing political intrigue against the current Diaz government and it fascinated him, but he also liked to read the advertisements for the "Gran Corrida de Juarez," the bullfighting arena right across the border.

Despite his seeming indifference to the people around him, Carlito was an item of interest, especially to young ladies. As beautiful as a man can be without being womanly, he had light smooth skin and black wavy hair. But it was the shape of his Roman nose and short, sensuous upper lip that many found irresistible. His eyes, though, were steely, dark, and almost frightening. On occasion, his eyes would soften and his face would light up with a childish grin, betraying his true age.

Since the young age of fifteen, Carlito had been no stranger to women. Because he was well developed and tall for his age and because he was brave, women of all ages made themselves available to him. Mostly he viewed them with scorn, as people with little self worth, but there were times when he had taken advantage, if the woman was attractive enough.

The only passion Carlito had ever displayed was his passion for fighting bulls. It appeared to consume his every waking moment and occupy his dreams.

Carlito started training at the bullfighting academy when he was six. He had absorbed the tales of the matadors who often visited his family. His uncle was one of Diaz's trusted generals and they entertained the most celebrated in all walks of life. It was the matadors' bravery and manhood that made the largest impression on him. He begged his aunt and uncle to train with them until they gave in, with the caveat that he do it only as a hobby. He must go to University and become a lawyer. About that they were adamant. And he was never to be a professional *torero*. That was out of the question for someone of his station.

But that promise had been forgotten of late. Carlito had a natural gift that showed itself at an early age. His career as a matador took on a life of its own and by the age of eleven he was known around Mexico City as *Al Joven Matador, Carlito Intrepido*. Still, his aunt and uncle clung to the hope that he would forget about being a matador and the trip to El Paso was their last-ditch effort to take him away from the environment of the *corrida* with the hope that his passion would fade.

Shortly after they arrived in El Paso, though, Carlito walked across the bridge into Juarez and presented himself to the *corrida* officials. He convinced them of who he was by fighting a bull and killing it with a beauty and intensity that could only come from a trained *torero*. Soon he was appearing regularly at the *Gran Corrida de Toros de Juarez*. He performed without his usual matador attire, which he had left at home. Entering the *corrida* arena dressed in only a white shirt and tan *torero* pants, he won the hearts of the spectators, for he was not only exceptionally courageous, he was humble as well. A legend began to grow around the name of Carlito Intrepido that summer. His uncle's hopes were fading to nothing even though he was not yet aware of it. Unlike other matadors, Carlito was becoming the *paisanos'* champion at a time when they needed one. And all of this happened under his aunt and uncle's noses without their knowledge.

This evening, Carlitos' head was buried in the *La Revuelta* newspaper's interesting piece about the Teresitas, although not as well-written as the pieces by his friend, Cinco. The two young men met soon after Carlos arrived in town and had been friends ever since. Cinco worked for *La Revuelta* and he was only allowed to write an article one day a week. In Carlito's opinion, it should be every day. Cinco was by far the best writer.

"Put down the newspaper," Mariani said to her son. "You are being rude."

He rolled it up, stuck it under his arm, and surveyed the small crowd before him, hoping to catch sight of Cinco.

Charlotte's attempts to rein in her headstrong foreman often got blunted by his attempts to sidestep them. They seemed to go round and round, never landing on a solution to the awkward position they were in. Lyle had been her father's foreman for almost ten years. He knew the lay of the land and he knew that no one was better at his job than he was.

Before sunrise that morning, Charlotte had ridden out to the north pastures in the foothills of the Franklin Mountains, looking for Lyle and the other men. She followed the scent of sweating cattle and cowboys until she saw their dust, then she rode into the camp where they were circled around a fire, branding calves. The odor became even more pungent, mixed with the smell of singed cow hair and seared flesh.

Lyle stood off to the side, keeping "tally" of the animals. He glanced up at her and looked back at his paperwork, as if she were an intruder. No doubt he felt she had undermined his authority the previous day when she told him to step aside at the meeting.

"This is no place for you, Charlotte ... why don't you jes' let us do our work? We don't need you here to supervise, believe me."

"I know that you know what you're doing. I just wanted to make sure ..."

"To make sure of what? That we know how to be cowhands?" Lyle took off his hat and hit the chaps on his upper thigh with it. A cloud of dust floated from it. "Well, what is it you want?"

"You must stop talking down to me in front of the men, Lyle."

"Charlotte, I have an idea. Why don't we have dinner tonight and talk it over then. Instead of you interruptin' the work and calling me out ... why don't we jes' ride into town and have a talk over dinner?"

So it was a conciliatory dinner. The ambience in the J&J Café was a bit rough-and-tumble—a bit loud—but the food was good and Josephina, the cook and owner, always managed to get fresh vegetables for her table. How she did it was a mystery because El Paso's only nearby truck farms were along the fertile bottom soil of the Rio Grande and those farms, though convenient, were few because they were totally dependent on irrigation from the river.

When she migrated north from the highlands of Durango, Josephina brought with her the restaurant's red clay pottery painted with white designs made by her Tepehuan Indian relatives, who also wove the colorful blankets hanging on the walls.

She brought some of her most popular recipes such as the corn meal crusted pie filled with cooked *chiles*, vegetables, and shredded pork. She called it "Timkaul," based on the Indian word for tortilla.

Josephina and her siblings were considered *mestizo* but her mother and her relatives were descended from the Tepehuan and Tarahumara, primitive mountain tribes who had lived in log houses or caves high up in the Sierra Madres for centuries. They were Catholicized years ago, about the same time that many of them were rounded up by Spanish colonizers and made to work the mines.

Recently, the Indians in the Durango area, including the Tepehuan and the Tarahumara, had been in revolt against the Diaz government. With the help of in-migrating Apaches, the local tribes protested Diaz's support of the heavy-handed mine owners and land developers with frequent skirmishes with Mexican troops. Josephina had left the area to seek a better life, but she heard often from her relatives about the injustices—and sometimes killings—that took place regularly.

On one wall in the restaurant hung a photo of Saint Teresa, who herself was of Indian descent. As one of Teresa's staunchest followers, Josephina crossed herself often when she passed by the photo.

Lyle watched Josephina's crossing ritual with a sneer on his face. "Can't seem to get away from 'em ..."

"Away from who?" Charlotte asked.

"The *insurrectos* ... they're everywhere."

"She's harmless, Lyle. She's just a religious woman."

"I don't know. I hear she has ties to some of the worst

of them. Her brother, they say, is an out-and-out bandit and raider named Salinas. Mateo Salinas. They call him *El Fantasma*, the ghost."

Charlotte took another bite, hoping the subject would be dropped. She didn't like to hear others spoken of with ill will, especially someone like Josephina who seemed to be a good woman.

After dinner, Lyle sat back with a beer bottle in his hand and adopted an off-hand tone. "Charlotte, the Copper Hills Ranch jes' about runs itself. Your daddy set it up that way. He knew what he was doin'. Jes' trust us to take care of the cattle ... and it'll continue to be profitable jes' like he wanted it to be."

Charlotte considered his words. The atmosphere in the café wasn't conducive to a long, drawn-out conversation so she just said, "I understand how you feel, Lyle. You're a good foreman ... I know that. But my father left the ranch in my care. Not yours. Not the hands. Mine. I'm responsible."

He screwed up his face like a man who'd heard those words before and decided to change the subject. "How about we go down to the band concert while we're here? It's cooled down ... should be a nice evenin'."

They walked down to the plaza, an uneasy silence between them. Outsiders probably thought the two of them were a good match. Charlotte was a pretty woman and Lyle was a masculine-looking man with a strong presence. Many in town thought they eventually would somehow put aside their differences and recognize the attraction between them. But this evening, their body language put a lie to that thinking. It appeared that there was a wide valley between them, as wide as the Rio Grande's.

The last edition of *La Revuelta*, printed only hours before the newspaper office was raided and squirreled away in a hiding place, contained an even more inflammatory article than El Pasoans were used to. It was a rebel manifesto, written in Spanish and aimed at the citizens and officials of Mexico. It began by recounting the recent outrages of the Diaz government, the massacre at *Tomochic*, the death of seven Yaqui Indians in the Teresita rebellion and the subsequent display of their mutilated bodies, and the killing of five men, pulled off a train and shot to death in a ditch by Mexican *rurales*.

It condemned President Diaz for suppressing a free press and persecuting reporters and editors. It advocated the passing of term limits so that Diaz could not run for re-election. But it saved its strongest words to denounce the Mexican government's collaboration with capitalists from the U.S. who subjugated and "enslaved" the native population, forcing them to work in mines and on ranches for almost nothing. The *coup de grace* was a call for redistribution of the land and other resources of Mexico.

It was a rash and yet courageous thing for Alberto Salazar to publish, given the persecution that other journalists in El Paso had suffered both from Mexican government agents and American federal courts. Editors had been routinely jailed in the last decade under America's law prohibiting advocating the overthrow of a foreign government. The manifesto seemed to be brought on by the recent killings, which happened the same day as the virtual banishment of Saint Teresa. It included an open letter to her, begging her to return.

Juan Lopez had let his guard down, the thought of being in character somehow slipped from his consciousness. He looked nothing like Señor Lopez. The affectations gone, he looked younger and wore the open, vulnerable countenance of Juan Miguel. Annabelle loved the rare occasions when her father was completely himself. She treasured them.

Annabelle whispered to him, "Look, *Papá*, there is that woman we saw at breakfast." She pointed to Charlotte, who stood to the side by herself. "Go talk to her ... go on, introduce yourself."

Juan sighed a deep sigh and adjusted his hat. For once in his life, he felt inclined to take his daughter's suggestion about meeting a woman. "Only if you go with me," he said, smiling down at her.

"It is a deal," she said, pulling him by the hand.

Charlotte looked surprised but pleased when they approached but she was whisked away by another man, who took her by the elbow and escorted her to the front of the crowd where he'd found some seats.

"Don't worry, *Papá*. We will find a better time to meet her," Annabelle said, patting his shoulder.

Suddenly fire works erupted from every direction, a cacophony of booming and pounding and hissing noises and streaks of colors shooting through the sky overhead. At the height of it all, the McGinty Band came marching down the street, straining to be heard over the noise and dressed in full regalia. They had on new, pressed black uniforms trimmed in gold braid and long gold and blue streamers flowing from every trumpet. Ahead of them a hapless peon led an aged donkey pulling a cannon. The procession reached the bandstand and proceeded to march some more in a precision formation that soon became comical as they turned in on each other and dissolved into a chaotic mess.

Juan tried to stifle his laugh but he soon realized it was as much a spoof as a band. Although the band members could undoubtedly play their instruments, the grandiosity of their presentation seemed to be tongue-in-cheek.

The crowd erupted in applause and the group of thirty or so band members took their caps off of their middle-aged balding heads and bowed. Then they launched into a lively rendition of a popular ragtime song, *Bye Bye Ma Honey*, which the crowd had obviously heard before. They swayed to the rhythm, not at all bothered that the song's composer never meant for it to be played by a brass band.

Three or four songs later, the band sat down for a rest, and some speech-making about civic matters ensued.

On the fringes of the plaza were hand-drawn carts where *mestizo* women sold their fresh baked goods and candies. Eyeing one of them, Annabelle asked, "Can we have some *pan dulce*, *Papá*? It looks so good."

He put his hand on her wavy hair and stroked it. She had a sweet tooth just like her mother. "I'll get you some. You wait here," he said.

He reached in his pocket for some change and he heard a teasing chuckle behind him. He turned and the woman with the dark hair stood watching him buy handfuls of pastries.

"Someone likes sweets, I see," she said, laughing as he tried to juggle them in his hands.

He looked chagrined. "They are for my daughter ... mostly. That is her there with the red hair." She reached out and rescued one of his pastries, which was about to escape onto the walkway. "You keep that one," he said. "It is for you."

She put the *pan dulce* in her mouth and looked across the way at the young woman. "I would like to meet your daughter. She is very beautiful."

"Yes, beautiful and hungry for pastries ... as her mother often was."

"Was? Are you a widower?"

"Please forgive my manners, *Señorita*." He shuffled all of the pastries into one hand and stuck out his other one.

"I am Juan Miguel del Valle."

"I had heard your name was Lopez ..."

He had shocked himself by uttering his own name, but it was too late to turn back now. "*Si* ... Lopez is my business name ... so to speak."

"Well, Mr. del Valle or Mr. Lopez, introduce me to your daughter."

"*Si ... si ...* "

The two women began to chatter about all manner of things, from the latest fashions to their trips to Paris to where to shop for clothing in El Paso. Juan Miguel stood back and watched them. He couldn't believe his good luck at finally meeting the woman he'd been watching from afar since he arrived in El Paso, one of the most beautiful women he'd seen in quite some time.

It felt good and natural, the three of them standing together. But then Charlotte noticed Lyle out of the corner of her eye, made her apologies, and returned to sit next to him. All through the evening, she cast glances at Juan and the very thought of it made him fall silent. He recognized the dangerous sweet feeling he'd first felt for Margaret Barone. He didn't take it lightly. How could he? It changed the course of his life the first time he felt it. This time he would be much more careful, but not too careful, he thought, looking at the lovely dark waves falling down her back. Not too careful.

General Cordova was in a complacent mood, some-what bored as he had been since he came to this Texas town. And he didn't particularly like the American custom of listening to music in the square. He preferred a more martial beat to his music and the disorderly crowd made him nervous. He sat next to his wife, letting his mind drift, when he noticed a man in the crowd looking at him intently—staring at him. He sniffed and wiped his brow with his handkerchief. He stuffed it back in his back pocket and stole another glance at the man. He didn't look familiar but the man seemed to know him.

Mariani Cordova looked at her husband and said something but he only saw her lips moving. He didn't hear what she said. He nodded and looked straight ahead. But he couldn't prevent himself from taking another look. He put his arm over the back of his wife's chair and looked again. This time, the man was gone, disappeared behind the crowd, perhaps.

Juan Miguel was the man who was staring. Throughout the concert, he stared because the man reminded him of someone from his past whom he hated. Someone he had spent years struggling to forget and then struggling to remember.

Then suddenly the peaceful evening was interrupted by a contingent of *federales*, probably the same company of soldiers who stopped the train, appearing from a side street and riding up to the plaza. They dismounted with their rifles in their hands. An officer walked to the front of the audience and held up one of the handbills that had been posted that evening.

"Who did this?" he asked.

No one answered. Some people shrugged their shoulders. Others looked at each other.

"Come now," the officer said, sounding sarcastic, "it's a small town and everybody knows everybody. With most of the editors in jail, that leaves very few people who have access to a printing press. I'm sure you have a good idea who it is ... tell me so we can get on with the entertainment."

Annabelle turned to her father and said, "Tell him this is a free country and we still have freedom of the press."

Juan Miguel shook his head and shushed her. "Not now, Annabelle ... be quiet."

The officer paced up and down in front of them, waving the handbill in the air. Then he stopped directly in front of Juan, threw the paper down on the ground, and stepped on it. "Harboring *insurrectos* is against the law ... even here," he said. "Is that not true, *Señor*?"

Juan said, "You, sir, are the authority. Not I."

"Pick it up."

"*Señor*?"

"I said, pick it up."

The people gathered in the plaza were dead silent. Juan bent down and picked up the handbill. He crumpled it in his hand and handed it to the officer.

The officer smiled wide and took it in his hand. "A

friendly word of advice, my friend. Don't make enemies with the wrong people. You and your daughter are like shining rays of light … let's keep it that way, shall we?"

They mounted their horses and rode away, but the incident had put a damper on the evening. Most of the people in the plaza drifted away.

Juan lay awake most of the night worrying about the impudent *federale* and wondering what he was up to, but also about the man who looked so familiar. Were they connected? Was the mysterious man the warden who tortured and mistreated him years ago in a Monterrey prison? He hoped to God he wasn't. He crossed himself, even though he was alone in bed in the dark. "God, do not let it be so," he whispered.

The next morning, the monsoon season hit with full force. A storm parked itself over the town and it rained for hours. Juan Miguel awoke with a headache and stomachache from his insomnia that only became worse as the day wore on. But after lunch the sun popped out, reflecting off of the huge puddles here and there on the downtown streets, and he felt renewed.

"The sky has cleared," he said, peering out the windows across the buildings to the mountains beyond. "I think I'll take a ride." He rolled up his shirtsleeves and put on a hat. "There are horses for hire down the street. Surely one of them is worthy."

He walked out without inviting Annabelle and that was unusual. Undoubtedly she would think it had something to do with Charlotte Borden. He turned his head and saw her at the window, smiling and watching him cross the street. He dodged a puddle on El Paso Street with liveliness in his step that hadn't been there for a while. He felt a strange force propelling him—something a bit manic, something out of control and frantic, but he didn't identify that until later.

He knew exactly where he wanted to go. He just didn't know how to get there. The old steed with the mangy mane he was riding seemed steady enough although a bit slow. He had directions to the Copper Hills Ranch, based more on landmarks in relation to the mountaintops than anything else. After wandering around the countryside across some muddy pastures and down a few horse paths, he found a well-used road winding through the foothills and low mesas. Finally, he saw a gate, wooden and falling apart, but holding a sign with the ranch's brand, a pair of longhorns atop a circle, seared into it. It reminded him of his family's brand, the cross within a circle of the del Valle rancho.

He dismounted, opened the gate, and rode through.

It took a little courage to walk up the porch steps and knock. He wasn't an invited guest. But he'd had some time to prepare his reason for being there. Although, at this point, it was beginning to sound lame as he rehearsed it in his head.

A middle-aged woman answered the door with a wary expression.

"Is Miss Borden in?" he asked, hat in hand.

"Miss Borden?" the woman said. "No Miss Borden."

"Miss Charlotte Borden?"

"Oh ... Charlotte ... well she's Señora Peterson. Not Miss Borden since last December."

When she appeared, smiling, his mouth got very, very dry and his head light and heavy at the same time. His heart started to race. Freckles across her milky cheeks softened the impression of a lean, sleek thoroughbred. He felt more intimidated than he thought he would—surprised and nonplussed— and he felt the headache returning.

"Señora Peterson, may I trouble you for a drink of water?" He sounded far away even to himself.

She reached for him as he slumped into a nearby chair, sweat soaking through his shirt. She took his hat from his hands and put her cool, competent hand on his forehead.

"You have had too much sun, Mr. Lopez. Mina ... bring some water ... Mina."

"I am so embarrassed," he said, shaking his head and wiping his face with his hand. "I shouldn't have come ... I just was out for a ride."

She smiled and left the room for a cup of water. His head was still spinning but he could hear the argument in the next room. Voices were raised with no thought of hiding the discord.

"What is he doin' here, anyway?" Lyle shouted.

"He just appeared at the door. He's come for a visit … do you expect me to put him on a horse and send him on his way?"

"That's 'xactly what I expect, Charlotte. For one thing … he's a Mexican, for God's sake."

"Shh, keep your voice down. So what, what has that got to do with anything?"

"Mexican, Charlotte … Mexican. You know how I feel 'bout 'em. They're dirty and ignorant. Not fit to be here … in your father's house."

He heard a scuffle and then her voice. "Let go of me. Go on back to work, Lyle."

Then the quarrel stopped and Charlotte returned. "Come with me," she said.

Behind the Copper Hills ranch house a trail followed a rivulet fed by a natural spring higher up in the mountains. The spring was said to have healing waters by the descendants of the local Indian tribes. Charlotte's mother had made regular treks up the trail to the spring's source, a mysterious grouping of stones from which clear, sweet water trickled onto a rock, flattened by eons of water erosion.

Charlotte put on a hat and boots and started up the trail to fetch some spring water for her visitor. She lugged a heavy bucket of it back down about an hour later. Juan

Miguel sat in the warm sunlight on a wooden chair on the house's back porch watching her descend the trail. He had thought about dissembling and making some excuse about his strange behavior but then he decided to own up to his brash, ill-conceived visit.

She plopped the bucket down almost in front of him, raised up, and rubbed her raw palms together.

"What have you brought, *Señora*?" he asked.

She lifted a ladle from a nearby hook and offered him some. He sipped it and made a face at the salty mineral taste.

"Drink it down," she said. "Then we'll talk."

He did as he was told. "What is it?" he asked.

"Just something to heal the body ... and the spirit too, the Indians say. Spring water has a calming effect."

"And you think my spirit needs to be healed?" he said before taking another drink. "It seems I'm fairly calm, *Señora*."

"I have an Indian grandmother and I inherited her gift of second sight. As she would say, your hurt is sticking out."

He smiled and drank some more. "Perhaps you are right."

Not in a long time had Juan Miguel been caught so un-prepared and unprotected. He had thoroughly embar-rassed himself. He had no doubt that she guessed one of the reasons he rode all the way out to the Copper Hills Ranch. But he was still prepared to talk about the other reason.

"I wish to apologize ..." he began, "for allowing you to misconstrue the situation ..."

She shrank back and crossed her arms. "It is my fault, Mr. Lopez ... I should've told you I was married when we were introduced."

"Please call me Juan Miguel, *por favor*. Why didn't you ... tell me you were married?"

Her brown eyes flashed with uncertainty when she looked into his eyes for a moment then looked away. "I suppose I'm not quite used to it ... the marriage that is. We've only been married for six months and I can't get the hang of it."

He drank the last of the water and handed her the ladle.

"Did you enjoy being married?" she asked, looking shy suddenly.

He took a deep breath and furrowed his brow and said, "That is a complicated question, *Señora*, because, well, I had a complicated marriage. May I tell you about it some other time?"

"Certainly ... some other time."

Juan Miguel felt the need to change the subject. "May I ask about your cattle, *Señora*? I too own a ranch, the del Valle Rancho south of San Antonio. I notice your brand has a Longhorn on it. Is that the breed you run here?"

"Yes ... some Longhorns ... some Herefords. Also, we breed bulls for the *corrida*, bullfighting bulls. My father bought a breeding steer years ago from a ranch in Mexico. He was from a long line of Spanish *toros*, brought to the new world centuries ago."

"And the line has remained pure?"

"Yes, and they were bred to be aggressive ... which some people find objectionable. But it's a tradition on the Copper Hills Ranch so I've continued it."

"And you are a fan of the *corrida*?"

"I didn't really understand it until I attended a bullfight when I was in Spain. I admire the bravery of the matador ... and the bull. Once you know the history, it's easier to admire."

"May we see you again, Charlotte ... some other time?"

"We?"

"Annabelle and myself. We are greatly in need of a feminine presence, *Señora*. Perhaps that is the 'hurt' of which you speak. Annabelle's mother has been gone for eight years and we have each other but we sometimes get ..."

"Lonely?"

"*Si* ... lonely ... that is a good word for it, I suppose."

"I know the feeling," she said. "I would like to see Annabelle again. Your daughter is one of the most charming girls I've met. Well let's get you fed and back on your horse and back to your daughter. I'm sure she is worried."

"Señora Peterson ... Charlotte ... wait, I have another reason for my ill-conceived visit."

She stopped and turned. "Another reason?"

"*Si* ... I would like to talk to your hands, ask them about the ones who were killed ... particularly the man named Tomás. He was the nephew of my friend and I promised to inquire about the circumstances of his death."

"I don't think Lyle would agree to that ... but perhaps you could talk to Manny. He's one of our most trusted workers ... a good *vaquero* with a wife and children."

"*Si ... por supuesta.*"

Manny was a short, solid man who brooked no nonsense. He reminded Juan of the *vaqueros* he had grown up with. He was not talkative. In fact, he said nothing until Juan asked him directly, "Why were the Copper Hills hands and Tomás killed?" Then a floodgate opened and he talked freely.

"They were Teresitas, all of them. They went on raids down south to fight the *rurales* and other *federales* who aid the mine owners. Tomás escaped from his life as a miner at the Taxcoco mine and he talked about the hard lives of those who are enslaved there."

"Enslaved?"

"*Si* ... enslaved. Slavery still exists, *Señor*. And the rich and powerful get away with it. Some, like me, come north and feel only gratitude. Others want to continue the fight. Tomás was one of those."

"So ... his resentment grew?"

"*Si* ... and then the flooding of the homes in Smeltertown, the poor who were made homeless. He could not stand the injustice of it."

Annabelle had been worried while he was gone, not

knowing where he was or why he left without talking to her. He saw it in her eyes when he returned. For the next few days, she watched him, pampered him, served him his Bergamot tea, and brought him anything he asked for. He was fragile, there was no hiding it. Seeing the familiar man in the plaza and the headaches and the stomachaches and the trip to the Copper Hills Ranch were all connected. He knew that. Something had knocked him off center, made old fears return, but he didn't know what it was. So, he waited, hoping to feel himself again.

CHAPTER FOUR

Because the feast of *Nuestra Señora del Carmen* fell on a Friday that year, it provided a perfect excuse for the community of Juarez to plan a fiesta for the following day. The *paisanos* and their families would make their way from the surrounding countryside into the town for the feast day mass, then stay on for the festivities.

When the monsoon rains abated, early on Saturday morning, Juan Lopez and Annabelle walked across the bridge for their first visit to the huge open-air *mercado*.

Already the Juarez market was bustling and it seemed the entire populations of Juarez and El Paso were there.

"Look at the *chiles*," Juan said with his hand over his heart. "I've never seen so many kinds." He headed straight for the food booths on the northern edge of the market where it was a tradition for the truck farmers from the valley to sell harvest. Laid out in rows, four or five deep, were baskets and clay bowls of tiny red *arbols*, vivid yellow *habaneros*, and dark green, almost black, *poblanos*. And next to that, there was every kind of bean and rice, and next to that, the fresh tomatoes, avocados, gourds, yams, and ears of corn. In the back of the stall, the women cooked tortillas over an open flame then stuffed them with fire-roasted *cabrito* they kept wrapped in *maguey* leaves to keep it warm.

Juan picked up one of the bright green *serranos* and sniffed it several times. The woman selling them cut off a piece of one, speared it with her knife, and handed it to him.

He took a bite and nodded. "*Si* ... it's *picante*, as it should be, but not too *caliente*. I will have a bag of them. And also the *poblanos, por favor.*"

"For *salsa* and chicken *poblano*," he said to Annabelle. "Beatriz's is almost as good as Celita's."

"You should have been a cook, *Papá*," Annabelle teased.

"*Si*, or a farmer, perhaps?"

Juan and Annabelle held their tortillas filled with meat and vegetables as they strolled through the noise and people and familiar odors of *barbacoa* and *pan dulce*.

When they reached the part of the market where the native women sold their handmade clothing, Annabelle stopped suddenly, shifted her tortilla to one hand, and waved to someone up ahead.

"Who is this you greet?" Juan asked.

But before she could answer, Cinco stood in front of them, sticking out his hand then bowing then sticking out his hand again.

"I am Cinco, *Señor*. Ricardo Morales but everyone calls me Cinco. I met your lovely daughter a few weeks ago while she attempted to ride the bicycle."

Juan shook the young man's hand and said, "*Si* ... Señor Cinco." He couldn't help smiling at the boy's bubbly nature.

"May I walk with you ... be your guide, so to speak?" Cinco said, taking his place next to Annabelle. "I have been coming to this market since I was a baby. I was practically born here. My mother has that stall ... over there ... the one with the beautiful silver work."

"Let's go see, *Papá*. Let's look at her jewelry."

Cinco's mother and aunt were true silver artisans, a craft they learned from their mother and she from hers. Annabelle picked up a bracelet with a hammered surface on one side and a smooth polished one on the other. She put it on her wrist and held it up in the sunlight to admire it.

From behind them, someone said, "Lovely, isn't it?" The man's voice was soft and mellow with a hint of sarcasm in it. "You would never imagine the horrible conditions of the men who mined that silver."

"Carlito ... let her enjoy," Cinco said.

She turned and looked at the man Cinco called Carlito,

an expression of innocence mixed with astonishment on her face.

Juan put his arm protectively around Annabelle's shoulders and pulled her back. "Do you have a problem, *Señor*?" he asked the rude stranger.

"This is my friend, Carlito ... he didn't mean anything by what he said ... did you, Carlito? Apologize to these nice people."

"*Pardoneme, Señorita y Señor*," Carlito said, "but I happen to know the silver miners suffer greatly under their burdens. It is not your fault ... I know that."

"No, it is not our fault ... so if you will excuse us," Juan said.

Carlito bowed slightly, looked Annabelle in the eyes, then walked on.

"He is full of *bravado* these days," Cinco said, "Ever since he's become a popular *torero* ... his head has grown to the size of a watermelon."

"A *torero*? You mean ..."

"*Si Señorita*, a matador ... one of the best and quickly making a name for himself."

"Here in Juarez?"

"*Si*, every Saturday at the *corrida*. Carlito Intrepido they call him. He has quite a following among the poor ... he is their champion. He's starting to take the role a bit too seriously, I think. Next thing you know, he will be elected a successor to Jesus Christ himself."

Something about the way the young man, Carlito,

looked at his daughter bothered Juan. And something about the way she looked at him, as well. He had an uneasy feeling, watching Carlito walk away.

"*Papá*, let's go to the *corrida*," she said. "Could we?"

"Bullfights are bloody, *mi amor* ... someone dies. Either the bull or the matador."

"I want to see one. It's part of your culture, isn't it? Isn't that what you've always told me?"

"*Si ... si ...* it is. But it's not for the faint of heart."

"I want to ... I want to see it."

Cinco stopped walking and put his hands on his hips. "If you really want to ... I can get you in. I can get you good seats. I know one of the *banderillas* ... the ones who stick the bull. He is a friend of my uncle."

Against his better judgment, Juan gave in. He told himself they could leave if the bullfight became too disturbing. The truth was that Juan Miguel del Valle missed the *corridas* of his youth—the running of the horses, the bronco riding, even a bullfight occasionally. He missed the pageantry and the pitting of men against animals. It was an age-old tradition, part of his culture, and it was also in his blood. The thought that he might see Charlotte Peterson also entered his mind, if only for a fleeting moment. She did say she supplied the bulls for the *corrida*. She might be there.

Annabelle could smell the cigar breath and heavy

cologne of the military officer seated behind her. The west side of the wooden box bullfighting arena was packed. On the other side, the poor and the peasants only partially filled the seats. It was evident to Annabelle why the seats Carlito procured were considered the "good" ones. They were in the middle of the late afternoon shade as the sun set behind them.

Her father leaned over to her and whispered, "If you don't like it, we will leave, *mon ami*. There's no reason to stay if you are uncomfortable."

"I know, *Papá*. I will tell you ... "

All of a sudden, the trumpets announced the Parade of the Matadors with the ancient Spanish fanfare, echoing through the clear summer air as it had for centuries. It changed to a mellow slow, almost requiem-like march as the first of the bullfighters appeared at the far end of the arena, sitting atop their steeds in colorful coats and white flat sombreros and carrying long spears. These *picadors* would be the first to confront the bull on horseback and weaken it with their lances, her father said.

Next came the *banderillas*, the helpers, who chased the bull on foot and stuck their lances into his neck muscles to lower his head and lessen the danger to the *torero*.

Then the trumpets announced that day's *toreros*, the *artistes*, the heroes, the ones who slew the bulls and put their own lives at risk in the age-old ballet of the bullfight.

"Not only must they save themselves and kill their rival, the bull, they must do it artfully and with respect," her father explained. "If you do not respect and understand your opponent, *mi amor*, then you have lost already. Remember that."

"But killing him? Do they have to?"

"He will die anyway, my love. It is a great truth. It is his valor in life and confronting death that matters. *Comprende?*"

Carlito Intrepido was in the center of the toreros as they entered the arena, not one of the most honored but not one of the least either. He wore a white collared shirt and the high-waisted tan britches the *toreros* train in. Across his shoulder was a bright blue and pink cape, wrapped around him in the same manner that matadors had done for centuries. The breeze blew a lock of hair in his eyes but he stoically ignored it, giving the impression that his mind was already in the bullring with the bull.

"Is it dangerous, *Papá*?"

"*Si* ... very dangerous. Do you not have the stomach for it, my love?"

"No, I want to stay. I might want to write about it someday."

The first bullfight was somewhat of a farce. The *torero* was aging; the bull was listless. The crowd grew restless and finally the *banderillas* were allowed to dispatch the bull. Annabelle looked away when the bloody carcass was dragged from the arena by a set of mules.

The next bullfight was better but not thrilling and the matador received only polite applause at the end. In a rare decision, the crowd took the side of the bull and voted by standing and clapping to let the bull live.

Then it was Carlito Intrepido's turn. He had already made a name for himself among the people of Juarez, so when they realized he would be next, they got attentive. The gates opened and a brown bull smaller in size than the others stood at the far end of the arena surveying his situation. The *picadors* approached and goaded him with their lances and taunting shouts of "*ole!*" He stood still for a few moments and then he began to charge with a fierceness they hadn't seen yet. The *picadors* withdrew with caution and it took more than a few attempts for them to insert their lances. Still, the bull raged, not at all quieted by his wounds.

The crowd was excited and already on their feet when the *banderillas* were finished with their work and Carlito stepped into the ring. He held up his hand to silence them. He unfurled his cape and took a few tentative steps. At the other end of the arena, the wounded bull waited, his head twitching and twisting from the many lances in his neck.

Carlito took a step then waved his cape to one side. "Hey ... Hey," he said, not loud but soft and sensuous like a man wooing his sweetheart. "Hey ... Hey."

The bull looked confused at the tone of voice. He took a few steps then bowed his head in submission.

Carlito once again sounded soothing. "Woo hoo," he

said, "shh, shh, shh."

He raised his cape and approached the bull, walking up almost to him. Then he snapped the bright pink cape in the animal's face and the bull charged it.

After a few passes of the bull, man and animal seemed to become one in a dance only they understood. Carlito's movements were graceful, like a ballerina's, his back arched, his shoulders squared. The bull's movements also had a certain grace. Yes, he was charging, but he was also withholding something. Annabelle sensed he could have taken down the *torero* at any moment, if he wished to. They passed closer and closer to each other until the dance became deadly, the bull's horns only inches from Carlito's torso. Annabelle grasped her father's arm and gasped every time the bull passed through the cape.

He patted her hand and looked at her face to make sure she was well. At one especially close call, she buried her face in his shoulder.

"Do you wish to go?" he asked.

"No ... I must see ... I have to see."

Then the moment of reckoning came. The crowd on the opposite side that had been on its feet shouting "*ole*" at every pass became quiet and sat down, out of respect for what was about to happen. The *torero* fetched a sword from the sidelines, hid it behind his cape, and approached the bull.

Sensing the dance had ended and his own ending was near, the bull got a puzzled expression in his wide eyes. His passes became furious, not graceful, and he aimed at the presumptuous *torero* in front of him. Suddenly, so quickly that the crowd almost missed it, Carlito himself charged the bull and plunged the sword into his neck at a strategic, vulnerable spot. The bull stood there looking stunned, then his knees buckled and he began to fall.

The crowd on both sides of the arena leapt to their feet, shouting at the *torero* as if they knew him, clapping together in rhythm. Carlito draped his cape over his arm, raised his other arm in a beautiful dancer's pose and marched around the arena in triumph.

"What do you think, *mon ami*?" her father asked, raising his voice over the noise of the crowd.

"It was horrible ... horrible," she said. "Yet it was beautiful, too. But I want to go now ... can we go now?"

Her father took her by the elbow and led her from the arena stands.

"I never want to see a bullfight again," she said once they were outside.

"I understand, little one. I understand. You just did not like it."

"No, *Papá* ... I did like it. I liked it too much."

Walking back across the bridge in the late evening sunlight, Annabelle and Juan were silent. He had been so concerned about his daughter's reaction to the *corrida* that he hadn't had time until now to think about Charlotte Peterson. Two rows below them and off to the right she had sat with her husband, surrounded by their friends. Juan could see the dark waves and part of her face if she turned a certain way. But he had no thought of speaking to her. There were just too many other people around. He stole a glance when he had the chance, just to see her pretty face.

She was the most attractive woman he'd met in many years but this time he would not pursue it. He had lost the brashness of his youth and he knew how difficult relationships could be—how difficult marriage could be. He would have to admire Charlotte Peterson from afar.

That evening after dinner, Annabelle came to him in the parlor and sat next to him, looking like someone with something on her mind.

"What is it?" he asked.

"I have written down my thoughts about the bullfight. It is my way of dealing with it."

She handed him a piece of paper with her writing on it. He read through it and handed it back.

"It is good. You are a very good writer," he said.

"*Gracias*, but I would find it more interesting if ..."

"If? If what, *mi amor*?"

"If I could try to get it published. Please don't forbid me, *Papá*. I want to try to get a position at one of the newspapers."

Juan nodded and looked into her eyes. They were young, brash, passionate eyes. They were his eyes when he was her age.

"I will ask around. That is my condition ... that you let me choose the situation and the newspaper. Do you agree?"

"You can't do everything for me, *Papá*. I'm almost a grown woman."

"Woman is the key word. You are a woman ... and therefore, you face dangers that men do not face. I will ask around and choose a suitable position for you."

"*Papá* ..."

"That is the condition, Annabelle Margaret. Now perhaps you need to refine the wording a bit. Do that and I will have an example to show to an editor."

El Pasoans were used to their modern, booming city existing alongside the wild frontier town it once was. The city fathers were proud of their new opera house, a showcase courthouse, even a telephone system, but there were still almost a hundred saloons along El Paso and San Antonio streets, ranging from the most basic tequila bars to the fancier honky-tonks. Not far away, a row of whorehouses lined Utah Street as it had for years.

Juan Lopez didn't take much notice of them because there were plenty of saloons and whorehouses in every Texas town. He walked down El Paso Street on his way to the hotel from Juanita's store where he bought a package of fresh chicken for Beatriz to cook with the *poblano* peppers from the *mercado*. The afternoon was warm so he walked close to the buildings in the shade.

Passing the Opal Saloon, he heard the plinking of a piano. When he reached the door, he smelled the whiskey and sweat of the cowboys and traveling salesmen inside. He stopped and peered in. They were clapping in time to the music and a few were singing some bawdy song about an errant woman named Kate. *But we don't hate Kate*, they sang.

He pulled one of the English cigarettes he just bought out of his pocket and lit it. He hadn't heard a good drinking song in awhile. This must be a new one.

He had just taken a drag and begun to exhale when he heard the unmistakable hiss of a pistol shot close to his ear. He ducked inside the saloon doorway, waiting for another shot, but it didn't come. He drew the pistol from inside his jacket and peered through the front window. The street was deserted. There was no one in sight except an old peddler standing next to his donkey cart.

A voice behind him asked, "Are you hit, *Señor*? Did it hit you?"

He turned his head and saw a young Mexican priest in a black robe.

"Were you outside, father? Did you see where it came from?"

"I was walking behind you but I did not see a thing. It

must have been a stray bullet ... or simply someone who does not like the Opal and its patrons ... unless perhaps you have an enemy, *Señor*?"

"Possibly ... I'm not without enemies. I just don't know which one."

The priest smiled and offered his hand. "I am Francisco Romo. Father Francisco Romo. And you are?"

"Juan Lopez, father."

"I invite you to have a drink with us, Señor Lopez." He took Juan by the arm and escorted him to the bar. Juan Lopez had not drunk in a saloon in quite a long time, but it felt familiar when the line of drinkers parted and allowed him to take a place at the bar.

He couldn't help stealing a glance or two at the young man next to him. He was short and looked to be fairly rotund underneath his black robe. He had thick black hair and a neatly trimmed mustache and his skin was dark, the color of the Indians in western Mexico.

Father Romo raised his glass to toast him. "You are an honest man ... I like that, Señor Lopez." Then he drank a few times and added. "If I were you, I would be considering who it might be. Whether it was a stray bullet or not, you surely would not want a repeat of that scene."

"No, father, I was ill-prepared, to say the least."

"I think I will have another drink. Care for another, Señor Lopez?"

Juan Lopez's nerves were sufficiently rattled that he decided to break his rule about only one drink. He tapped the rim of his glass with his thumb and the barkeep poured him another drink.

"Now that we have calmed our nerves, I invite you to meet my *compadres*. In the back room, *Señor*."

Juan picked up his glass and followed Father Romo. He was surprised to see a contingent of people sitting around a table and leaning against the walls. He recognized the newspaper editor, Alberto Salazar, sitting with the last edition of *La Revuelta* spread out before him.

"Señor Lopez ..." Salazar said.

Juan bowed his head but he felt as if he'd been waylaid. The scene reminded him of a similar scene several years ago in Galveston at the luxurious home of Miss Bettie. This dusty, foul-smelling saloon was anything but luxurious. Nonetheless, he recognized the same earnest faces of people with a purpose and the atmosphere of conspiracy, and in his mouth was the bitter taste of having been compelled to shed his complacency, all of which made him uncomfortable.

"Señor Lopez, you know Alberto Salazar," Father Romo said, "and this is Josephina Huerta, the owner of the J&J Café. This is Jim Redding, the American journalist. The others are from various parts of Mexico. Won't you have a seat, *Señor* ... someone get up and let Señor Lopez sit down, *por favor*."

It was with reluctance, and only because good manners dictated it, that Señor Lopez sat down at the table and placed his glass carefully in front of him and next to it, the package of chicken. He felt the gaze of dozens of pairs of eyes—expectant, hopeful eyes.

"I am happy to see you are no longer in jail," he said to Salazar.

"So ... you saw Cinco's handbills. I told him not to print them but he is young and foolish. My wife has managed to raise bail ... now, it's either cross the border where things are even more dangerous or stand trial."

"Which will you do?"

"The border ... of course. The newspaper office was raided only a few minutes after you left. I'm certain that they saw you there, Señor Lopez. You, too, are in danger."

"Perhaps that explains the stray bullet, *Señor*," said Father Romo.

"Perhaps ... perhaps not. I have enemies of my own. *Señores* ... whatever it is you have in mind does not interest me," Juan said. "I am simply an American rancher ... nothing else."

"But an American rancher with connections ... and with influence."

Señor Lopez picked up his glass and took a drink. It tasted horrible and the look on his face betrayed his dislike of cheap whiskey. "May I trouble you for a glass of wine ... Spanish wine if that is possible?"

He succeeded in buying himself some time to think while the barkeep searched for and found a bottle of wine and opened it. The others in the room watched him with fascination. None of them had ever seen anyone with his

manner, or his elegance, or his grace. They looked mes-
merized.

After he'd taken several soothing drinks of the surprisingly good *beaujelais*, he crossed his hands in his lap and
sat back. "I do not wish to hear anything about your cause.
I only want to inquire about the death of the *paisanos* on
the train. Why were they killed?"

"They were aiding the Durango rebels ... buying arms
for them."

"Ah ... I see," he said. "And who allows the Mexican *rurales* to come this far north?"

"No one stops them. Diaz and his men run rough shod
... even this far north."

"So there is some sort of agreement?"

Salazar sat back and put his palms on the table. "We
suspect ... but we have no proof ... that the government in
Washington is in cahoots with the Diaz government. And
there may even be agents here in El Paso, keeping tabs on
the *insurrectos*. From time to time, we have suspected
strangers in town of being such agents."

"From Washington? Agents of our government?"

"*Si, Señor* ... as I said, it is only a suspicion."

Señor Lopez nodded his head. "I promised my friend,
Beatriz, that I would find out what happened to her
nephew. Now that I have, I am satisfied." He rose and put
on his hat. "Besides, *amigos*, my chicken threatens to turn
foul in this heat."

He smiled and looked at their serious faces. "It is a

joke, my friends ... just a joke. Please excuse me, I must go."

"I will walk you out," Father Romo said.

When they were outside, the priest touched him gently on the shoulder to stop him. "I ask a favor ... in memory of your friend's nephew ... come to the Socorro Mission and visit."

"Why, father?"

"To talk to the poor people ... to hear their plight. Just this one favor, *por favor*. Then I will not ask anything else."

Señor Lopez felt his heart being tugged but still, past experience had taught him that fighting for causes creates as many enemies as friends. "I will think about it, father. Where is this mission?"

"South of the city ... ask anyone the way. Will you come?"

"*No contenga la respiración.*"

"*Si, Señor*, I will not hold my breath, but I will hold out hope," the priest said to his back as he stepped off the porch and looked around cautiously before walking down the deserted street of saloons in the midday heat.

Annabelle inherited her creativity from her mother. But every other attribute she possessed came from her father. Kindness, compassion, passionate purpose, cunning intelligence, the ability to see all the avenues that were open to her, and, most of all perseverance, that stubborn unwillingness to give up.

That summer in El Paso, she had set two goals for herself. First, to ride her bicycle well, which she accomplished by practicing almost every day. Up and down the streets near the hotel, she rode until it became second nature to her. The second goal required more time and research. But perseverance paid off and she succeeded in getting accepted to the St Joseph's academy, a boarding school for girls on north El Paso Street.

Then she enlisted the help of an ally to convince her father to let her finish her schooling in El Paso.

Juan opened the door to the blessed sanctuary of his hotel rooms with relief and eager to plan a dinner of chicken and rice *poblano* with Beatriz. He stepped inside only to find more *conspiradores* awaiting him. Annabelle and Charlotte sat on the sofa with their heads together, chatting and smiling. Whatever they wanted from him, he was inclined to give them. How could he resist two beauties like them?

"Where have you been, *Papá*? We've been waiting for you."

"You don't know how happy the sight of you makes me," he said. "Hello, *Señora*, will you stay for dinner? I have something special planned."

"*Papá*, we want to talk to you about something. Please sit down."

He sat and listened to the well thought out plan. His daughter impressed him like never before. She spoke with confidence and conviction about her desire to learn to write better and do it as a career. Sitting across from him in the afternoon sunshine coming through the windows, she looked more mature than he had realized. He saw the woman she would become. Tears burned his eyes but he managed to hold them back and not embarrass himself.

"St. Joseph's has accepted me, with Charlotte as my patroness. She will watch over me," she said. "I only need your signature and I am enrolled."

Charlotte sat up on the edge of the sofa, her hands clasped on her lap. "You said yourself that Annabelle is in need of a feminine presence. Let me be that presence."

He stood, walked to the window, and looked out at the small provincial city and the barren landscape. The stray bullet that missed him only a few minutes ago was a reminder of just how dangerous the world could be. This town is not what he would choose for her, but he must let Annabelle make some decisions on her own. She will learn from her mistakes just as everyone does. And also perhaps there were things about becoming a woman that he hadn't been able to teach her.

"Fine, I will consent, but only for one term. At the end of it, we will assess whether it has been a good idea or not."

When the conversation was over, Charlotte asked to speak to him alone and he sent Annabelle from the room.

He sat in a chair by the window, pulled a cigarette from his inside pocket, lit it, and waited. Charlotte Peterson looked lovelier than ever, her long hair loose and hanging in waves across her shoulders. Her dark eyes looked at him with a directness he found compelling, so he looked away, out the window, at the late afternoon sky.

"Señor Lopez," she began. He blanched slightly at the formality of it and put the cigarette to his mouth again to hide his displeasure.

"Señora Peterson," he said, blowing the smoke between his teeth—between the words.

"Juan ... is that what you wish me to call you?"

"You can call me whatever you like, *Señora*."

"My only qualm about being Annabelle's patroness ... while she is here ..."

"*Si*? ... what is this qualm you speak of?"

"I sense ... that is, I have a feeling ..." She stopped herself and took a deep breath. "It seems there are feelings in the air when we are together."

He leaned forward and put out the cigarette in a small bowl on the table by the window.

"I have not had the feelings you speak of for a very, very long time, *Señora*. My heart ... my heart ... belongs only to Annabelle.

"I'm sorry ... I've embarrassed myself."

"No ... no ... *Señora*, you have not. You are most ... attractive. Of course, I take notice of that. But nothing more, I assure you. Does that make you more comfortable?"

She got up to leave. He stood. He walked her to the door. She looked back and smiled slightly at him. He took her hand, bowed over it, and kissed it, barely touching her glove with his lips.

Autumn was approaching and the grasses along the *acequias*, the irrigation canal running parallel to the river, were starting to turn deep gold in some places but were still a dark military green in others. The ditch was wide at one point and zigzagged across the open meadows then disappeared into groves of trees. It was full from the summer rains and its still surface reflected the blue-gray clouds spreading across the sky in soft billowy rolls. Underneath, the water sped along its way to the groves and fields, taking advantage of the slope of the land.

Here and there small groups of men made sure the water was flowing free and not hampered by fallen limbs or deposits of silt. They worked lovingly. The livelihood of the people in the farms and villages along the Rio depended on the ancient system that fed the citrus orchards, cotton and grain fields, and vegetable patches—a series of oases in the arid south Texas landscape.

Once more, he rode a hired nag. She was a slow buff colored old girl with a dark mane who was more accustomed to the streets of El Paso than the dirt road he followed along the *acequias* south to Socorro.

Late in the morning, he rode into the tiny village. Along the main street, old women sat in the shade of the adobes grinding walnuts on their *metates*. It was September 15, the day before Mexico Independence Day and the *abuelas* of the community were preparing to cook the traditional *chiles en nogada*. A dish invented for the occasion, it incorporated the green, red, and white of the Mexican flags, which were draped across the doorways and fluttered in the slight breeze from wooden flagpoles. The thought of *chiles en nogada*, an exquisite concoction of *poblanos*, pomegranate seeds, and walnut sauce, made his mouth water.

In front of the mission church, a line of *paisanos* with their donkey carts sold batches of limes and pears and other fruits of the season, alongside the usual *chiles* and nuts. He dismounted the weary mare, took off his hat, and nodded at the men. They all looked alike, with black bowlers over long braids and colorful serapes over their shoulders and smoking tiny cigars, puffing out their cheeks as they exhaled.

"Is this the Socorro Mission church?" he asked them.

Almost in unison they said "*si*" then continued their smoking and puffing.

"Is Father Romo about?"

Two of them shrugged. The others just stared at him.

He walked to the door and pushed it open. A rush of incense assaulted his senses. It reminded him of the small rancho chapel that had only one window and one door. The incense Father Moreno burnt sometimes became suffocating.

Inside, Father Romo was waiting for him, looking like

one of the church's many statues sitting on top of and next to a tall painted altar behind him.

"Father, I am here … as you asked," Juan said, walking up the aisle.

Then he noticed they were not alone. Sitting off to the left on the second row of benches were several men dressed as *bandidos*, who were obviously not local residents.

"Meet the Jalisco brothers, Señor Lopez. They are from Durango and they dare not show their faces in the city."

"I thought you wanted me to talk to the parishioners … the poor …"

"We will do that later," Father Romo said, motioning for him to sit down.

One of the Jaliscos stood and began a long protracted plea for his support of the revolution—the revolution they hoped was coming to overthrow President Diaz and restore what they considered to be a real democracy.

Juan felt betrayed. He had not ridden all the way from El Paso to this rural village to hear what he could easily have heard there. When the speech was finished, he said, "Shall we cut to the chase … get to the point, gentlemen. You are trying my patience."

"You understand the forces against us …"

"*Señores*," Juan said, interrupting before the man got started again. "Tell me exactly what it is you want. And, please, no more political speeches."

"Use your influence …"

"Specifics, *amigo*, specifics."

Father Romo walked over to him, his arms folded across his black Jesuit robe. "We want you to go to Washington and find out what transpires between the Diaz government and the U.S. government. We want you to use your good offices to convince the people in power to stop supporting Diaz."

"So you want me to spy and to lobby? Am I understanding you correctly?"

One of the Jaliscos started to protest but Father Romo held up his hand to stop him. "Yes ... that is what we are asking. There is no danger to you. You are simply acting as an unofficial ambassador ... a curious businessman ... looking for information that any citizen has the right to know."

"When would you want me to go?" he said.

"As soon as your schedule will allow it. As you probably know, tensions between our government and the Spanish government are rising. This could complicate our cause but we don't know what effect a Spanish American war would have ... if it breaks out. These are questions only someone of your standing can answer for us."

"Now that I know what you want, we can dispense with the rest," Juan said, standing up and running his fingers through his hair. "I will consider it and let you know."

"We are prepared to pay you ... it would not be much ..."

"If I do this, it will not be for money, *Señores*. Give me

a week. You will have my answer in a week."

The row of seedy looking men stood and filed into the aisle and out of the church. Father Romo raised his voice and said, "*Entrar.*" From behind the altar, another row of men and women walked in. They were the poor of the parish, dressed in plain homespun pants and blouses and carrying their straw hats. One woman had a baby in her arms.

"They want to tell you their stories," Father Romo said. "They are from the village of Tomochic. They all lost relatives when Diaz's soldiers attacked the village several years ago. But to save time, they have asked Jaime to speak for them."

One of the men stepped forward, looking proud but also humble. "There were rebels in the mountains ... it is true. But the villagers and farmers were innocent. Their only crime was kissing the icon of Saint Teresa in the chapel ... that is all. The soldiers rode in and killed almost everyone ... babies, women, grandmothers ... then they burned the village. Only those who ran away or were already gone survived."

"And you were survivors?" Juan asked.

"*Si* ... but my wife, my three little children ..." The man began to weep. He hung his head and his shoulders shook with silent weeping.

Juan looked at the line of people standing before him. Their faces were sincere. Their eyes were transparent, as the eyes of the blameless usually are. Their hands, though, were rough and cracked and aged. He was reminded once again how much he owed to people such as these. "*Gracias, mis amigos, gracias* ..." he said. He stood and shook the man's hand. Then he shook the hands of the others and patted them on the shoulder.

He watched them walk away, his heart feeling the compassion he had tried so hard to keep at bay. Then he glanced up at a statue tucked inside a cove of the wall of the nave—the statue of a man clad in armor and holding an uplifted sword. He'd seen this saint's statue before many times, but never one quite like this one. It was beautifully carved and the original color was still vibrant. It was St. Michael, the archangel—the prince of heaven, the protector of the people.

"That is a beautiful statue, father," he said. "Who made it?"

"St. Michael? He came here strictly by accident centuries ago. He was on a cart being drawn by oxen from Mexico to Santa Fe. The cart got stuck in the mud, the oxen couldn't pull it out, so the monks accompanying the statue decided that St. Michael wanted to live in Socorro. He has been here at the mission ever since and the people of Socorro consider him their patron saint."

"Will you leave me alone with him, father, *por favor*?"

Father Romo nodded, turned, and walked out of the church.

Juan went down on his knees on the hard wood floor in front of the statue of Saint Michael and bowed his head. "*Si, Padre*, I get the message. You have used a mallet to get my attention. I have not forgotten what Sister Michael told me ... what Priscilla told me ... about St. Michael. But St. Michael, he had the heavenly hosts to back him up. He had advantages I do not have ..."

He raised his head and looked up at the statue. The face of St. Michael always had an uncanny resemblance to his own face. It was disconcerting. He put his fingers on the faded scars on his cheek, what Priscilla had called the "sign of St. Michael."

"Why, *Padre*, why do you choose me? Can someone else not take up the mantle for once? What about someone younger like ... Carlito, for instance ... someone with the hubris and swagger of the young?" But God didn't answer and the statue of St. Michael remained frozen, his carved wooden face locked forever in a perpetual expression of resolve.

Juan smiled at the *naïvete* of his own questions. He rose from his knees, picked up his hat, and left the church.

The Mexican Independence Day celebration in El Paso's San Jacinto Plaza the next day was subdued. A Mexican band played and a small crowd carried the red, green, and white flags but Mexico's independence from Spain had led to a tortured relationship between the Mexican government and its people. El Pasoans of Mexican heritage longed for the day when their country of origin would be truly free, not just independent from Spain.

Juan and Annabelle walked from the hotel to the Mc-Murray home for a dinner party. The next day, Annabelle would move to St. Joseph's and begin her last year of school and Juan would return to the rancho for fall roundup. They walked side-by-side, passing by the square where a Mexican flag still hung on one of the railings by the band box.

"Will you miss El Paso when you get back to the ranch?" Annabelle asked.

"Yes ... and no. It is a strange little town. Backward and progressive at the same time. However, I will not be staying long at the ranch this time. I have decided to go to Washington ... on business."

"Will you be there long?"

"*Si* ... possibly."

"What sort of business, *Papá*?"

"Government business, that is all I can say."

"Does it have something to do with the men who were murdered on the train?"

"*Si* ... everything to do with it."

"I knew you would not disregard it. I knew you would do something about it."

"You know me too well, little one ..."

"I will miss you so much," she said and she took his hand and held it as they walked.

"And I you, *mi amor* ... and I you."

More than twenty people sat at four tables arranged end to end in the McMurray's hallway. The same Mexican band that played at the plaza strummed guitars and mandolins softly while the guests ate their tamales and corn chowder with *chiles*. Juan and Annabelle sat together at one end and across from them were Charlotte and Lyle Peterson. It was warm in the hallway that night. That and the free-flowing wine made their faces flushed and the conversation became animated.

At the other end of the table, General Cordova and his nephew had been arguing, keeping their voices down so no one would notice. But as the argument wore on, their voices rose and everyone else got quiet.

"A newspaper should be able to print the truth," Carlito said.

"Ha, the truth ... who is to say what is the truth?" the general responded.

"President Diaz ... whatever he pronounces is the truth, I suppose." Carlito sounded sarcastic. "Meanwhile, people die ..." He stood up, threw down his fork, knocking it against one of the china dishes, and left the table.

Although some of those present agreed with Carlito's views, they were relieved to see him leave. It was, after all, a social event. But soon he returned, the dictates of a young man's appetite overcoming his political views.

That evening, Juan Lopez was dressed in a fashion reminiscent of Martin Zamora, an identity he used in the past but hadn't needed recently. A charcoal gray three-piece suit, white tailored shirt, dark gold silk tie pinned just so with a diamond encrusted *fleur de li*, and his hair slicked back, which always made his light brown eyes and thick black lashes seem more prominent somehow. He had not been Señor Zamora in awhile but he still knew how to use all of it to his advantage and he felt that he needed the protection of a disguise more than he had in some time.

Charlotte kept stealing looks, raising her eyes from her plate, when she thought he wasn't looking.

But of course, he was looking and he noticed. "Are you enjoying the evening, *Señora*?" he asked, sounding a bit more arrogant than was his usual manner.

"I was just thinking," she said before taking another sip of wine, "that we will miss the elegant Señor Lopez. You have raised our level of discourse ... and fashion."

He laughed and raised his wine glass in a toast. "*Gracias* ... you are too kind. I am bound for Washington on business and I doubt there will be anyone as gracious as you there."

"But there will ... a dear friend of mine will be there in December. The princess Pilar Constanzia of Spain. We met in France several years ago and we've kept in touch since."

"She is a Spanish princess?"

"The sister of the former King, who died ... the aunt of

the current king. She travels the globe, representing the crown. I will write to her and suggest she receive you while she's there."

He bowed his head in gratitude but meeting a Spanish princess didn't sound very interesting. Spanish royalty were notoriously stuffy and Spanish ladies were notoriously stiff-backed and religious. On the other hand, it could be an entrée to the world he needed to infiltrate.

"I would love to meet her, *Señora,*" he said.

Another guest, General Cordova, was stealing glances at the refined gentleman at the other end of the table but he looked as if he just wasn't sure of his identity. The man who called himself Juan Lopez was relaxed, sophisticated, confident—all calculated to make sure that General Cordova would convince himself that he'd never met him before.

Juan Lopez, on the other hand, became convinced once and for all that General Cordova was indeed the man who tortured and raped him years ago in a Mexican prison. Just as he had suspected from the first moment he saw him in the plaza that evening several months ago. Juan Lopez recognized the beady eyes, the oily manner—much like the devil himself. And now that he knew his name was Cordova—well, it was a different first name but how hard is it to change a name? Certainly, it had never been difficult for him.

Juan raised his wine glass, took a drink, and put it down. When he looked up, and then down the row of tables at the man at the other end, he was looking through the eyes of Señor Zamora—placid and serene. Inside, he was still Primo, the *desperado*, and his soul was a boiling cauldron of pure loathing.

Annabelle hardly noticed her father's subtle transformation that night and that was not like her. She usually noticed every nuance of his behavior. The presence of Carlos Cordova, who was sitting a few people away from her, was distracting. His brown hair shone in the candlelight and his high cheekbones gave him a serious look. She longed to smile at him or catch his eye, but he seemed bored and only once looked in her direction. His eyes lingered for a few moments, as if he recognized her, and she held on to that small bit of hope.

She thought she would never meet someone who was as brave as her father—until that day in the Juarez *corrida*. Carlito Intrepido—a silly name, but a gallant *matador*, and one of the principal reasons she conspired to stay in El Paso.

CHAPTER FIVE

The sun was about to set in Washington on a bleak early December day. It had not shone all day so it wouldn't be missed. He lay on the bed and looked out the window of his room in the Hamilton House, one of seven row houses on M Street in Georgetown. The Potomac, visible over the rooftops down the hill, was almost frozen over. Only the middle of the river had not succumbed to the early winter.

He preferred to look out even though the scene was bleak. Inside, gaudy metallic gold filigree wallpaper clashed with mauve upholstery on the chairs and offended his sensibilities. A small fire crackled in the fireplace. He had to feed it every half hour or the room was unbearable. He reached over and picked up a glass of wine from the bedside table and put it to his lips. When he realized it was empty, he sat up and looked around the room for the wine bottle.

Two days ago, he had to start paying extra when the proprietor of the boarding house threatened to move another boarder into his room. He was loath to share the bed with a man from Poughkeepsie who belched garlic nonstop and was suffering from a cold, so he paid the extra. Also, these days, he needed his solitude.

He'd been in Washington only six days but long enough to know he hated it. The people were provincial, even compared to Texans. The elected officials were old men, for the most part, who were married to sad, stale wives. He caught himself. He had no right to be such a harsh judge. Still, the social scene was definitely lacking. He longed to be back in San Antonio, or in London, or, *Dios no lo quiera*, even El Paso.

So far, his trip had yielded no hint of information about a conspiracy between Washington and the Diaz government. He'd hit brick walls everywhere he turned. But two days ago, he did receive an invitation to a social gathering at the Spanish embassy hosted by the Spanish ambassador and The Infanta Pilar Constanzia of Spain. He had resolved to stay on three more days, attend the embassy affair, and then return to Texas although undoubtedly he would return empty handed. He owed it to Charlotte to honor the invitation she probably arranged, and there was a chance—however small—that meeting the ambassador might produce a lead.

He was registered at the Hamilton House as Juan Lopez but Martin Zamora had made a number of appearances since he arrived—at local restaurants, night spots, a play, and a concert. He felt comfortable slipping into Señor Zamora's skin, taking on his mannerisms and accent. He was a very convenient fellow to have around. However his invitation to the reception was addressed to Juan Lopez, so going as Juan Lopez was a necessity.

The Spanish Princess Pilar, who the Spanish called 'The Infanta,' was a sturdy soul who spoke dozens of languages and took a daily constitutional. She was legally separated from a husband whom she detested from the moment she met him. She had the good sense not to merely languish in a terrible, arranged royal marriage, and had determined to make something of her life.

Traveling in Europe and North and South America had made her worldly and she had taken many lovers and collected many friends, all of whom she was genuinely fond of. One of those friends was the princess Alexis Victoria also of Spain, who was royalty by birth and by marriage. Her father was The Infanta's cousin, a Spanish don, and her mother was a Russian princess. She had married another of The Infanta's distant relatives, a man born to Spanish royalty who was also a great grandson of the English Queen Victoria.

Princess Alexis and her husband were gay companions with whom Pilar looked forward to traveling or visiting with when she was in Russia or Spain. A year ago, though, tragedy changed all that when an assassin, a notorious self-proclaimed anarchist, blew himself up next to her carriage and murdered the Princess Alexis's father and husband. Both men were mutilated beyond recognition.

The princess herself would have been blown up had she not dallied, talking to a friend just inside the restaurant where they had all been dining. She witnessed the explosion and since that day, she'd been a mere shadow of herself.

On the night of the reception, almost immediately after Juan Lopez walked through the door of the embassy and took a glass of wine, The Infanta approached him and introduced herself. She wasted no time in asking a favor of him, that he would escort her friend, Princess Alexis, around the city and show her the sights.

"She has just now come out of mourning, *Señor*," The Infanta said. "She needs a friend such as you to make her feel at home."

Then she reached around, put her arm on someone's back, and brought her forward. "Señor Lopez, may I present Princess Alexis of Spain and Russia. Princess, Juan Lopez of Texas."

His first impulse, before he laid eyes on her, had been to make excuses, the chief one being his plans to return to Texas. But then—she stepped forward and all plans, all thoughts, all misgivings went out the window. She nodded at him and smiled, the corners of her lips barely moving, as if she hadn't smiled in months.

She put out her hand. He bowed and took it. It was like cold porcelain.

"*Excusez-moi, s'il vous plait*," she murmured in a breathless voice, and she seemed at a loss for words.

The Infanta began an explanation of who she was and how she was related to the royal families of many countries.

He was aware of the words but not the meaning. His eyes took in every exotic detail of her appearance. Her hair, pulled back in a tail that flowed past her waist, was the color of expensive dark champagne. Her eyes were pale gray with flecks of gold. She had refined features and buttermilk skin and a demeanor of soft velvet.

She wore an ermine-trimmed blue dress, cinched in at the waist to display her bosom, and a jewel encrusted tiara wrapped around her forehead. From it an enormous faceted gold topaz dangled between her eyes. And she was tall. She looked straight into his eyes. It was quite evident to him that her unusual appearance was a façade. Her real essence, he guessed, was more like a wild gazelle, graceful but vulnerable.

Again she murmured, "*Excusez-moi, s'il vous plait*," and slipped away.

When she was gone, The Infanta said, "You see the problem, *Señor*? She is out of place ... and so sad. But she is beautiful, no?"

"*Si*, Princess, *si* ..."

"So, do you agree to befriend her? *Por favor, Señor*."

"I ... will do my best ..."

He waited a polite amount of time and then he found her sitting alone in the next room, in front of a fireplace, staring into the flames, her cheeks rouged from the heat.

"*Puis je me joindre à vous*?" he asked.

"I speak English, *Señor*," she said without looking at him. "And yes, you may join me."

"How did you learn English?" He sat down on a couch across from her, leaning forward with the wine glass in both hands, feeling suddenly as if there were no position that felt comfortable to him.

"As a child. I was tutored with the king and his sister. We learned to speak every major language."

"Well ... you speak well."

She turned and looked at him and her expression started to relax. "Do you ride, *Señor*?" she asked out of the blue.

"*Si* ... I *am* from Texas ... we value our horses almost as much as our pistols." He laughed and she almost laughed, but not quite.

"What sort of horse do you have?" she asked.

"My horse? His name is Jícama. He was sired by Umberto, a Spanish Arabian. So, he is half aristocrat and half mustang, I would say."

"Mustangs ... are they not wild horses?"

"Yes, princess ... wild, free, untamed."

"And does that describe Texans, *Señor*?"

He smiled and took a drink of wine. He relaxed and sat back. "*Si* ... we are a wild bunch, compared to Europeans, I suppose."

"I also ride. My horse is named Cecil. He is an English thoroughbred. I miss him when I'm away. Does that sound foolish?"

"No ... no, princess. A horse can be a good companion. No one knows that better than I." He put the wine glass on the table and took out a cigarette. "Do you smoke?" She shook her head no. "What else do you miss, princess?"

"I miss ... the Spanish wine ... and Russian *borscht* ... and the sleigh rides ..."

"Well, as far as I know, we don't have sleighs but we do have carriages. May I take you for a carriage ride ... to see the sights of Washington?"

"Did Pilar put you up to this? Did she ask you to do this?"

"*Si* ... she did. But it would give me great pleasure to be your friend ... and frankly, I could use a friend also. I, too, am a stranger who misses his home."

"What do *you* miss about Texas?"

"My daughter ... first and foremost ... but also the people. They are jewels. Beautiful inside like precious gems. Generous. Open. Also, a little rough around the edges."

Her eyes misted over and she blinked back tears. "You describe my people, too."

"Ah, another thing we have in common."

"Then, yes, I would like to take a carriage ride with you. I would like that very much."

"Would tomorrow be too soon?"

"No ... tomorrow. What is your other name, Señor Lopez?"

"I'm not sure I know what you mean."

"You must have other given names."

"I was christened Juan Miguel, if that's what you mean."

"May I call you Juan Miguel?"

"Yes, you may. And what shall I call you?"

"My friends call me Alia." She stood. He stood as well. "Thank you, Juan Miguel. I look forward to seeing you again."

"Princess ..."

As she passed by, he had the impulse to take her in his arms, but of course, he didn't.

It struck him like a howling winter storm, cutting through his body, touching every organ, whisking away every previous notion, emptying his mind of extraneous ideas, and replacing it all with a lump in his throat. He stood there with no notion at all what to do next. He stood there for what seemed like hours. Slowly, as the gale subsided, he once again saw the landscape before him. He put his fingers through the hair over his forehead and pulled it back. He adjusted his tie. He took a deep breath. He was thunderstruck.

"Princess," he repeated under his breath. "My god, she is a princess, and not just any princess ... a Spanish princess *and* a Russian princess. My god ... my god ... my god."

He went through the motions of the rest of the reception. He had the presence of mind to ask the Spanish ambassador for an appointment, which he was granted. He saw the princess, out of the corner of his eye, leave the party. When he realized she wouldn't return, he made his regrets and said good night to The Infanta.

His room at the Hamilton House seemed cheerful suddenly—not so cold—not so lonely. He lay in the lumpy, rickety bed staring at the snow falling in the lamplight outside the window. But he was seeing the princess. Did he think she loved him, too? That she fell in love with him in only the few minutes it took to have a conversation? Yes, he knew she did. He felt it in his loins.

The desk clerk scoffed when he called for her the next day at her hotel.

"I will pass the message to her bodyguards," he said with disdain.

It hadn't occurred to him that she would be traveling

with a contingent of bodyguards, but that made sense. He sat down in the lobby and balanced his hat on his knee and waited. Almost an hour passed and he was beginning to doubt himself. To doubt that he actually met a princess named Alexis. To doubt that they agreed to go for a carriage ride.

Finally, she appeared at the head of the hotel stairway dressed in a stuffy, formal looking suit with a fur stole and muff. Her hair was pinned up and she wore a woolen scarf around her head. She smiled when she spied him and it was the first time he noticed that she had dimples. She rushed down the stairs and stood before him, then stuck out her hand.

"Thank you ... thank you for waiting. It took such a long time to convince Major Garza to let me go."

"Hello, princess ... it sounds like he's very protective."

"Protective? No, he's obsessed."

"How did you convince him?"

"I told him you were a cowboy. But let's not talk about him."

He held out his arm and she took it.

The day was sunny and warmer than it had been. The snow was melting. Their carriage rolled through the dirty slush and slid over slick patches of ice. He covered her lap with a blanket that was lying on the seat. She drew close to him and leaned against his arm for warmth.

They rode past the White House, the Smithsonian, the Washington Monument. He explained each landmark to her. She asked questions. At some point, she put her hand on his. He took it and held it.

In spite of the sunshine, by mid-afternoon he was chilled and he knew she must be.

"Princess, would you like to stop in that tea shop for a warm drink?" he asked.

"No, I want to go some place more private," she said.

"Private? Such as?"

"Such as my hotel suite."

"Do you really think that that's a good idea, princess?"

"I've never had to be subtle, Juan Miguel. I don't know how."

"I see ... driver, take us back to the hotel."

The fireplace in the hotel room was too large, really, for the space. Within only minutes after he stoked it, the room was almost stifling. She closed the drapes and took off her jacket and threw it on the bed. She motioned for him to do the same.

They sat on a settee in front of the fire and she poured them both a cup of tea from a china pitcher.

"Sugar?" she said.

"No, I like the taste of the tea. Especially Bergamot. I usually grow the plants myself and make my own."

She handed him the cup. "I cannot have tea ... without thinking of that day."

"That day, princess? What day?"

"The day my husband was killed. We had stopped in a restaurant for afternoon tea."

He took a drink then put down the cup. "Tell me about that day," he said. He put his arm on the back of the settee and touched a blonde tendril that had escaped and was falling over her ear.

"I was just talking to Georgette ... and I looked up and the carriage exploded."

"And what you saw was horrible?"

She looked into his eyes and he saw the hurt. He drew closer to her and held her lightly.

"Yes ... I saw my husband ... and my father ... body parts flying through the air."

He drew closer still and held her tight. She clung to him and said no more.

"Princess?"

"Yes?"

She pushed back from him and looked into his eyes.

"Let me kiss you ... Alia ..."

She nodded. "I was so hoping you would ask."

He kissed her and he could feel himself breathing new life into her. So he kissed her again.

The princess Alexis was blonde and pink all over—and beautiful—and soft and supple like unformed clay. She bent like a new twig, her yielding presence a counterpoint to her taut body. When he stood by the bed and took off his clothes, she looked him up and down, as if his maleness was something totally new to her. "You are beautiful," she said. He blushed then lay down beside her.

And when they were through, she straddled him and kissed him, her long hair falling across his chest.

She put her hand on the scar on his cheek and asked, "Were you in love with your wife?"

"Yes, very much," he said.

"Passionately?"

"Yes, princess, passionately."

"I knew that was true. I knew you wouldn't marry someone you didn't love passionately."

"And you, Princess?"

"I must tell you something, Juan Miguel. This is the first time I've ever ... done this with a man."

He took a strand of her hair and wrapped it around his hand. "I know. I sensed that."

She lay back down next to him and snuggled close. "My husband and I had known each other since we were children. We grew up together. We were like brother and sister."

"How long were you married?"

"Three years. On our wedding night, he told me he was in love with someone else."

"Another woman?"

"No ... another man. He said he could never find me attractive. He even tried to procure another man for me ... one of his butlers ... but I refused."

"Did you love him?"

"He made me feel safe, I suppose. But love? I never

knew that until yesterday when I met you. And ... Juan Miguel, if you don't love me, it's fine. You don't have to."

He turned to her and smiled at her and looked into her eyes. "You know that I do." He put his hand on her cheek and his thumb on her lip.

For two days, they dodged the unit of bodyguards and made excuses to her other attendants. They hid around corners when The Infanta was in the hotel lobby. They went out to dinner at a Russian restaurant so she could have *borscht*, which she pronounced to be quite good. They walked in the parks. But mostly they spent time in her hotel room with the fire roaring and the wind outside wailing around the building. He continued to call her "Princess" even though she told him over and over to call her Alia. It was as if he needed to keep reminding himself of who she was.

Inevitably it had to come to an end. The Infanta's tour of the United States, Cuba, and then Canada continued and the princess had to go with her. "I could tell her I want to stay," she whispered to him on their last night together before she was to leave early the next morning.

"You know you can't do that. It would create an international incident," he said holding her next to him. "I think it will be easier if I go tonight and let you rest for the journey."

She raised her head and looked at him with alarm.

"But I'm not prepared to say goodbye. I thought I would have more time."

"Have you heard of the Great Horned Owl who lives on the steppes, princess?"

"Yes ... why?"

"The owl is a great strategist who remains patient while waiting for what he wants to come along. Then he uses all his senses and all his intelligence to capture it."

She frowned. Their conversation had become strange, all of a sudden.

"But you have captured me, Juan Miguel ... you have me."

"There are a million fences between us."

"So ... you are giving up already?"

"No, I will never give up. Do you trust me on this?"

"Yes ... I trust you. I've never trusted anyone as much."

He put on his clothes while she sat on the bed watching him. "I will find you again, princess. Nothing will stop me," he said then he walked to the door. He hesitated and looked back at her. She had a stricken, bewildered expression on her face but no tears. "I will tear down the fences, princess. I will," he said and he left.

On the train back to Texas, he allowed himself to consider the web in which he'd become ensnared. He was in love and this time, he wouldn't let her go. She needed him and he felt it in every inch of his body. But if it became public, he was bound to be recognized as the once-notorious outlaw of dime novels and Wild West shows. And if that didn't happen, he would be recognized as Juan Miguel del Valle, his real identity. The thought of never seeing Princess Alexis again was not an option but neither was having his identities revealed.

He thought about the princess traveling to Cuba with The Infanta. He should've just packed her up and brought her with him. That's what he did the first time he fell in love. But Margaret Barone was not the princess of a powerful foreign nation. Princess Alexis was. His meeting with the Spanish ambassador had opened his eyes to just how dangerous travel to Cuba could be for anyone, particularly a Spanish princess.

The ambassador had explained the unspoken American policy of stepping in the middle of conflicts in Latin American countries, so that the U.S. could maintain some sort of control, so that the real revolutionaries in Mexico and South America would never get the upper hand, which would be bad for American capitalists. The U.S. purposely walked the middle ground between royalists and rebels, forever thwarting a "real revolution," he said.

He also indicated that that was about to happen in Spanish-owned Cuba. The Spanish Crown and the American government would go to war, he predicted, effectively freezing out the Cuban rebels.

"I tell you this in confidence," he had whispered. "The U.S. is no less an imperialist nation than Spain."

Several days after he saw the ambassador, as he was about to make plans to return to Texas, he received a note from the office of Texas Congressman Joseph Bailey. The Congressman had agreed to a 15-minute appointment the next week, which Juan assumed was the result of much back-stage finagling on his part. He delayed his trip home.

The Washington snows of early December had given way to a cold blustery rain. Only his discovery of a couple of good local restaurants made staying on bearable for him after the princess left town. For days, it seemed, he sat in his room watching the rain and only ventured out to get some *huevos rancheros* at the café down the street that had a Mexican cook or to revisit the Russian restaurant for a warm bowl of *borscht*.

Finally the Wednesday of the appointment arrived. He dressed in his best clothes, those of Martin Zamora, although he no longer felt the need to call himself by that name, and walked in the rain to the corner to hail a public carriage to the Capitol.

He was in a horrid mood by the time he found the congressman's office and sat in the waiting room in damp, chilled clothing, on an errand he found distasteful.

Congressman Bailey was an overweight, blustery Democrat, who was soon to become the Minority Leader of the House of Representatives. He greeted him from behind his desk with a limp handshake and a mere nod to politeness.

"What can I do for you, Mister Lopez? South Texas

ranchers always have my support, you know that."

"It's your support of the Cuban rebellion I wish to ask about," he said.

Bailey was caught off-guard. He was rarely asked about that subject by fellow Texans. Usually it was the national press who brought up his involvement in the Cuban problem.

"As I have said, Mister Lopez, I'm not for war just for the sake of war, but there is a grave injustice that's being done down there. The Cuban people suffer under the tyrannical rule of the Spanish Crown and the northerners of the Republican Party ... the same ones who have their boot on the neck of the South ... turn a blind eye to it."

"So you are for American intervention in the Cuban struggle?"

"Why, yes, I would say I am. There's a moral stance to be taken. We should help the poor people of Cuba with our military might, don't you agree?"

"What I think about Cuba is not important, Congressman. I'm only here to gauge your opinion."

"I don't understand where your interest comes from, Mr. Lopez."

"A war with Spain might have profound consequences on many things in Texas. The economy ... the relationship with Mexico and other Central American countries."

"Well now, Mexico is a different story altogether. What's going on down there ... with the revolutionaries trying to overthrow the duly elected government of President Diaz. Well, I can't support that and no good Texan can."

"So you don't see any conflict in your view of supporting the Cuban rebels and not supporting the Mexican rebels? Are the Mexicans under President Diaz not just as oppressed as the Cubans under the Spanish Crown?"

Bailey bounded out of his chair, his round belly protruding from between his pants and his vest and his face turning scarlet. "I might'a known you were a Mexican *revolutionario*, being named Lopez and all. Your actions, sir, border on criminality ... coming here to advocate the overthrow of a foreign government. This country has laws against that."

Juan stood also. "Congressman, I'm not advocating anything ..."

But the Congressman put his fists down on the desk and leaned over menacingly. "I'll thank you to leave this office, sir ... before I call for the Sergeant at Arms to throw you out. Now, good day, sir."

He picked up his hat and walked out. There was no arguing with a man who's been caught in the web of his own hypocrisies. Bailey more or less confirmed what the Spanish Ambassador had told him, that the U.S. government would take whatever pragmatic approach to foreign affairs would further its imperialist ambitions, which meant that there would be no American support of the Mexican rebels in the foreseeable future. But more than likely, war with Spain over Cuba was imminent.

It was a troubling visit but what waited for him at his hotel was even more troubling. The door to his room was ajar when he returned and the contents of the room had been turned upside down. When he complained to the woman who ran the boarding house, she looked skeptical and asked whether anything was stolen.

"No, nothing," he said. "But the door was open."

"Perhaps you left it open yourself," she said.

She looked at him as if he was simply a chronic complainer and it occurred to him that maybe he was. However, it left him with the unsettling feeling that he was being watched and spied on. He left the next day for Texas.

CHAPTER SIX

The entrance to the villa del Valle, a stone walkway bounded by a low adobe fence leading to a double wooden door, was lined with the red poinsettias that Beatriz and Jose brought back from Mexico. In front of those were Juan and Annabelle's favorite Christmas decoration, the lit candles called *luminarias*, casting a red glow. It was like a welcome beacon he saw for more than a mile, riding through the dark cool December evening with Pedro. He rode at a slower than usual pace so he could savor the landscape he loved and had missed.

Every few minutes, he bent down and rubbed and patted Jícama on the neck. The horse reared his head in recognition.

"He has been out of sorts since you've been away,"

Pedro said more than once.

"*He* has been out of sorts?" Juan said, smiling. "Or you have been out of sorts?"

"You have been gone for a long time. That's all I'm saying."

They rode on. The soft, fragrant southern breeze blew at their backs. He pulled on the reins and stopped. Pedro did also and he looked back at his old friend, trying to discern why he stopped.

"*Que paso?* I was not complaining, *amigo*," Pedro said.

"No ... of course not. I'm at a loss ... I owe you so much."

"Is that all? You stop short of the house ... and reuniting with Annabelle ... to tell me this?"

"*Si* ... I don't know how to express ..."

"*Ai, ai, ai, poco*. Let's go. ¡*Vámonos!*." Pedro nudged his horse and rode on.

Juan yelled after him. "You are a stubborn old goat. *Comprende*?"

"And you, my friend, are as slow as a pregnant heifer."

When they rode up to the house and tied their horses to the front railing, Juan once again attempted to talk to Pedro. He put his hand on his shoulder and pulled gently. "Pedro ... I have much to tell you. And I'm going to need your help."

Pedro turned and stood in front of him, blocking his way. "Listen, my friend. I have something to tell *you* before you go in."

He got that sinking feeling he usually felt whenever he

thought Annabelle might be in jeopardy. "What ... what is it? You've been trying to tell me something since you met me at the station."

"*Si* ... Annabelle is ... well, perhaps 'changed' is the right word."

"What do you mean changed?"

"You will see for yourself, but be prepared to meet a new Annabelle."

He laughed somewhat derisively and then looked into Pedro's face. The man was dead serious.

"Just tell me."

"I think it has to do with a boy she has met. That's all I can say."

"No ... she's too young."

"She's older than you were when ..."

"*Si, si, si,*" he interrupted, "you needn't remind me. Well, then let's go see this new Annabelle."

"As for my help with your plans, you have it, *como siempre*. There is a bottle of *mescal* waiting. We can discuss it after dinner."

Inside the villa, Annabelle was not waiting by the door for her father's return, as she might've done when she was younger. She sat in the darkness in her room upstairs with only one *luminaria* candle she had taken from the porch burning on her table by the window.

She was anxious to see her father but her mind was

on something—someone—else. The *luminaria* cast strange shadows in the room, long eerie shadows, like the moonlight the night she said goodbye to Carlos. Underneath a spindly new Chinese elm tree in the plaza, the moonlight slanted through the branches at their backs. Their shadows were entwined, almost one. They sat looking at them, feeling reluctance to part, she for the rancho and he for his family home in Mexico City.

"I will see you in a few weeks," he reassured her.

She nodded and put her cheek to his.

He stood and took her hand. "You go first," he said.

"You won't walk with me?"

"If they see you with me, it will only cause you more trouble. Just walk fast and you'll be fine."

It had only been a month since they first became acquainted. Her father had kept his promise to her before he left town. He asked around and found that the *El Paso Times* was the legitimate newspaper of the city, a place where real journalists, not propagandists or *insurrectos*, worked. He used his contacts to meet the editor and asked him to give Annabelle an opportunity. "If her skills are not sufficient, then you can let her go," he said. "Just give her a chance to show what she can do."

The editor agreed to let her write three articles, one a week, during the month of November. Her last article was an interview with Carlos Cordova, the new bullfighting sensation in Juarez. With Cinco's help, she arranged to meet with him at the J&J Café on a Sunday afternoon.

He was disdainful when he walked in, acting as if he could barely tolerate her presence. He sat across from her, gazing out the window and answering most of the questions with one word or a nod. Finally, frustrated at his lack of cooperation, she closed her tablet, stuffed her pen in her bag, and stood, almost knocking the chair over in anger.

"You are no gentleman," she said. "Don't you wish to have an article about you in the newspaper?"

He smiled and looked at her as if seeing her for the first time. "So, you're not all business, then?" he said, smiling.

"What do you mean, all business? I came here to do an interview."

"Do you have to act so stuck-up? Your nose is in the air like a ... like a bull. Why don't you relax?"

"If I relax, will you answer the questions?"

"*Si* ... how about a beer?"

"Fine ... let's have a beer."

Josephina served the two hot heads a couple of beers. They seemed to relax a bit. Carlos took a few drinks, put the glass of beer down, and wiped his mouth with his sleeve. "Annabelle Palmer," he said. "You have beautiful hair."

"So do you," she said. She picked up the glass and took a few drinks, even though she hated the taste. "I have seen you fight the bulls. You're very brave."

"Ah, I remember you. We met one day at the *mercado*.

I saw you later sitting in the stands at the arena. Your hair … it was very distracting."

After a few more drinks and a few more questions, they forgot to feel self-conscious. They sat and talked for hours.

Charlotte and the nuns didn't approve of the young man who came to call on Annabelle. "He is a bit of a wild card," Charlotte told her. "Your father would not approve." But nothing deterred her from seeing him. She was smitten and he was, too.

Remembering how he looked when she glanced back at him standing in the moonlight that night, she felt a longing in her heart. His brown hair hung over his eyes, making him look much younger than he did in the bullring. She missed him already.

When she heard her father's voice downstairs, she jumped up and ran down to see him. He was, after all, the man she loved and trusted above anyone.

He was waiting at the bottom of the stairs and she nearly leapt into his arms. He lifted her and twirled her around and around the room. "Ah, *mon ami*, little one, I'm so happy to see you," he said into her ear.

"*Papá* … I love you so," she said, just as she always did when she saw him.

"I love you so too," he said, smiling down at her and holding her close.

"Did you see the tree? Beatriz and I made the decorations last night. We made the mistletoe balls like Mama used to make. Come ... see."

They had a dinner of tamales and chicken soup with *chiles*. Whatever tension Pedro predicted between Annabelle and Juan didn't materialize. Beatriz and Jose had many stories to tell about their trip to Mexico. Juan talked a bit, but not too much, about his time in Washington. Annabelle said nothing about a young man. Juan began to think it was just Pedro's imagination until the dessert dishes were cleared and he and Annabelle were left alone. Then she told him.

"He has invited me to Mexico City for New Years eve," she said, looking at her father across the dinner table for his approval.

"Annabelle, you are too young. You're not out of school."

"But you were younger when you met Mama and fell in love with her."

"First of all, there's no comparison because times have changed. Second, I had known your mother for years, since I was a child."

Tears came into her eyes—tears of anger. "I can't believe you ... you have always followed your passions. You told me many times that life is nothing without passion."

"Passion, *si, mi amor*, but not this kind of passion ..."

"How do you know what kind it is? You don't know him. Give him a chance."

Beatriz peeked her head in the door from the kitchen. She had never heard Juan Lopez and Annabelle argue before. It had just never happened.

"It is fine, Beatriz," he said. "We are just discussing ..."

"There's nothing to discuss," Annabelle said. Then she put her hand over her mouth and started to sob. She ran from the room. He followed her to the stairway, but she turned and yelled, "Let me alone, *Papá*. I want to be alone."

He followed her. She slammed the door to her room in his face. "Annabelle," he said quietly, knocking on the door. But she didn't answer and she didn't emerge for the rest of the night.

The two old friends had long faces, sitting by the fire passing a bottle of mescal between them. The mood in the house was somber.

"She's just being emotional," Juan said sitting back in the chair, looking into the fire. "Isn't she?"

"Well ... I don't know," Pedro said between drinks. "She is a woman."

"She is a girl, Pedro."

"It seems to me ..." Then Pedro hesitated, gathered his courage, and proceeded. "It seems to me that you have forgotten what you were like at her age."

"What does that have to do with it?"

"Everything ... *amigo*. Everything. She is just like you. There is almost no difference. You are the same person."

"That's not true."

"No? Well, you are a man and she is a woman. But other than that ..." and he shook his head and took a drink.

Juan took a deep breath and let it out slowly. "What, then? Just let her run wild with this ... *matador*?"

"She is in her room crying. I do not call that running wild."

"What should I do?"

"Leave her be until morning. Everybody calm down ... then, a few kind words wouldn't hurt ... maybe a little gift. Women love gifts."

"Since when did you become an expert on women?"

Pedro shrugged. "Perhaps not an expert. But I know when I've lost an argument with one ... unlike you."

"I've lost already?"

Pedro took several long drinks and passed the bottle back to Juan. "*Si* ... you have."

After Pedro left, Juan let his mind wander back to the time when he first fell in love with Margaret Barone. They had stormy times and he couldn't stand it when she cried, either. He gave her anything she wanted to make her happy. Remembering her made him smile. His love for her would never fade. It just became his love for Annabelle. The thought that he would have to let Annabelle go brought unbearable pain. He felt the tears. He put his fingers to his eyes and wiped them away. It wasn't fair to

Annabelle to cling to her, but when she left him, he would have nothing left of Margaret.

"Marguerite," he whispered. "Marguerite ... my love. I have never been able to part from you ... never. Even with someone new in my heart, I still can't let go."

The tears and the familiar wave of grief subsided. He was struck by the injustice of it. Annabelle didn't yet know about his feelings for the princess Alexis and even when she did, he doubted she would object. Ever since her mother died, she'd encouraged him to find someone new.

He was tired and his head had been throbbing since he left Washington. Maybe that's why he acted so badly, he told himself. He put his head back and went to sleep by the smoldering fire.

"I have fallen in love again and it is very real this time," he said to Pedro the next morning in the sun room off of the kitchen. They sat at a small table by the window, the winter sunshine filtering through the tree limbs, the glass, and the smoke from Pedro's pipe. Juan lifted the coffee cup to his mouth and looked over it at Pedro's expression, then took a swig. What was he expecting? Pedro never betrayed his feelings on his face. He put down the cup and continued, "She is a princess ... a Spanish princess ... so you see that complicates things."

Pedro puffed a few times, took the pipe from his mouth, and scooted up closer to the table. "No ... I do not see. Explain it to me, *poco*."

"She was widowed about a year ago. Her husband, a Spanish don, was murdered by a political activist right before her eyes. I met her at the Spanish Embassy ... we fell in love. But ..." He took a deep breath and let it out, put his hand up to his hair and ran his fingers through it. "You know the problem. I am not who I pretend to be."

"You are respectable enough. People know you as Juan Lopez."

"That is true. I will have to go plead my case to her family in private, though, get their blessing, so that there is no scandal ... no publicity."

"Who might that be?"

"The Spanish king himself. Her mother, her cousins, perhaps even the Russian tsar ... God knows."

"So you intend to marry her?"

"Yes, for the first time in many years, I want to live my life with someone else ... someone besides Annabelle."

"When will you go?"

"As soon as she returns to Spain from her tour with The Infanta Pilar. In a couple of months."

"Why do you need my help? You have thought it out. I have no doubt you will charm the whole Spanish aristocracy."

Juan smiled. Pedro was getting dangerously close to complimenting him, something he almost never did. "Now the bad news ... someone has been taking shots at me and breaking into my hotel room looking for something. At first, I thought it was coincidence but now ..."

"Any clues as to who ... or why?"

"Pedro ... I am almost sure that the jailer ... the Monterrey jailer you thought you killed ... still lives."

Pedro turned ashen. He looked genuinely startled. "That can't be. I felt for his pulse with my own hands. He was dead."

"We were in a hurry to get out of there. Who knows what happened? I met him in El Paso. He's now an army general, someone close to Diaz himself. And his name is Cordova."

"Did he recognize you?"

"I did not think so but now I don't know, but here's the strangest thing of all. He is the uncle of the young man with whom Annabelle is smitten."

Jose had slaughtered and butchered a pig weeks ago. It was a messy process best done in late fall before the cold of winter. He selected the fattest one, pierced it quickly with a lance, lassoed the feet and tied it upside down for bleeding, soaked the carcass in salt water in a wooden trough, separated the meat, and hung the pieces in the smokehouse to cure them. The ground, his clothing, every tool were covered with blood and offal. Buckets and buckets of water were needed for cleaning up.

Beatriz and Celita had spent the days before Christmas making pork and chicken tamales to distribute to the *va-*

queros and other rancho workers and their families. This, too, was best done outside. Over an open fire, they cooked the meat, then ground it, stuffed it inside corn mash and wrapped it in corn husks, then baked the tamales in a huge cast iron oven suspended from two logs over the fire. They also cut the large hams into smaller ones and the belly meat into strips and wrapped them in cheesecloth.

For the last few years, Annabelle had played the part of Joseph, approaching each home to ask for shelter, which the people of course offered with grace and humility. Juan followed with boxes of food, a satchel of money, and gifts for the children. They started making their rounds after breakfast and usually didn't finish until late in the day. After that, Juan and Annabelle had their private dinner and gift giving by the tree.

Juan and Annabelle put aside their disagreement to do the Christmas tradition they loved the most. Seeing the smiles of the people was a gift beyond measure for both of them. When they were finished, Celita was waiting for them with a bowl of soup and fresh bread to restore their energy. They sat down in the parlor by the fire, unusually quiet and careful with each other.

Juan broke the silence by reaching around behind his chair and picking up a box. He offered it to Annabelle and said, "Merry Christmas, *mi amor*, and please forgive me for my … insensitivity yesterday."

She rose, took the box, and kissed him on the cheek. "I love you so, *Papá*," she said. "But I also love Carlos."

"Let's ... talk about that subject later. Just open your present."

She nodded and opened it. It was a gilt-edged, leather covered journal much like the one he gave Margaret years ago, but this one was for writing, not for painting.

"*Gracias, Papá,*" she said. "I love it.

He put out his hand and said, "Please come sit by me, little one." She moved closer and sat at his feet with her hands on his knee, looking up into the face she adored. "I've been unfair to you, clinging to you, asking you to take the place in my heart that your mother filled and that only you can fill as she did." Tears came into her eyes as they often did when he emptied his heart to her. "I promise I will cease doing this ... but I ask this in return ... that you use your fine mind to guide your beautiful, open heart. I don't want you to suffer for your passionate nature ... as I have."

A tear spilled and rolled down her cheek. She brushed it away with her fingers and smiled at him. "You told me yourself ... many times you told me ... life is suffering as well as joy. *Papá* ... you cannot protect me all my life. You must let me go."

"Annabelle, if I saw you suffering, I don't think I could bear ..." She rose and embraced him, kissed him on his curly brown hair, and then his scarred cheek. "Now, you know how I have felt all these years watching you put yourself in danger for the sake of others."

They dried their tears with a handkerchief Juan pulled

from his pocket and continued with their gifts.

Father Ramirez was nearly eighty, and probably should've retired by this time, but he was active for a man his age. Born in Veracruz, he left that southern Mexican state when he was only seventeen to enter the Franciscan seminary in Mexico City. Most of his priesthood was spent in Chihuahua, the barren northern state that borders Texas and New Mexico. The dry air and extreme temperatures of the Chihuahuan Desert had made Father Ramirez's skin look like ancient leather. Set within the wrinkles and folds were two milky eyes, overgrown with cataracts and no longer serving him well.

Recently, Father Ramirez had taken on the tasking duties of traveling from one south Texas rancho to another to perform mass in the rancho chapels. It was a difficult job, one for a much younger man, however Father Ramirez had earned the right to choose his own placement. So that is what he chose, to be close to the common people in his last years.

Juan and Annabelle had no quarrel with the old priest. He was known to "shoot from the hip" when speaking but Juan was tolerant of that. They just didn't feel close to him as they had to other local priests such as Father Moreno and his successors. Father Ramirez made no secret of his grudge against landowners and often talked about the need for a general rebellion and redistribution of the land, political ideas he came to espouse while he worked in Chihuahua where revolt fermented and occasionally erupted.

On Christmas evening, the old priest arrived to perform mass late in the day. Juan and Annabelle put on their jackets and walked out into the calm night air when they heard him ringing the small bell that hung from a rope in the chapel.

With thousands of stars over their heads and the moon shining in a cloudless sky, the people of the rancho had gathered outside the chapel listening to a group of children sing *La Rama*. Carrying branches decorated with ribbons and shiny objects and banging on their noisemakers, they chanted the song about a tree branch, loud and sincere. The melody was lost in all the noise, but it didn't matter, their beaming faces were filled with pride.

One of the singers was a young boy, not more than six or seven, they had never seen before and who had terrible burn scars over his face and appeared to be blind. The boy stepped forward and the purest, clearest soprano voice they'd ever heard rang through the clear night air. He sang the old Castilian carole, *Brincan y Bailan*, which means "They jump and dance." The haunting melody and the story of the enthusiastic celebration of simple fishermen pierced their souls, and they stood transfixed.

Once inside, they noticed the boy sitting on the second row in the chapel, seemingly alone. "*Papá*, who is he?" Annabelle whispered. "He looks so lonely."

"I don't know, *mi amor*. I will find out."

Later that night, after Annabelle was in bed, Celita walked into the parlor with Father Ramirez trailing behind. He was giving her a long explanation on the meaning of the mass and Christmas traditions. Celita looked long-suffering as she always did.

"Father, what brings you here so late?" Juan asked, rising to meet him.

"*Pardon, Señor*, but I have been asked to deliver this to you before I return to Bandera." And he reached into his cassock and pulled out an envelope. "I hope it is not bad news, but it is marked 'Urgent.'"

Juan took the envelope, which contained a telegraph cable, and tore it open. It was from the princess Alexis, from Havana, Cuba. It said,

Juan Lopez,

We return to Spain within weeks. Please make plans to visit as soon as possible.

Princess Alexis

He wadded the cable in one hand and sat down as if he'd been hit over the head.

"Can I be of service?" asked Father Ramirez who stood by the fire, going largely unnoticed. "I am a priest after all. Why not take advantage of my ear and tell me your troubles?"

"*Pardon*, Father, please sit down."

"Bad news?" he asked, taking the chair closest to the fire.

"Not bad news, father, just impossible ... a request that

borders on the impossible."

"From a woman?"

"How did you know?"

"I've heard much over the years. I know how these things go."

"What things, father?"

The old priest chuckled and raised his cassock to warm his feet. "This is why I choose to be a priest. It's easier. Well, I leave you to figure this out alone," he said, standing to leave.

"Father, before you leave ... who is the boy who sang? The blind boy?"

"That is Michelito. I brought him with me from Chihuahua."

"What happened to him?"

"He was trapped inside his parents' house when the soldiers came to town and burned it."

"Diaz's soldiers?"

"Who else?"

"But why?"

"They dared to shelter a rebel ... the woman's younger brother."

"The parents were killed?"

"The father was killed. The mother was taken and is still being held by the soldiers."

"What was she convicted of?"

"Nothing, *Señor* ... nothing."

One last thing ... the boy's name, Michelito, that is

French, is it not?"

"I believe his name is Michel. Yes, his mother is French."

"The name Michel is French for Miguel. Isn't that right, father?"

The priest put on his hat. "Yes ... Michael, the noblest of names," he said, preparing to walk out.

"Wait, father, *por favor*, what is the sign of St. Michael? Have you heard of it?"

"It is only an old folk tale, *Señor*, to explain away birth-marks and scars."

The priest walked toward the door. Juan followed him, unable to let him go. "What was a French woman doing in the middle of Chihuahua, father?"

"A political activist, I believe. I have heard reports that she is raped by her captors almost daily because of this."

"*Ai, ai ai, padre.* Aren't there efforts to rescue her?"

"There is no way, Señor Lopez, no way."

He lay in his bed that night, with visions in his head of a woman he didn't even know being raped over and over again. Her despair became his despair. He felt every hu-miliation, every painful act. His own suffering at the hands of General Cordova rose to the surface like a rotten *chile* in a boiling cauldron. His heart raced and his stomach churned. He slept not at all.

When he wasn't thinking about the captured French woman, he was worrying about Annabelle. Before she re-tired for bed, his daughter had broached the subject of her love for Carlos once again.

"Please don't object, *Papá*," she pleaded. "You are like some unreasonable old patriarch who dispatches the *abuelas* to walk ten paces behind us as they did in the old days."

"That is not a bad idea," he teased. "But must you say 'old'? You wound me, *mon ami*."

In the end, he forbade a trip to Mexico City. It was just too dangerous.

Juan Miguel del Valle was not yet old. He was only thirty-seven, but he had lived several lifetimes and, indeed, several lives. Even now, after all that had happened to him, he felt the push-pull of conflicting ideas, of passions at cross-purposes. His daughter and her awakening to romance—the Mexican rebels and their just cause—the woman he fell in love with only weeks ago. Then there was the other matter. Either he had gotten quite mistrustful or someone really was following him.

He remembered the advice of Father Moreno, his friend from many years ago. "The victor and the vanquished are one and the same," he said. "You are either part of that or you are part of nothing." It was Father Moreno's way of telling him that inaction only makes things worse.

CHAPTER SEVEN

In mid January 1898, a sullen blanket of freezing air seeped down from the north and lay across the south Texas plain. The birds had sought refuge south of the border, so the early Sunday morning silence was striking and the sun hid behind a layer of low clouds.

Already Father Ramirez's donkey clomped up the road, burdened under the weight of the old man and his young charge, Michelito, who sang a wistful song about the cactus bush in his clear soprano voice.

Father Ramirez stopped in front of the rancho chapel, reached around to help Michelito off the donkey, and dismounted, looking around for a place to tie it up.

"Why is it so dark still?" he asked Michelito.

The little boy shrugged his shoulders.

146

The priest patted him on the head lovingly. "*Pardon*, my child, I know … it is always dark to you." Then he bent over and kissed Michelito on his hair.

Juan had awakened early that day. In truth, he had hardly slept for a week. Just for something to do, he saddled Jícama and rode out a little way to check the fences. He hoped the frigid air would clear his head and allow him to see the way forward.

He noticed Father Ramirez struggling with the donkey's reins, so he called out to him. "Father Ramirez, let me help you." And he pointed Jícama in that direction.

Juan slid off of Jícama and took hold of the donkey to tie it to a nearby limb. Father Ramirez had just opened his mouth to say something, when the sharp, sure sound of a rifle shot sliced through the quiet. Father Ramirez slumped then fell onto the hard cold dirt.

Juan grabbed Michelito, swept him up into his arms, and ducked behind the north wall of the chapel. He pulled a pistol from his inside pocket and waited and watched. Only silence ensued.

Pedro and the other *vaqueros* came running and they searched the rancho in every direction but they found no one. By the time they carried Father Ramirez inside and laid him out on the floor by the door, he was dead.

Michelito cowered sobbing in the corner, the trauma of losing his friend, the priest, adding to his other unbearable sorrows. Annabelle rushed into the room, held the little boy, and tried to comfort him.

Juan looked up from the priest's dead body to Pedro. "Put out sentries," he said. "Now I know someone is out to kill me and I fear he will kill anyone else who gets in the way."

Once the turmoil of what happened that morning subsided, Juan and Pedro sat down by the fire in the parlor to talk it over.

"Who sent him, *poco*?" Pedro asked, leaning over with his elbows on his knees, tossing a match into the fire.

"It ... could be several people. General Cordova, President Diaz's henchmen, American spies working on behalf of the Mexican government ... I just don't know yet."

Juan felt himself shaking inside, in fear not so much for himself as for Annabelle and Michelito and the other innocent people around him. "Pedro, I know what has to be done and it isn't going to be easy." He sat back in the chair and sighed heavily. "I have to send Annabelle away. Not to El Paso, but far, far away. Europe possibly."

"*Si* ... that is what I was thinking."

"She will think it is to keep her away from this Carlos fellow. But that is only a small part of it."

"I know ... *comprende*. Do you want me to take her ... escort her to safety?"

"*Si ... gracias, gracias*." His eyes filled with tears as he laid his head back and stared into the fire. "And the boy can stay here with Jose and Beatriz."

"Where do you wish us to go?"

"Madrid, I think ... I have friends there."

Pedro rose and patted him on the arm. "Annabelle is secure. As long as I have breath in my body ..." He walked out and left his old friend alone to mourn Annabelle's departure.

That day, Jose traveled to Bandera to send a cable from Juan to Princess Alexis, who was still in Cuba. He would be unable to meet her right away, it said. The cable ended this way: *I have a great favor to ask; will send by letter.*

It was an imposition but he needed her assistance. He sat down to write a letter to the princess, in care of The Infanta, asking her to meet Annabelle once she was back in Madrid, befriend her, and help her get settled. Perhaps in the back of his mind, it was a test of sorts. A test of her strength and willingness. A test of her character. A test of her love.

Despite the brewing rebellion in Cuba and the chilly January weather, the people of Havana turned out to welcome the Spanish Infanta and her entourage with a parade and program. The princess unwittingly wore a blue and gold gown, the colors of the Cuban rebel flag, but it only seemed to endear her to them. She rode through the streets in an open coach pulled by four white Spanish Arabians followed by a band playing Cuban music. The Infanta was in her element. She loved a good party and many young men around to admire her.

With her was Princes Alexis, who found the day tedious. Every minute, her thoughts were on the man she loved. She felt almost sick with her yearning for him and besides that, she had no idea when she would be with him again. She went through the motions of the parade, the reception, the dinner, the special entertainment, and finally, begged The Infanta to excuse her.

The next morning, Pilar appeared at her door with a cup of tea to check on her. "Why go to your room and sulk when you are here to represent the king, your country?" The Infanta asked, sitting on the princess's bed in a familiar manner that was unusual for her.

"Pilar ... I am in love with Juan Lopez."

"I know ... did you think I did not know? Ha, everybody knows. Everybody in our entourage, that is. I hope word has not gotten back to Spain. That would be trouble for you."

"We intend to marry. It is a serious relationship."

The Infanta doubled over with laughter. She howled at the idea, then when she'd calmed down, she reached over and patted Alexis on the leg. "No, no, no, my sweet Alia ... no, no, no. He is beautiful ... someone to enjoy ... take to your bed if you want. But to marry? No, no, no."

"But why? He is from a prominent Spanish family in Texas. He's not a nobody."

"It doesn't matter, *mon ami*, it doesn't matter. The king's mother, the queen consort, is a racist, as most royals are. Everybody knows she is. She hates Jews ... she professes to hate anyone who isn't Spanish, even though she is Austrian. She even commands everyone to speak Spanish ... even members of her family who speak nothing but English, French, and German have to suddenly pretend to speak Spanish."

"I think she could be reasoned with ..."

"No, no, no ... she will not see him the way you do. To her, Señor Lopez is nothing but a Mexican, the lowest of the low in his own country. Besides, you are a widow. No doubt, she's plotting to marry you off, make a good, advantageous match. Not just for you, but for Spanish politics."

"But if she could meet him. He is intelligent and charming ..."

"*Si*, all the more reason to be with him, but no, my sweet Alia, even to mention marriage with him would put you in grave disfavor with the king's mother. No, no, no, you must not pursue this. Promise me that you won't."

The princess Alexis looked stricken but also convinced. The Infanta's arguments rang true with her. The queen consort was a narrow-minded woman. She knew that. She'd known her since she was a baby. Tears came into her eyes and she lay back against the pillows.

"I also came to tell you that our journey has been cut short," The Infanta said. "We must return to Europe and we leave as soon as the next German steamer puts into port in Havana. It will take us to New York and from there, we must board a ship and cross the Atlantic as soon as possible."

"But why? I thought we were to remain in America for several more months."

"The ambassador in Washington cabled me. Relations between Spain and America are heading to war. The people who want war ... and there are many ... have all the advantages, so it will happen. For our own safety, we must go home."

Annabelle bore the news without complaint, looking stoic, saying nothing. He explained the danger not only to her, but also to Michelito. "It is nothing to do with Carlos ... well, almost nothing."

"I will do as you ask, *Papá*," she said. "How long must I stay there?"

"As soon as I have resolved the situation, you may go back to El Paso and resume your schooling. If this Carlos loves you, he will wait. I promise, Annabelle. I promise."

He watched the wagon receding down the rancho road with Pedro riding behind it, on the way to the train station in San Antonio. He turned to Beatriz and said, "Before we bury the priest, I want you to strip off his cassock and clean it as best you can. I'm going to need it."

He would do many things but walking across the Chihuahuan Desert of West Texas was not one of them. However unlikely it would seem for a lowly monk, he would ride on Jícama and use Father Ramirez's donkey as a pack mule.

The sun was going down behind the far mesas, backlighting a crowded stand of agave, their tall thin flower stalks shooting straight up into a lavender sky. The evening cold was brutal. Wrapped in two layers of clothing covered by Father Ramirez's Franciscan cassock of heavy wool still left him frozen. He stopped and built a fire of dead creosote bushes, which quickly burnt red hot but had to be fed with new ones every few minutes. He looked around for something—anything—that would burn more slowly. Nearby were some mesquite limbs blown up against an old barrel. "Aha," he said, "God provides." He gathered up limbs and stacked them near the fire then started to tear apart the wooden barrel. When he had enough wood to last the night, he sat down to cook his bacon wrapped around a stick and munch on a dried biscuit.

He had waited until he was sure that Annabelle and Pedro were safely on board the ocean liner, bound for Cuba then Europe. He also received a letter from Princess Alexis telling him that she was returning to Europe as soon as possible.

Now, he sat alone, miles from anyone, in the desert. Or at least he had thought he was alone. He could see a rider in the distance, catching the last glow of the already set sun. It appeared to be a man with a tall hat riding on a large grey spotted horse. He was headed straight for the campfire. "He wishes to take advantage of my fire building abilities, Jícama," he said. "Should I let him?" He reached over and took his pistol out of his saddlebag and tucked it away underneath his cassock.

The man rode up with obvious caution, sat looking down at the monk by a small fire in the middle of nowhere, and asked, "Where you headed, father?"

Juan stood and folded his arms, one of them inside the cassock. "I am on my way to the mission south of El Paso. And you?"

The man dismounted and threw the reins over a nearby bush. He walked up to Juan, into the firelight, and put up his hands to show good faith. "I ain't lookin' for trouble, father. Jes' some warmth ... maybe some company."

"You are welcome to share the fire ... and the food."

Sitting across the fire from each other, passing a bottle of whiskey the man offered up, the two men looked at each other with suspicion. "What is your name, father?" the man asked.

"I am Father Estéban from Chihuahua," Juan said, reaching for a name out of thin air. "I am on my way home by way of El Paso del Norte. And you are?"

"Name's Hendrick. Matt Hendrick."

"And what are you doing out here, Señor Hendrick?"

"On the lookout for ..." He hesitated, took a drink of

liquor, looked Juan in the eyes, and continued. "For *bandidos ... insurrectos ...* bad guys."

"For whom do you work?"

"For Mr. Pinkerton hisself. It's jes' a job, far as I'm concerned."

"And who does Mr. Pinkerton work for?"

The man looked surprised that a priest would ask such a probing question. Juan could see the suspicion growing behind his eyes. "Mr. Pinkerton? He contracts with a whole lot of people ... has many clients."

"And in this case," Juan said, his hand gripping the pistol, his finger feeling for the trigger. "Which one is it?"

The man put the whiskey bottle down and put his hand on the rifle butt by his side. His eyes darted from side to side. His cheek muscles twitched. "What is it to you, father?" he said.

Before he could blink one more time, the priest produced a pistol and pointed it at him.

"Which one is it?" Juan said, smiling.

The man started to pick up the rifle, but Juan shot the rifle butt and moved it just out of his reach. The man put his hands up again.

"Just tell me and all will be well," Juan said, smiling.

"Someone in Washington ... that's all I know." He raised his hands even higher.

"In Washington? Or in Mexico City?"

"Washington ... I swear."

"You swear? You sound like a man who protests a little

too strongly, my friend."

"Someone in Washington. Now, who he works for is somethin' else."

"Ah, *si*, that is how it always is. 'Who he works for is something else.' I want you to get on your horse and ride north and don't look back. If I see you turn, I will shoot you off your horse with your rifle. *Comprende?*"

The man did as he was told. But when he had ridden out beyond the agave, he jumped from his horse, ducked behind one, drew a pistol, and shot at Juan, hitting the ground close to the fire. When he emerged again to take another shot, he was picked off by his own rifle, shot between the eyes and killed instantly.

Juan rode up to where the man lay dead, his head exploded by the rifle shot. "He has been following Juan Lopez for weeks," he said to Jícama. "But it took Father Estéban to reel him in for a closer look. At last, we are rid of him, but we are not rid of the man who hired him ... whoever that is."

By the time he rode into El Paso, his beard was grown out, covering the scars on his cheek. His curly light locks had grown long. One might have said he looked like Jesus, the man himself.

It was almost twenty years ago that he first impersonated a priest to catch a horse thief in San Antonio. He had spent the last few days as he rode through the desert remembering the mannerisms, the speech pattern, the unique way of walking of a priest. He was ready now to be Father Estéban.

He rode up to a small hotel off the main street and rented a room on the second floor with a view of the saloons along San Antonio and El Paso streets. He pulled a chair to the window and sat down, rifle in his lap, waiting. Hours later, he saw Father Romo enter the Opal Saloon. Then the editor Alberto Salazar entered. Then several other men he recognized from the meeting of *insurrectos*. He waited. He watched. He waited. About an hour later, a man emerged from the whorehouse opposite the Opal and walked across the street, looking both ways and in all directions. "He looks a little furtive for my taste," Juan said to himself. "I should see what he is up to."

Father Estéban retrieved his donkey from the stable behind the hotel and led it out into El Paso Street across from the Opal. He stopped and rearranged the items in one of the packs, all the while watching the man lurking outside the saloon windows out of the corner of his eye. When the man walked away, he followed at a safe distance. It was the middle of the day and the traffic conspired against him. He lost sight of the man on San Francisco Street. So, he backtracked to the whorehouse, tied up the donkey, and walked in.

He squinted to see what was before him in the dark parlor. Heavy cologne and a pungent odor he was loath to identify lingered in the oppressive smoky air. His eyes began to adjust and he saw a row of women in various stages of undress leaning against the far wall. An older, more portly woman sitting in a chair by the door asked, "What can I do for you, father?" Her words were slurred and almost lost in the loud banjo music coming from the back room.

One of the scantily dressed women sauntered up to him and looked him up and down in a most embarrassing manner. "Too bad you're a priest," she said. She attempted to lure him with a strange, almost comical look on her face. The portly woman pulled her roughly and pushed her back to the wall.

"I would like to ask about the man who just left," he said, "the one with the black mustache."

"We don't talk about our clients, mister. 'Client privilege' we call it."

He reached in his pocket and pulled out several folded bills. He peeled one off and handed it to her. "I will pay for information," he said.

She pursed her dark red lips and took the bill but said nothing.

"What is the man's name?"

"Name's Scott. Wendell Scott."

"Where from?"

"Up north ... an easterner, I'd say."

"Where does he stay?"

The woman said nothing. He peeled off another bill and handed it to her. "Stays at the hotel down the street on the corner when he's in town."

"Anything else?"

Again, she said nothing. He peeled off another bill. "Usually eats dinner at the J&J ... almost every night."

He uttered "*Gracias*, madam," then hastened out the door before he was overcome by the sight and smell of the place.

That evening, he waited outside the J&J in the cold night air until almost midnight. Finally, the man walked out and got into a nearby buggy. He mounted Jícama and followed him down the streets of El Paso and out of town, south to the river.

Passing clouds raced across the moon, making it difficult to keep sight of the man he followed and discern his surroundings at the same time. Gradually, the road started to seem familiar. The clouds parted, the almost full moon shone, and he could see the Santa Clara winery looming in the distance.

He hid behind a small outbuilding and watched the man ride up to the house of his friend, Francisco Diablo, and go in the front door. Then two officers of the Mexican *rurales* in long blue coats appeared and went in the door. Last and most surprisingly, a priest in the black robe and pink sash of a monsignor, accompanied by two lesser priests, went inside. He felt confident that the meeting was meant to be secret. It was almost 2 o'clock in the morning when the last person had departed.

Father Estéban sat against the wall shivering in the

cold, smoking his last cigarette as he watched them ride away. Some of them went north to El Paso and some went south to Juarez.

He put out the cigarette in the damp earth with his heel and stood to untie Jícama. "I have had enough of spying in the cold," he said to the horse. "And so have you, I would wager. It's time to approach this problem from a different angle."

Waiting for the meeting to break up, he had had plenty of time to think. His best guess was that it was a group of counterrevolutionaries whose fortunes would suffer from a change in power. There was only one way to confirm it. He would have to ask Señor Diablo himself.

But before confronting Señor Diablo, the sleepy, tired Father Estéban had one important stop to make, the back room of the Opal Saloon.

"Juan Lopez sends his regards," he said to the group that Father Romo assembled. "He returned to his rancho in south Texas a month ago, to spend Christmas and the new year with his family."

They looked at him with suspicion as he stood before them as Father Estéban. What aided him more than anything, though, was the dark room, lit only by an oil lamp in the corner.

"Juan Lopez asked me to report what he found out in Washington. War with Spain is imminent and the American government will continue to take the side of the Diaz government in Mexico City. Beyond that, he found out very little."

One of them sat forward and opened his mouth to ask a question, but Father Estéban cut him short. "*Señores*, there is a conspiracy against you ... and I think you knew that. It is, shall we say, the highest of the high ... of government, the military, even the church. So you sent the unsuspecting Juan Lopez to Washington for what? To smoke them out? Because if that is true, you have put an innocent man in jeopardy. Well ... what do you have to say for yourselves?"

Father Romo spoke up first. "We might have needed Señor Lopez as a decoy ... but he was never in danger as far as we knew."

"Hmm ... a decoy. You must explain this to me. I know much too much for you not to trust me, *comprende?*"

"Sit down, Father Estéban, sit down."

When he was seated, Father Romo looked around the room at the others and proceeded. "They are a cabal composed of *cientificos* ... rich creoles in Mexico City, *hacienda* owners, American capitalists, and the Catholic political party, both in Mexico and in Washington. They thrive off of the slave labor of the poor *Indios*, treat them with no respect and pay them almost nothing."

The intensity in Father Estéban's eyes shone in the lamplight. "Go on, father."

"The military ... Diaz's military makes all of this possible. They persecute, they maim, they kill, they intimidate ... all in the name of religion and order but really to keep the *paisanos* in line. It is in the interest of all of them that Diaz stay in power and they will do whatever it takes to make sure that happens."

"And is General Cordova one of those who supports this cabal?"

"General Cordova? Why do you bring up his name?"

"Personal reasons, father. Is he a supporter or not?"

"If he is close to Diaz, then he is a supporter. Otherwise, he would be dead by now."

"You fight a formidable enemy, *amigos*, you have my sympathies," Father Estéban said, picking up his hat and putting it on his head. "*Gracias*." He started to walk out but Father Romo stopped him.

"Father Estéban ... what do you think we should do?" the priest asked.

"Oh, father, I never divulge my thoughts. Spilling information is your *forte*, not mine."

Juan Lopez was a bit too exotic for El Paso society but not exotic enough for Juan's new purposes. He needed the help of an old friend, Martin Zamora. Foreseeing that possibility, he had packed Señor Zamora's necessities, his *artículos de primera necesidad*, on the mule that he had led all the way across the desert from south Texas. In his hotel room, he unbound the packs, took out the suits, the ties, the jewelry. He trimmed the beard. He pulled back the hair.

"*Buenas Dias*, Señor Zamora," he said to the reflection in the mirror. "First things first. Back to a decent hotel—the St. Charles—and then the best meal money can buy in this town." The image smiled back at him, threw a wad of money on the bed, and descended the back stair.

It would be the biggest test of acting ability that he had undertaken so far. It required different clothing, to be sure, richer fabrics, gold jewelry, the finest leathers. But he would also have to change his accent, his mannerisms, his speech pattern, and his outlook on life. Not to mention the lighter skin tone and the trimmed beard and spectacles to shield his eyes. He even gave himself a manicure in the European style.

He looked forward to the challenge of fooling Francisco Diablo. He was up to it. He'd had weeks to plan and think about it. He had known this time would come and he had suspected it would be with Señor Diablo. The man was just a little too accommodating and ingratiating that evening in July and he pushed Juan Lopez a little too hard to drink enough wine to loosen his tongue about his political views.

He was feeling the loss of sleep, it is true, but he was ready. He sat on Jícama outside the winery gate and prepared himself in every possible way then rode up to the house.

An old *abuela* of a housemaid showed him into the

parlor, which looked out on the patio. The fountain was off and the potted plants were pushed up against the east wall to catch the morning sun. Leaves from a nearby elm tree piled here and there, hiding in corners and around table legs. It was a bright, stark day—cool, still, not unpleasant for late January.

Señor Diablo walked into the room and only glanced at him before sitting down behind an ornate desk by the window. "Señor Zamora ... please sit down," he said, gesturing with his hand and shuffling papers at the same time. "I see from your letter of introduction that you know General Cordova?"

"*Si* ... we have met ... but I don't know him well." Martin Zamora had an accent seldom heard in west Texas, a bit Italian, perhaps a tad French. Señor Diablo looked up at him, surprised at his way of speaking. "Where are you from, Señor Zamora?"

"Oh, many places, *Señor*. I am a traveler ... a man of the world, so they say."

"What can I do for you this morning?"

"As the letter mentioned, I am an investment capitalist. I look for opportunities to make a profit. Señor Cordova has recommended the company in which the two of you share an interest ... I believe it has an American name, which escapes me at the moment."

"Concordium?"

"*Si* ... that is it."

"He suggested you invest in the silver mines?"

"To add to my portfolio ... to diversify my investments."

"What would be the advantage to us? To the other investors?"

"Well, an influx of money, of course ... a great deal of money. For further exploration, better equipment, more laborers."

"It is a private company, *Señor*. We do not sell stock."

"*Si*, I understand, but perhaps a part ownership, a small percentage."

Señor Diablo sat back in his chair and eyed Señor Zamora more carefully than he had until that moment. He looked to see whether the man was as well-heeled as he claimed. If so, he could be a good source of money.

Señor Zamora felt a lull in the conversation, which he always found dangerous when portraying someone else. He decided to make small talk to take Señor Diablo's mind off of his persona. So he asked about the patio fountain, the grape harvest, the process of making wine until finally, Señor Diablo became impatient and looked as if he might stand and cut the appointment short. "Do you have the time, Señor Zamora?" he asked.

"*Si* ... of course." Señor Zamora reached in his vest pocket and pulled out his watch. He cupped it with his hand and opened it then stuffed it back in. "It is 10:45, *Señor.*"

When he looked up, Señor Diablo was ashen. He looked stupefied. He mumbled something about having another appointment and left the room, at which point the maid showed Señor Zamora to the door.

It had been a failure. Not his portrayal. That had gone well. But something spooked the man and made him flee before the conversation was over. Señor Zamora felt panicky riding back to town. He rode not so fast as to arouse suspicion, but not too slow either. Something was wrong. Something was horribly wrong.

"Either the man is a fraud ... or," said Diablo, who hesitated a moment then sat down. "Or he is actually Juan Lopez."

"That is ridiculous," the monsignor said. "No one changes identities like they change their coat. Perhaps they have the same watch."

"No, it is a rare and expensive watch. It's too much of a coincidence. Either they are friends and the watch passed hands ... or, *mi Dios*, they are the same man."

"To what purpose?" The monsignor sat in the same chair where Señor Zamora had sat that morning and looked out at the late morning sun shining on the cobblestones. "He is a double agent ... of whom? The *insurrectos*? But why? He is a successful rancher. What reason would he have?"

"What difference does it make what his reasons are? His snooping could lead to trouble ... upset our plans ... reveal the silver trafficking."

"What do you propose?"

"Remove him from the scene. A murder would be too messy. And ... he might draw a handsome ransom ... who knows?"

Juan Lopez felt uneasy but not as uneasy as he should have felt. He tried to convince himself that all was not lost, that Diablo was simply a suspicious man. He proceeded to his next step, which was a meeting with Charlotte Borden. He had arranged for Juan Lopez to meet her in the St. Charles hotel restaurant to find out what she knew about the secret cabal and the Concordium Company but also to talk about Annabelle.

The hotel restaurant was packed with people who just arrived by train. Five different railroads ran passenger trains through the small city and sometimes it seemed they all converged at once. Juan sat back and sipped a glass of wine, craned his neck to see over the heads of the chattering crowd, and then felt the impatience of waiting for someone who was late. He took out his watch.

Before he even opened it, he knew. A wave of anxiety went through him. It was the watch that gave him away. How could he have been so careless? He thought he had gone over every detail but he ignored a basic, the individuality of jewelry. He took another sip of wine, took a deep breath, as his impatience grew to near panic.

Charlotte touched him on the shoulder from behind and he jolted forward, and stood to greet her.

Once they were seated, he put his hand on hers and leaned toward her. "Please forgive me, *Señora*, for foregoing lunch but I must be very swift in what I say to you."

A look of concern came on her face. She nodded.

"I ... must disappear for awhile and I cannot tell you why."

"Disappear? But why?"

"Just listen, *Señora*. When I am gone, I ask you to contact Pedro Garcia on the steamer *Wohlwollen* and tell him to proceed to Europe. Tell him I will be in touch, that I am safe, and that I will be gone for ... perhaps months."

"Pedro Garcia ... who is he?"

"Please, my friend... just do this. I need your friendship now more than ever."

"Of course. I will cable him right away."

"Remember the name ... Pedro Garcia. Make sure no one else knows about the cable. Not even Lyle ... *comprende*?"

"I will ..."

"Now, I must go," he said, standing. "Please stay seated until I am gone." And he disappeared into the crowd.

He tossed the packs of expensive clothing and jewelry onto a burning pile of garbage on the outskirts of Juarez and rode south on Jícama. He had only the clothes on his back, the worn Franciscan cassock of Father Ramirez over an old coat, the lining stuffed with a small amount of U.S. currency. He was entering a hostile place with virtually nothing except his wits and his skills.

Part II

Chapter One

The week before Juan Lopez arrived in El Paso disguised as a Franciscan, newspaper headlines across the nation screamed the sensational news that a letter written by the Spanish ambassador—the same man that he had visited in Washington—was seized by Cuban rebels and exposed to the public. In the letter, the ambassador made fun of the American President William McKinley, calling him weak and indecisive. The insulting letter became an international scandal and ramped up public opinion against Spain and for war.

The very day Juan Lopez disappeared, February 15, the U.S. battleship *Maine* exploded and sank in Havana harbor. The next day, newspaper editors across the nation called for the U.S. to intervene in the Cuban struggle for independence from Spain. With cries of "Remember the Maine," war fever spread quickly and it was obvious to everyone that war with Spain was inevitable.

Even in as remote a place as El Paso, American citizens rallied for war and against the faraway, unknown Spanish Empire. The McGinty Band members hauled their cannon up a nearby foothill of the Franklin Mountains and fired it off several times, just to show their patriotism.

Pedro and Annabelle arrived in Havana shortly after the sinking of the *Maine*, but they had no trouble booking passage to New York where they boarded the *SS Campania*, an ocean liner of the British Cunard Line, bound for Europe. They didn't know until two days into the voyage that the princess Alexis was also on board.

The Campania was a well-appointed ship with trappings of the British upper class in the first-class staterooms and public rooms. It was a level of comfort that Pedro Garcia was unused to, although Annabelle had been on several voyages on luxurious liners with her father. Pedro spent his time sitting on a deck chair, staring at the rolling sea, keeping his charge in sight, and left the socializing to Annabelle.

She first noticed the princess one morning on the promenade deck, surrounded by four Spanish military officers making a fuss over her. They seemed to cater to her every whim and she flirted with them—not serious flirting, just demure looks and winsome smiles. Still, it was something Annabelle had seldom witnessed. She was from the southern United States, a place that was no stranger to feminine wiles, but in this instance, the imbalance was quite striking. As she watched, Annabelle viewed it with repugnance. She didn't approve of a woman using her beauty in such a way.

At dinner that evening, she pointed out the princess to Pedro and wondered who she was.

"That should be easy to find out," he said.

Being the straight forward sort that he was, Pedro asked one of the ship's officers. When he learned her name, and he realized she was the woman his friend fancied, he hesitated to repeat it to Annabelle. In the end, he couldn't deny her anything, even a scrap of information.

"Her name is Princess Alexis of Spain," Pedro said as they sat inside looking out the windows at a cold, breezy day. "She is someone your father knows ... he met in Washington."

"He knows her?"

"*Si* ... quite well."

Annabelle turned her head and looked at Pedro's face. The jaw muscle below his ear was twitching, and his brow was furrowed. "What do you mean, Pedro?"

"I mean they have had a ..."

"A what? What have they had?" Her voice sounded harsh and high-pitched. Her heart was racing.

"They have been together ... socially. They have been together socially."

"Are you saying they have been intimate?"

"I must let your father tell you about it later. For now, I would not advise making an enemy of her."

Annabelle stood and pulled her scarf up over her hair then reached inside her purse and pulled out a pair of white kid gloves and put them on. She walked out the door onto the deck to get some air.

Chapter Two

The snow was several feet deep in places along the isolated mountain pass high up in the Sierra Madres. He used snowshoes to make part of the climb and he carried a backpack. The effort to ascend the steep walls of the canyons and cliffs and carry a heavy pack kept him sweating in spite of the below-freezing temperature.

"You are *loco* to go up there at this time of year," the guide told him before they started out from San Bernardo, a small town nestled among the foothills. "No one is up there except *bandidos ... cabrones*." But when he offered American dollars, he relented. "I will take you but if you cannot keep up, then you are on your own," he said.

"I will keep that in mind," he said, although he knew the man's reputation as a mountain guide would be ruined if he were to abandon a client on the mountain in the middle of winter.

The man spoke in the strange accent of the mountain people, almost devoid of the hard sounds of some consonants. Although Spanish was his native tongue, at first he struggled to understand him. After a few days, he understood him all too well.

"They call me Panchito ... but I don't know what my real name is," the man said, giving a running commentary of his life as they climbed. "My mother died before I could talk and my father ... well, he was a *tonto*, a no-good, you see. My auntie sold me into the mines as soon as I could lift but I escaped as soon as I could run away. Many die in those mines without seeing the light of day. I was not going to be one of them."

He stopped and adjusted his own pack and then his client's pack, both of which were tilting from the sideways slope of the path. "In my village, a man had three choices—be a priest, be a mine worker, or be a *bandido*. To be a priest ... well, I'm just not the type. I hated the mines and *bandidos* die very young ... so I had to think of something else. It came to me ... hit me over the head like a falling boulder ... one day when I was helping a man carry his lode up the mountain trail. I am fit. I can climb well. I can find my way. So ... here I am."

Panchito was a small, wiry fellow who had not an ounce of fat on him. He must have had a roaring furnace inside because he wore only light clothing and never seemed to be cold. But he had good boots, he always made sure of that, because without good boots a man could die. He had a shock of gray hair sticking out in all directions and a scraggly beard and almost no teeth. Perched on top of his hair was a brand new straw hat several sizes too small. He had the laughing, joyful eyes of the truly free.

"I fell in love right away … as soon as I started to make money. I married my Chiquita when I was only fifteen and she is still mine. We have stayed together … all these years. Want to know the secret? We hardly ever see each other." He put his head back and howled with laughter. Then he coughed and sputtered and put a handkerchief to his mouth and spit into it. "When we do … *ai, ai, ai* … is hot, *caliente*."

"You're a lucky man," his client said. "Lucky indeed."

"So you, *amigo*, do you have a lover, a wife?"

"*Si* … far, far away, over the ocean in a foreign land. I miss her terribly."

"Is she … beautiful, comely … shapely?"

"*Si* … beautiful, comely … shapely. All of that and more."

"So, what are you doing here, then, so far away from her?"

"I have some business to take care of …"

"Some might say you are on the run … is that so?"

"On the run, *si* … but not from the law. From some selfish, corrupt people who want me dead." He surprised himself. He hadn't been inclined to talk freely with anyone since he left Texas.

"Why are you climbing this mountain, then?"

"Ah, that I cannot tell you."

"Well, *Señor*, you come at the worst time of year. Any other time would be better. And this year, we have more snow than usual. Bad for you."

They reached a summit of sorts and went over it. On the other side, they saw pine and oak forests stretching for miles—perhaps a hundred miles. "Ah ... we have reached the top without you falling off the side of the mountain," Panchito said. "Once you fall ... well, that is it. The snow is too deep, the walls are too steep. You are lost forever."

A shudder went through his body when he realized that he had been in real danger for miles. He took a deep breath, adjusted the heavy weight on his shoulders, and took a cigarette out of his shirt pocket. He lit it and rested his foot on a nearby rock. "So ... the way down will be easier and safer then?"

"What way down? We will walk among the mountain tops for awhile to reach the valley. So ... watch your feet. Don't slip."

"I'll make note of that, *Señor*," he said, smiling and taking a long drag from the cigarette.

"And put out the smoke, *amigo*. You will need all the air you can get up here," Panchito scolded, so he put out the cigarette on a nearby tree trunk.

Panchito heaved his pack to one side and rested it on the ground. "We rest a short time ... and eat a small amount. Not too much. Can make you sick up here."

By the end of the day, they had walked along narrow, almost non-existent trails on the sides of the mountains. At some points, he could see lush tropical jungles far, far down below them and up above, snow still falling on the tallest peaks.

They slept in a cave-like dwelling with a log front set into the side of a mountain. In a pit in the middle of the floor, Panchito built a fire, which ventilated through a small hole between the overhanging rock and the wood wall. It became stifling in the night and he had to take off his shirt to stand it. But it was preferable to the freezing temperature outside the cave, so he didn't complain.

The next morning, they washed their faces and upper bodies in ice cold spring water trickling down the rocks next to the dwelling. They cupped their hands and sipped the sweet, pure water, which almost made up for the horrible dry tortillas fried in grease, the only food they had left.

Panchito had been unusually silent since he woke up that morning. Finally, after they ate and put away their gear, he spoke. "I must part company with you before we reach the valley," he said, looking chagrined. "I don't want to see these men who live up there. They are bad *hombres, amigo.* You can turn back and return with me if you wish to. I will not hold it against you."

"No … I must go on," he said, picking up his pack. "I have no choice."

"You always have a choice, *Señor*. If someone should come looking for you and you have not returned after ... say, weeks, who would they be looking for? What is your name?"

"I see ... in case I get killed up there. My name is Juan Miguel del Valle. Don't divulge it unless you know I am dead. *Comprende*?"

"*Si, comprende.* Another thing ... the *Tarahumara* ... the *Indios* ... they can be trusted to help you."

"Where will I find these Indians?"

"They are all around ... they have been watching and following us for days."

He looked around for them. Panchito laughed. "You will never see them unless they want you to or unless you let them know that you need them."

"How would I let them know?"

"Do this," he said and he put his hands to his mouth and made a vibrating, keening sound with his voice. "Go on, try it."

After a few tries, he had it down.

"... '*ueno*," Panchito said. "... '*ecuer'e*. Do not forget it, whatever you do."

As they parted, Panchito couldn't resist one last piece of advice, "Remember, *amigo*, if you live in a pigsty, you will get dirty." He turned and waved and was off, back down the trail.

It was a foregone conclusion that the two nations would declare war. It was just a matter of when the formalities were over and the hostilities would begin. The *SS Campania* took a northern sea route and was never in danger, however the two Americans felt uneasy about entering a country hostile to their own. In fact, the question arose whether they would even be permitted to enter Spain at all once the war began.

The day before they were to reach port in Ireland, Annabelle decided to introduce herself to the princess Alexis. She found her on one of the upper decks, wrapped in several layers of coats and scarves against the cold north Atlantic gales. The ship had encountered the leading edge of a storm system that morning and the sea roughened and the wind gusted. The princess looked lost in thought and a bit queasy from the rolling motion. She stood by the railing then walked a bit, then stood by the railing again. The deck was high enough to protect passengers from the sea spray but a fine mist was beginning to fall.

Annabelle walked up and put her hands on the rail only inches from the princess's and looked out at the thick clouds hanging over the ice blue sea. "I wish to introduce myself," she said. "I am Annabelle Palmer, the daughter of Juan Lopez."

"I know ... it has been pointed out to me," the princess said, her voice sounding strangely distant and unruffled. "The Infanta ... she told me. She is aware of who you are."

"I suppose we should try to get to know each other ... be friends, if possible," Annabelle said, casting a glance sideways to catch the princess's reaction. The two women gripped the rail as the ship pitched leeward and knocked them back.

"*Si* ... let us try to be friends. Shall we have tea later today ... in the drawing room?"

Annabelle left her standing there, and wondered whether she was intent on riding out a storm on deck or whether she might have been seasick.

Later that day, she went to tea with the princess in the ship's drawing room, which was designed as a gathering place for women in particular. It had sumptuous mahogany paneling and a functional fireplace making the atmosphere close and slightly smoky and warm enough to be uncomfortable.

The princess looked pale and appeared to still be a bit queasy. Sitting next to each other on a velvet sofa, the two women attempted polite conversation, and when that didn't work, they somehow got to the subject of the impending war. The tea service slid on the tray and the cream pitcher spilled. The muscles in their legs tightened and they reached out to steady themselves with every roll.

It was an uncomfortable situation and the conversation turned contentious. Annabelle expressed the opinion that the Cuban people were oppressed by the Spanish crown. She said she had read a newspaper article before she left New York about how the people were treated, that they were rounded up and made to live in guarded camps near the city. The princess took offense and said she had known the King of Spain since he was a baby and that he would never be brutal to his people. Annabelle reminded her of the sinking of the Battleship Maine in Havana harbor only weeks earlier. The princess quickly responded, "But it was an accident. I have been assured by The Infanta that it was an accident." Annabelle told her about witnessing the brutality of Mexican *rurales* who murdered her fellow train passengers in cold blood, simply because they were powerless peasants. The princess said, in her opinion, it had nothing to do with the situation in Cuba. They glared at each other and seemed to be in a standoff.

Soon, the afternoon tea ended and Annabelle took her leave. For the first time, she was aware of questioning her father's judgment.

"Is he blinded by his feelings?" she asked Pedro.

Pedro smiled—a rare occurrence—and put his fingers on his mustache. "*Si*, blinded, deafened, and muted. Love … it clouds all of the senses … and your father has a large capacity for love. But …"

"But what, Pedro?"

"But she is over here … and he is over there. We shall see. We shall see."

When the ship reached shore, the cable from Juan was waiting for Pedro. He imposed on The Infanta to take Annabelle into the protection of the bodyguards of the

King of Spain and allow her to accompany her entourage to Madrid. When he was sure that Annabelle was sufficiently safe, he left to return to America as soon as possible.

Before he left, he said to Major Garza, who commanded the royal bodyguards, "If anything should happen to Annabelle Palmer, I will find you and kill you myself. *Comprende?*"

"You have my word, *Señor*," the major said. "I will guard her personally ... as if she were royalty."

"I am no longer a priest, *Señor*," the man said. "Call me Cucho."

He had been searched and his pistol had been taken, along with the backpack and ammunition. But, of course, the easiest pistol to find is, simply, the easiest pistol to find. Nothing else.

Cucho pushed him along from behind, a rifle pointed at his back. When they reached an old log building, not much larger than an outhouse, the others started to appear. They walked out the door, from behind trees and bushes, and jumped down from the low cliff behind it.

"Who do we have here, Cucho?" one of them asked.

"I found him wandering around down the trail, whistling to himself," Cucho said. "We've had awhile to talk. He's *Americano* ... a rancher ... a sympathizer, he says."

"What's his name?"

"Juan Lopez. Manages a rancho in south Texas."

One of them, the one who appeared to be in charge, stepped forward and looked him in the eye. He was a tall European-looking man, obviously not *mestizo* and probably not Spanish. "What are you doing up here?" he asked.

"I am looking for you ... not you, personally, *Señor* ... but the *insurrectos* who have been harassing the military in this area."

The man laughed. "That is ridiculous ... what possible reason would you have?"

"Someone is after me, *Señor* ... trying to kill me ... someone connected to the Concordium company or perhaps the elite group that supports them."

"Go on. I'm listening."

"I don't know why they want to kill me ... that is the irony of it. I'm running from them and I'm trying to figure it out at the same time."

"Has he been searched?" the man asked Cucho. Cucho nodded.

"Could I trouble you for a drink, *Señor*?" Juan asked. "I am in need of a little fortification at this point."

The man laughed again. "Hand him a bottle," he said.

Around a fire in the clearing, they sat on rocks and boxes labeled "Bananas" in English and passed around a bottle of American whiskey. For the next half hour, Juan explained what he'd been told about the Concordium, how he'd been followed and shot at, how he killed a

Pinkerton guard who was trailing him across the desert.

"*Señores*, if I do not find out what's going on," he said, fiddling with his hat and pushing it down a bit more tightly on his head. "I will surely be picked off at some point. Not only that, but many other innocent people could be killed."

He was relaxed. He felt he was winning them over. Then after sundown, suddenly, without warning, the man in charge, an evil grin shining in the firelight, said, "Tie him up, put him inside." At which point, two of them grabbed him roughly from behind and dragged him into the dirty, dank log cabin, tied his hands and his ankles and left.

The smell of urine was overwhelming and he tried not to imagine what the reason for that might be. But the two drunken *tontos* who tied him up didn't do a good job of it. That was the first thing he noticed. When his eyes adjusted to the dark, he could see a stockpile of dynamite in the corner. And by some miracle, he had managed to keep his hat on. All in all, it was not a bad set of facts for someone who's just been kidnapped. The bad news was the door to the shack had a huge lock and one of the men who put him in there also locked it and pocketed the key. That was going to require further thought.

But before he made his move, he needed to take advantage of the opportunity they just gave him to do a little spying. He began to scoot himself closer to the door so that he could hear.

About an hour later, they were thoroughly intoxicated, hooting and cooing about a woman they knew down in San Bernardo who liked to display her ample bosom.

"I saw her bend over and pull up her stockings," one man said. "They jiggled in the sunlight like ripe melons swinging from a vine." They all laughed and then got quiet again.

"But I hear she belongs to an army officer ... that he visits her every night."

"She doesn't like him ... just his *pesos* ... that is all."

"Which officer?"

"All of them. Any of them." Once more they all laughed then got quiet.

"She knows the sister of the head of the mine, its *el director* ... that is how she gets so much business."

"The secret mine?"

"*Si* ..."

"That is enough, *estúpido*," the man in charge said abruptly. "Shut your mouth before you say anything more."

"The Taxcoco mine ... that's not so secret."

He heard a scuffle and then, "*Callate!*, if you don't want me to push you off the nearest cliff. *Comprende*?" The man in charge seemed to have a French accent, as best he could tell and though he spoke Spanish well, it sounded stilted. It was probably not a coincidence that Michelito's mother and this man were both French, but what was the connection?

He decided to sit back and relax as best he could for the rest of the night. He was learning more from these drunks than he'd learned from anyone else in days. But the fatigue of climbing overtook him and he fell asleep listening to the men outside tell about women they had known—or women they pretended to know.

He was jolted awake by another sound, the sound of rifle shots—four of them—up on the cliff in back of the shack where he'd been tied. He heard an unfamiliar voice, a Spanish speaker, shouting orders to the men and complaining about their overnight drinking party. One of the men called him "Señor Mateo."

Then the door swung open and the morning sunlight blinded him. He squinted and averted his eyes, trying to take peeks at whoever had walked in. A young man, not much older than Annabelle, grabbed his arm and pulled him up and out into the cold morning air. He pushed him against the wall and stepped back to face him.

"An American rancher?" the man asked.

Juan Miguel nodded his head.

"You know, *Señor*, we have no choice but to kill you ..." He walked up to him and looked into his eyes. "Unless ... unless, perhaps, we can use you somehow. What can you do?"

"I am a very convincing actor," Juan Miguel said. "I would make a good spy."

"An actor?" Señor Mateo put his head back and roared with laughter. "That is the last thing I expected to hear ... an actor ..." He shook his head and grinned. "Fine ... then do some acting. Show us."

"To do it justice, *Señor*, you will have to untie me."

"Untie him ... let's see this actor," he said to one of the *hombres* nearby.

He untied his hands first, which of course was a mistake, because as he bent down to untie his feet, Juan Miguel reached up to lift his hat with one hand and smooth his hair with the other. When he put the hat back on his head, he had a pistol in his hand. He kicked the man in front of him in the groin and then the jaw, sending him into paroxysms of pain.

"This is my best impersonation," he said. "A *bandido* named Primo. Perhaps you have heard of him."

Señor Mateo started to laugh, then stopped short. He raised his rifle, but Juan Miguel shot his hand. Then without hesitation, he shot him in the head, between the eyes.

The others stood back watching, their hands raised in the air. "You ... the one with the key," he said, "gather up all the guns ... and the knives ... every last one and put them in a pile."

The man stepped forward but he vacillated. Juan Miguel said, "By my count, I have four more bullets, *Señor*."

So the man did as he was told. He collected guns, rifles, knives, even the cooking knives, and threw them in a pile by the campfire.

"Now throw me the key to the building," Juan Miguel said. "And there is some rope in my backpack ... get it. *Bueno* ... now step back with the others."

He ushered all of them inside and told the man to tie up all of them, about a dozen men, together. When he had tied the last man's hands and feet and pushed him down, he lit a stick of dynamite in the corner. "I suggest you free yourselves before the dynamite ignites," he said, his voice calm as he locked the door.

He walked over to his backpack and picked it up. He slung it across an old mule and then mounted it. "*Adios*, my friends ... it has been lovely visiting with you," he called to them as he rode away.

As he descended the trail riding a cantankerous old mule, he listened intently for the sound of an explosion, hoping he wouldn't hear one. He really didn't want to kill all of them, but he would have if he needed to. It took only a few hours to ride down the same trail it had taken three days to walk up. It took only a few minutes to untie his hair and let it flow across his shoulders, put on Father Ramirez's cassock, and retrieve Jícama. He rode out of San Bernardo, his robe flying in the warm, dry desert wind, at a gallop.

"The queen consort will receive us on Thursday at the Royal Palace," The Infanta Pilar told her. "It will be in one of the small, inconsequential rooms in the back of the building. Expect her to be haughty because she always is. And ... just a warning ... she does not understand Americans, not in the least, and now that Spain and America are headed to war, well, prepare for the worst, that is all I can say."

Since she arrived there six days ago, Annabelle had felt frightened just being in Madrid. It was only a few days after the United States declared war on Spain and Spain reciprocated by declaring war, also.

"Why must I go at all?" Annabelle asked. She looked across the large sitting room of The Infanta's Madrid apartment at the woman who had been cordial to her on the ship, but once they entered Spain, became distant. "I would be only too happy to stay invisible ... or better yet, return to America as soon as possible."

"Well, my dear, neither of those is possible. An American staying with the king's aunt is likely to arouse suspicion and cause a scandal. We must do whatever we can to reassure her that you are not one of the Americans who wanted war with Spain."

She opened her mouth to protest, but The Infanta waved her away, which meant she should leave the room. She stood and found her own way out then walked through the hallways to the room she'd been assigned.

She'd seen the Spanish Royal Palace from the window of The Infanta's carriage one day when they were out for a drive. It was enormous, the largest building she'd ever laid eyes on, and she had seen palaces and cathedrals all over the world. She'd read that it had more than 200 rooms and the most elaborate and sumptuous appointments of any European palace. Even the thought of being summoned there intimidated her.

Never before in her life had Annabelle felt confined. In her father's home, in places they'd stayed when they traveled, even in her room at boarding school, she felt free to be herself, to express herself, and speak her own mind. When she arrived in Madrid, however, there were restrictions everywhere she turned. She was expected to stay in her rooms, except on rare occasions that she was summoned to see the princess Alexis or The Infanta.

Once again, she walked into the two-room suite in which she'd spent the last six days. They were comfortable enough, although they were sometimes drafty. The windows looked out on a small park and several other apartment buildings. The thought that spring would be coming soon and she would be required to view it from inside a stone edifice frustrated her. She longed to be back at the ranch where she could jump on her horse, Jorge, and ride out into the countryside any time she wanted to.

Someone knocked softly. "Come in," she said in English, forgetting where she was. Princess Alexis walked in, looked her up and down, and took her by the hand. "The Infanta has asked me to go through my closet and find you something acceptable to wear. Shall we begin?"

On all four walls, the room had the most intricate murals she'd ever seen. What made them strange to her, though, was the color—scene after scene in blue and white, nothing else. And above that, carved wood trimmed in gold leaf and above that, individual paintings of scenes from Spanish history, most of them incomprehensible to her, in row after row all the way to the top of the curved, domed ceiling.

At the end of the room was a large, empty desk. Two chairs, one behind the desk and one in front, sat on top of a marble floor covered in Persian rugs. If this was one of the small, inconsequential rooms, she wondered, what must the other rooms be like?

She had bowed appropriately and waited for the queen consort to ask her to sit. Queen Christina Mariana stared at her for an inordinate length of time. Behind her stood two guards at attention, dressed in strange, medieval clothing with silver plumes sticking up from their metal helmets.

Finally, without looking at her directly, the queen consort asked, "Who do you favor in the war between Spain and America?"

"Your Highness, I am loyal to my country as you are to yours. But I've never advocated war in any way."

The queen consort looked at her again for a long time then she said to a clerkish-looking man standing by the door, "She will be incarcerated ... under house arrest ... for the duration of the war."

"But Your Highness," she began. The queen consort put up her hand and the man said, "Silence."

"She will be allowed to stay in The Infanta's apartment but she is not to go out ... never. Search her belongings and read her mail before sending it. That is all."

After the necessary protocols, she was escorted out of the room and taken back to her two-room prison. She sat on the settee watching the policemen search her valises and trunk. When they were gone, she began to sob. She felt abandoned and alone. Thoughts of Carlito had gone out of her mind and she wanted nothing more than to be in the safety her father's arms.

"How do I reach the Taxcoco mine?" he asked a woman in a roadside café.

She didn't answer, serving him a glass of beer and a shot of tequila on the side. He picked up the shot glass and submerged it, tequila and all, into the glass of beer. He up-ended it and swallowed all of it without stopping.

She nodded at him as if asking if he wanted another. He tapped the glass with his thumb. "*Si ... de nuevo,*" he said. She took the shot glass out and poured more of both. He went through the ritual again and drank it down.

"Is there anyone here who can answer my question?" he said.

She stood looking at him, considering whether to answer. At last, she said, "Up the mountain a ways from San Merino, *padre*. Ask when you get to the town."

"Is San Merino down the road from here?"

She nodded. "*De Nuevo, padre?*" she asked.

He tapped the glass with his thumb and drank his third glass of tequila-laden beer. His head was swimming by this time, in the best possible way. He threw money on the bar and left.

The road to San Merino was moving—from side to side—making it difficult for him to follow it. He struggled to keep the horse pointed in the right direction then gave up and gave Jícama his head. His own head lolled down onto his chest, his eyes closed.

Like lightening streaking across the sky in an early spring thunderstorm, the story of Primo spread through northern Mexico. The mysterious man from Texas had shot and killed Mateo Salinas, who was called *El Fantasma*, "the ghost," and was one of the rebel leaders. The person who did the deed claimed to be Primo, a notorious outlaw who died almost twenty years ago.

"It is someone claiming to be him," was what most people said. But others said, "It is well known someone else was in the coffin when Primo was buried, so who knows?" Whether it was true or not true, it made a sensational tale and it was told over and over again in *cantinas*, in *mercados*, on ranchos, in the mines and small towns around the Sierra Madres.

Juan Miguel, disguised as Father Estéban, slept in stables and under hay bales in the farms near San Merino. He dispensed with the rather expensive habit of drinking in bars and cantinas and bought bottles of *tequila* and *mescal*, polishing them off one at a time almost every evening.

He looked hellish, not having bathed or shaved or washed his hair for weeks. And he smelled even worse. One morning, he stumbled out of a barn right after sunup to avoid getting caught in there by the owner. A group of young girls on their way to school saw him. They got frightened looks on their faces, screamed, and ran the other direction.

He found Jícama, by some miracle, still tied to a nearby fence post, and managed to mount him. Patting him on the neck and talking in a soothing voice, he walked him out into a nearby field to let him feed. "*Lo siento*, my friend ... my trusted old friend," he said. "I have become the town drunk and nobody except you will even talk to me." His stomach burned like hot irons. His head was the size of a boulder. His hands shook.

"If I do not get myself together, Jícama, all will be lost. The first steps, I suppose, would be a bath, some breakfast, and better clothes." He pulled on the reins and pointed his horse in the direction of the next town, Guanacevi, which he'd been told had a small hotel.

It was being held against his will—even for one

night—that brought back the feelings of terror he'd experienced in the Monterrey prison, where he'd been incarcerated unjustly and raped and persecuted by a sadistic monster, the monster he now thought was still alive and thriving as one of Diaz's generals. It made him sick. And the sick feeling gave way to the craving to obliterate his past. So he used alcohol to satisfy that craving, as he once had. Now, at least, he recognized it. He was conscious of what he was doing.

It was nothing more than a square building with cracking, flaking yellow paint and a sign over the door that said "Fonda San Saba," but it looked welcoming nonetheless to someone who'd been living like a donkey for almost a month. Just inside the door was a counter on one side and on the other, soiled, frayed sofas and a table or two. An elderly woman with a long gray braid over one shoulder rose from her rickety chair and looked at him as if he were the devil himself, instead of a priest.

"*Señor?*" she said, sounding wary.

"I would like a room ... and a bath, please, *Señora.*"

"Can you pay money in advance?"

"*Si* ... for a few days."

She quoted him a price, took his money, and handed him a key. "The bath, *Señor*, is in the back room. If you pay extra, we will fetch the water and heat it for you."

"*Por favor, Señora,*" he said. He bowed his head. "*Gracias.*"

"And a shave, *padre?*"

"*Si ... si.*"

The cold was bone chilling once he'd shed his cassock, coat, and other clothing. His skin looked like the desert floor, cracked and dusty. He stood in the middle of the dark room in his underwear shivering, waiting for the water to be heated. He could hear the woman shuffling around outside and then unlocking the door to open it.

But it was not the old woman who walked in carrying a large bucket of steaming water. It was a young woman who appeared to be pregnant.

"Let me help you with that, *Señora*," he said, taking the heavy bucket from her.

"It is *Señorita, padre*," she said.

She left the room and came back with a freshly laundered towel and cloth and a bar of soap.

He hesitated. Did she expect him to take off his underwear and get in?

"Get into the water, *Señor*, so that I can shave you."

He turned his back, shed his underwear, and eased into the warm water. He felt himself flushing and it was not just from the heated water.

Like an expert, she put the towel over the side of the tub, soaped her hands, and spread the lather onto his face. She began to shave him and she had the gentlest touch he'd ever felt. Her hands were calm and graceful, her face angelic. He was embarrassed, there is not doubt, to be sitting there naked in full view. She sensed it and said simply, "Relax, *padre*, I do this all the time."

"*Si … Señorita … but I don't.*"

He relaxed, put his head back, and let her do her work. The warmth of the water, the soothing touch, the feminine presence lulled him and he closed his eyes. "What is your name?" he asked.

"Anna Maria."

"When is your baby due?"

"My baby has died … it stopped moving in the womb. The doctor says it will have to be cut out."

His eyes popped open and he looked at her face. There was great sorrow in her eyes.

"I am trying to get enough money for the operation … I am saving for it," she said, cupping her hands with water and rubbing it over his face. She took the towel and lightly blotted the dampness with it. "What does God think of this, *padre*?"

"I am not much of a priest, *Señorita*, but I know God has nothing but compassion for you."

"That is not what the priest at the cathedral told me."

"Then he is wrong. You are blameless."

"He said being a whore is the reason … sleeping with the soldiers at the mine."

He tried to look into her eyes but she looked away.

"That is for a doctor to say," he said. "Not a priest."

She gathered the razor and towel and stood looking down at him. "You have a very handsome face, *Señor*. Why do you hide it?"

"Will you go to a store and buy me some clothes,

Señorita? I will pay extra."

"*Si* ... I know just what you should wear. I can pick out something nice for you."

Before he even finished buttoning the new black vest Anna Maria had bought for him, he knew what he would do. He still had the gun hidden in his hat but he needed a six-shooter and a holster. He wasn't worried, though. One way or another, he would arm himself, because one cannot rob a mine without a proper gun.

Annabelle balanced a china teacup on her knee and sat on the edge of the settee in her boudoir, as the two of them had afternoon tea in the manner of the English. She took a small bite of a fresh-baked scone, which was dry and flakey, not at all like a real English pastry. Her mouth felt dry already so the sandy crumbs stuck to the roof of her mouth and her tongue and she tried to swallow.

It was the first time she'd had a chance to talk to the princess in several weeks. Both Princess Alexis and The Infanta shunned her, for all intents and purposes, once the Spanish American War got under way. She wanted to take full advantage of the occasion to ask some questions.

"Princess, may I ask what you know about why my friend, Pedro Garcia, returned to America so abruptly? Did it have something to do with the hostilities between our countries ... or was there another reason?"

Princess Alexis looked quite overcome with the circumstances in which she found herself. She had a stricken look on her face. "He told us that a friend needed him ... was in 'danger,' I believe he said."

"Did he say who the friend was?"

"No ... he did not ... I assumed it was a woman."

"Oh, no, Princess, that is unlikely. Pedro has been interested in very few women since I've known him. The only friend he has, really, is my father."

Princess Alexis looked at her with a startled expression. "You don't suppose?"

Annabelle stood up and nearly knocked the teacup onto the carpet. "I do suppose, Princess. I do suppose. Why didn't you tell me this before now?"

"I assumed you knew ..."

Annabelle put down the cup and starting wringing her hands. She walked to the window and looked out at the expanse of courtyard that seemed to go on for miles. "I must go back and see if my father is all right. You've got to petition the queen consort to let me go back." She turned and faced the still seated Princess. "We both should go and make sure we're there for him if he needs us."

The princess looked sad and apathetic, like someone who has no will and no say in her own destiny. "I cannot go to America. That would never be permitted. But I will see what I can do to convince the queen consort to let you leave. If I know her, she would probably welcome the idea of getting rid of the responsibility of having you here."

"And do you feel that way also, Princess?"

Princess Alexis shrugged her shoulders. "I have lost faith ... in so many things. What seemed possible a few months ago seems only like a dream. I think you should return to your own life, Annabelle, and I to mine."

"But, do you still love him?"

"Yes, of course I still love him. One cannot quit loving him. But I don't have the strength to fight ..."

"We all have to fight for what we want, Princess."

She laughed for a few seconds then her face became passive. "That is an American idea ... and it is not for a European ... especially a European woman, especially royalty."

Annabelle felt a pang of disappointment go through her—for her father's sake. "Well, then, please petition the queen consort as soon as possible. Can you do that much for him at least?"

The princess looked offended but she nodded. "I will do it today," she said.

The queen consort consented to allow Annabelle to leave right away and she even offered to pay for her trip back to America. Just the day before that, the queen consort's advisers had told her that, in all likelihood, Spain would lose the war. The princess had been right. The queen consort welcomed the opportunity to get rid of Annabelle before the time came to sign a peace treaty, lest Annabelle be used as a bargaining chip in the negotiations.

It took ten days for Annabelle to travel to New York City, first by train then by boat. She boarded another train to Chicago and from there to Texas, tracing the footsteps of Pedro Garcia a few weeks earlier. At the train station in San Antonio, Beatriz and Jose told her that Pedro had gone to El Paso. Although she was weary and almost sick from bad food and traveling, she immediately boarded a train for El Paso because that is what her father would do for her if she needed him.

Charlotte Borden met her at the train station in El Paso and she nearly collapsed into her arms, sobbing and clinging to her. Charlotte patted her and held her close.

"Pedro will find him, Annabelle. Or we will find him, I promise."

Annabelle looked at her with pleading eyes. "Will you help me ... please ... will you help me?"

"Yes, of course I will. We will all help you ... all of us. But first, let's get you some good food and a good night's sleep." They rode out to the ranch in the buckboard with Annabelle's head on Charlotte's shoulder, tears of relief streaming down her cheeks and her hands and torso not shaky for the first time in days.

CHAPTER THREE

In a cantina down the street from the Fonda San Saba, Juan Miguel sat eating his *huevos rancheros* when he noticed a Mexico City newspaper lying on the other end of the bar. A headline said something about Spain, so he asked the man next to him to pass him the newspaper and he started to read the story, which was about a standoff in Havana harbor between the U.S. and Spanish fleets. But then the photograph accompanying the article caught his eye. It was a photo of the Spanish ministers and royal family reviewing Spanish troops before sending them off.

There was the queen consort, with her hand on the shoulder of the 12-year-old King, alongside the Prime Minister, several other ministers, The Infanta, and standing off to one side, almost alone, was Princess Alexis. She was identified and then after her name, it said, "recently engaged to Grand Duke Sergey Romanov of Russia, cousin to the Tsar."

He read no further. He could see it in her face, even in a photo taken from far away. She was a pawn in their political games and there was nothing she could do about it. Spain was in a precarious position, in danger of the same type of revolution that had brought down so many other European monarchies. The Spanish Empire needed the support and the good graces of the Russian Empire. What better way to solidify their monarchies than to arrange a propitious marriage? That's how it had been done for centuries.

He put down the newspaper and finished his eggs. His heart sank down into his gut and his head felt hallow.

"Where can I purchase a gun?" he asked the man tending bar as he stood to leave.

"There is a store one block from here ... the 'Durango Mercantil.'"

"*Gracias,*" he said. When he walked out into the bright morning sunlight, it was more than he could bear, hitting him in the face and making him teary eyed. He sniffed and wiped the moisture from his eyes.

Pedro Garcia picked up the trail of his old friend without much effort once he had put a gun to the heads of a couple of *insurrectos* in El Paso and found out that Juan had been impersonating a priest named Father Estéban.

He seemed to have gone south into the mountains, but Pedro needed to take a side trip first, before he continued his search. He boarded a train for Monterrey.

He found the city's records office and bribed a few clerks to look into the records that day instead of waiting the required seven days. They went to the back of the warehouse where the files containing information about the deceased were stored. They returned with a certificate confirming the man he thought he killed, the warden of the Monterrey jail, was officially dead. He was buried in the city cemetery, they said, in a family vault.

After much searching, he found the vault and read the man's name himself, carved into a stone along with the names of numerous other family members. It was just as he thought. The warden was dead. He had killed him.

But the information didn't allay his concern. Instead, it heightened it. He had known Juan Miguel all his life. He knew the signs. The man might be coming unglued.

By the time he crossed the country again and reached the Sierra Madres, the trail had gone cold. He surmised that Juan had changed identities again. But to whom?

Feeling rested and reassured, Annabelle ate her breakfast in the spring sunshine, coming through the windows and warming her insides like nothing she'd felt in a long time. She was thankful to be back among friends and to be back in Texas. The Franklin Mountains, stark and primeval, were more beautiful to her than the richest, no-blest, finest European palace.

"May I have another cup of coffee?" she asked Charlotte.

"Help yourself, my dear ... and pour me some also."

Annabelle picked up the simple metal pot with an old dishtowel hanging from a hook by the sink and poured them both more of the coffee, which was so dark brown it was almost black.

Charlotte blew on her coffee then took a sip. "Um ... too hot," she said. "Are you ready to get down to business, my friend? Let's talk about what you want to do."

"I want to find him ... that is all I know. Except ... well, I doubt very much he would have gone off on this 'adventure' if he'd been thinking clearly."

"What do you mean ... thinking clearly?"

"I mean, he is a wonderful man, compassionate, brave, intelligent ... but he has had some horrible experiences. His life has been a see-saw that started long ago when he fell in love with my mother ... who was already married and much older than he was."

Charlotte winced. The story was already gripping her heart.

"He is loved by everyone ... my father ... so it is hard to understand how he could've been mistreated the way he was."

"By whom?"

"My mother's first husband, authorities, jailers ... it is

a long story, but my point is this … there are times when these horrible memories come back to haunt him. That is one reason Pedro remains so loyal to him. He hovers over him like a mother hen."

"If you go into Mexico looking for him, would you only add to Pedro's woes? Double his worries?"

"Yes … that is possible. But I must … I must look for him. Will you help me?"

"I will give you money … but you must find someone to take you. That I insist on. I will not permit you to go alone. Your father would never forgive me."

Annabelle sat back and exhaled, looking relieved. "I'm going to ask Carlos Cordova and Cinco Morales to go with me. The two of them know Mexico and they're good, loyal friends. I only hope they will say yes."

"First of all, Carlos never came back to El Paso. He is still in Mexico City with his family … fighting bulls, I have heard. And Cinco … well, he's a good boy but not yet a man."

"What do you propose, then?"

"We take Cinco, yes … but also Manny. He's one of our hands and he's a good solid *caballero* who knows how to shoot a rifle."

"We? Do you mean you want to go with me?"

"I can't let you go by yourself and I can't keep you here. That is the only other choice."

Annabelle jumped up and wrapped her arms around Charlotte and hugged her. "Thank you, thank you so much

... but what about Lyle?"

Lyle Peterson interrupted the conversation by clanging a bridle onto the cabinet as he walked into the room. "I hope you two aren't plannin' to go chasin' after Juan Lopez in Mexico. Seems to me he's made his own bed. I heard ... well, I heard he poked his nose where it didn't belong 'fore he left. Spied on perfectly respectable people ... threatened 'em."

Whatever he did," Annabelle said, "it was for a good reason. My father always has a good reason."

"Oh, I'm sure he does ..."

Charlotte all but yelled at him, "Stop it, Lyle. Annabelle is worried about her father. Is that so difficult for you to understand?"

"Nope ... I just hope you're not plannin' to get involved in it, that's all," he said and he walked out.

Charlotte reached over and put her hand on Annabelle's. "Never mind him. He's not a problem. I will take care of him."

They had four fresh horses for riding, another one to carry packs, and enough money to live on for quite some time, but more important than that, they had Cinco and Manny's knowledge of the country. Charlotte was skeptical of just riding into Mexico to search for someone. She knew it was a wild idea but she went along with it to satisfy Annabelle and because she agreed with her when she said, "Doing nothing is always the worst idea. That is what my father would say."

Annabelle borrowed some men's clothing for the trip. She was used to that. She'd always worn men's clothing when she helped out at the rancho. Cinco rode out front, followed by Annabelle and Charlotte then Manny pulling the pack horse. They had ridden for five days in what seemed like wilderness. Besides the small towns, they saw only an occasional adobe *casa* surrounded by a small herd of sheep, or a way station for the *rurales* patrolling that part of Mexico, or once, a *hacienda* set far back from the trail up against the low mountains, foothills of the Sierra Madres. In the towns, they stopped and asked for information and had a meal if there was a cantina or café. Her father hadn't bothered to cover his trail. In fact, it seemed as if he wanted to leave a trail.

Annabelle and her friends tracked her father across the deserts of northern Mexico by following Jícama. Everyone remembered the man on the wonderful black horse.

Jícama's sire, the thoroughbred Umberto, was lean, graceful, tall, and broad in the withers. The people of Nuevo Laredo had given him to Juan Miguel to thank him for his generosity but also to show their love. Jícama looked exactly like Umberto except he had a quality that made him almost human—the same mindfulness of his owner—and his eyes were striking.

"*Si* ... I will never forget him," an old man carrying a

load of straw on his back told them. "Not the man ... the horse. I would give everything to have a horse like him ... everything."

But when they reached San Bernardo, the trail became obscured. The horse disappeared and so did the man.

They never imagined that the man they were following would make a trip up into the high mountains of the Sierra Madre. After they rested a day in the city of Guanacevi, they bought fresh supplies and decided to begin the long ride to Durango to continue their search.

The cobblestones were still wet from a shower and the April morning had started off cool, making the bright sunlight all the more vibrant, shining through the clear, clean air. It reflected off of the metal lamppost across the street and he put his hand over his eyes to shield them so that he could see the crowd in the street several blocks away. They started walking his way and he could hear the slow, dull beat of large drums, one answering the other, as they marched.

He had forgotten it was *Semana Santa*, the solemn procession commemorating Good Friday in Mexico. He recognized the eerie dirge-like quality of it and the solemnity in the people and on the signs they carried. The beginning marchers had icons framed in silver and mounted on velvet banners of purple and dark green and black. Followed by hooded men bearing the statues of the fallen bloody

Jesus lying on a bed of yellow chrysanthemums, and Mary, sobbing behind him.

He stood still watching it approach and then pass by. The faces of the people were earnest. The ritual was not done for show. He stepped out into the street to be nearer them. They passed him without expression—some of them brushing his arm as they walked—the ones carrying large, heavy wooden crosses, dragging them along the cobblestones just as Jesus had, and the ones walking bent over in supplication. Finally came the flagellators, men with bare chests and feet who were swiping leather straps over their shoulders and digging into their own flesh with metal hooks attached to the ends. Their flesh glowed red and dripped with blood.

The sight of it entered his soul and made it cry out for the passion of blind, unquestioning devotion. He bowed his head in shame. He had not paid a high enough price yet. His sacrifice had been too small. Tears formed in his eyes and he let them flow freely down his cheeks. The marchers didn't question his tears. They nodded as they passed him. They knew why he was crying.

It was because God sacrificed that they marched and it was because the marchers sacrificed that he owed them. Would there ever be an end to it? Would Saint Michael one day throw down his sword and take his foot off of the neck of the serpent and find it dead? No, never. It was unending, etched into eternity. The good would always suffer.

At the Durango Mercantil, he spent most of the last of

his money to buy a good balanced pistol with a holster and ammunition. He strapped it across his chest underneath the vest, put on the black hat, and looked down at the spurs he had just purchased. They were shaped like stars.

Then he waited. He knew the gang of *bandidos* would show up sooner or later.

They rode into town late the next day just after sunset on a couple of stolen, broken-down old nags and an ancient wagon. They stopped, piled out in the street in front of the cantina, and prepared to go inside. He stepped out from the shadows and planted his feet and smiled.

The Frenchman was the first to notice him. "Well, if it isn't the man who steals mules," he said. "That is you, isn't it, my friend?"

"I'm relieved to see you escaped from the stinking shack in which you confined me," he said, his smile beaming in the low light of dusk. "Can I buy you each a drink?"

The Frenchman smirked and looked back at his *compadres*. "I think we can tolerate that," he said.

Through the evening, they each had more than one drink and at one point, he gathered them around a table in the back. They were eager to listen. They hadn't been searching for him to kill him; they wanted to follow him.

"What is your goal?" the Frenchman asked.

"The San Vicente mine," he said.

"Oh ... my friend ... that mine is so well-guarded that no one can penetrate it ... no one ... not even Primo the Outlaw."

"We will think of something. A load of silver would go a long way in arming the *insurrectos*, wouldn't it? A lot of guns ... a lot of bribes. Perhaps, enough to free your sister?"

"My sister? How did you know about her?"

"Your nephew ... Michelito ... was brought to my ranch by Father Ramirez after she was taken. He is still there."

"Is he ..."

"He is doing very well. He's being taken care of. But he would be better if his mother were free."

The Frenchman's macho façade cracked and he got a vulnerable, almost helpless look on his face. "She is in a bad way ... we have heard ... tortured, raped ..."

"I know ... that is why we need to start now planning how to rescue her. Let's get down to business, my friends. Time is wasting."

"What about this man who is after you? Are you still being followed?" the Frenchman asked.

"*Si*, I am. I haven't seen him but he is there. He found me several days ago but I gave him the slip by escaping from a barn disguised as a priest."

"And now?"

"And now, he still follows. I will catch him. One way or another, he will show his face."

"Will that not be too late?"

"*Si* ... that is a good point. Perhaps you are right."

Once more the trail had gone cold for Pedro. He staked out Jícama, who'd been tied to a tree and left there. He knew Juan Miguel would return for him but when he awoke the next morning, the horse was gone, disappeared as if in thin air. The horse's tracks went out into a grassy field beside a small stream and stopped. No doubt he rode down the middle of the shallow water to hide his tracks. Which way did he go? That was the question.

Pedro chose to go upstream, into the low hills. Once again he lost him. Juan Miguel knew all of the tricks for alluding pesky followers. Pedro was the one who taught them to him.

He turned around to go the other way and the stream broke up into two streams, both of which flowed into irrigation ditches. He doubled back along the streams' low banks but he found nothing. He was too good. He had vanished. So he abandoned the idea of tracking him once again and headed for the nearest town to ask more questions.

It was obvious to Pedro that Juan Miguel thought someone hostile was following him, that he still believed someone was out to kill him. But it was also obvious that Juan Miguel wanted to be followed—that he didn't want to be totally lost. He played a game of allowing himself to be tracked while at the same time eluding capture. It was an old Comanche trick, one that any good Texan knew.

So Pedro continued to play the game right along with him. He followed faithfully but stopped short of showing his face. Then one night, on a rare occasion when he'd checked into a hotel, the thought occurred to him, "Maybe someone besides the warden is out to kill Juan Miguel."

The San Vicente mine was a well known, government-sanctioned mine, one of the largest in the country. Surrounded by a high stonewall, the only entrance was a wrought iron gate decorated with ornate copper plates. The grandiosity of the Spanish and the fine workmanship of the native Indians were evident in the intricate design, however it was also meant to be impregnable.

Just inside, four separate wenches operated by steam engines lowered and raised men and supplies and loads of silver through holes dug hundreds of feet into the earth. It was all connected by miles of tunnels that went deeper and yet deeper into the silver-laden rock hard layers of earth. Workers had painstakingly secured the walls and ceilings with rough-hewn stones along which hung gas lanterns at intervals. Still, it was dark and eerily silent. Nothing but the sound of the miners' tools working those areas deemed to be the richest, which were also the deepest.

Men from the Indian tribes of the region worked twelve-hour days and were paid almost nothing. Their choices were few because their economy had been ruined by the inroads of European society, taking their land and ruining their customs. Most of them rarely saw sunlight even in the summer. The average length of time for a worker was ten years and then he either became too ill and weak to work or died. There were few safety measures. The men were ill clothed and ill equipped.

The people who owned the mines were far, far away. Some in Mexico City. Some in America. Some as far away as Spain. Even though Mexico had won its independence from Spain fifty years earlier, the Spanish conquerors still held sway in the economy and through a political system governed by the elites of society, those who owned land, high-ranking priests, and government officials.

In between were the enforcers, the cruel overseers who did what the owners expected because if they didn't, they too would be forced to bend and hack twelve hours a day in the bowels of the silver mine. And making it all possible were the soldiers—President Diaz's soldiers.

It took only two days of surveillance to learn the schedule for transporting silver ore out of the mine. The problem was the military escort, a couple of dozen, armed with rifles.

"They have to sleep at some point," Primo said. "That is the time to take them."

So they shifted their attention to the nearby army post. The security was lax, to say the least, and whores came and went every evening. The soldiers drank until they passed out—all except the two sentries who had taken their turn at sacrificing an evening of revelry to stand guard.

They picked off the sentries one at a time and dragged them, passed out from a blow to the head, and hid them. They entered the barracks, pointed their rifles at the soldiers, demanded their uniforms, and tied them up.

Taking the silver was just as easy. No one at the mine even looked twice at them when they arrived in the uniforms of government soldiers and watched as the silver ore was loaded onto wagons and then escorted it out the gate.

The next day, two wagonloads of silver ore resided in an old abandoned shack near the foothills of the Sierra Madres. But the next day, they began the laborious task of hauling it up the mountains to an abandoned granary built eons ago by the Tarahumara Indians, a place so remote that very few white men had ever seen it.

More than a dozen descendants of Queen Victoria attended the St. Petersburg wedding of Princess Alexis of Spain. From England, Spain, Sweden, Norway, Prussia, Austria, Greece, Saxe-Coburg Gotha, and several other German principalities, they came to show their royal solidarity. Their governments may disagree, but they were family, and their family tree formed an intricate web of intermarriages and births.

The Russian Orthodox Church had granted a hasty annulment when the princess testified that her first marriage had never been consummated. So even though she had been married before, the bride wore a white silk shantung dress, decorated with Russian eagles embroidered in gold thread, with a ten-foot train. She had a diamond necklace and a tiara lent to her for the occasion by the Russian Empress Alexandra Feodorovna and across her bosom was the velvet scarlet sash of royalty. A white and gold net veil covered her face so that none of the distinguished guests saw the look of sadness or the red-rimmed eyes.

The day before the wedding, she confessed her indiscretions to her future husband. She had to. She was pregnant. She sacrificed her dignity by admitting the truth. Her fiancé, a cold man with hands of ice, could have taken the opportunity to use the information against her. Instead, he just became more distant.

"You are nothing to me," he said. "The marriage is a necessity ... nothing more."

His gray eyes were empty, devoid of feeling and reflecting the light like cold hard silver. There was no depth. She looked into them and saw an over-privileged, barely educated prince who marched to the drumbeat of the aristocracy. There was not an ounce of individuality within him.

She realized that this was to be her life but she didn't mind. She looked forward to the arrival in early fall of a baby—a very special baby—the child of Juan Miguel del Valle.

The day after the wedding, U.S. President McKinley approved war with Spain. America was hated and vilified by the nation of Spain, including its royal family, because to them America's zest for war was nothing more than a commercial enterprise trumped up by jingoistic self-serving businessmen and journalists, and they were right. Princess Alexis knew that no one must ever know the father of her child was an American and she would do everything in her power to make sure that never happened.

He was happy to leave the work of hiding the silver to his *compadres*. They gave him hard looks when he said, "I have other fish to fry," but they nodded and began to load the silver onto pack mules.

He managed to sell a large chunk of the ore, one in which the silver was particularly shiny and spectacular, to a local merchant who was accustomed to buying silver on the black market. He went back to town and gave part of the money to Anna Maria for her operation. She kissed his cheek and then his hand. *"Gracias, Señor, que Dios te acompañe,"* she said. "You have saved me. May God save you as well."

"I will be back next week, Anna Maria. I will try to come back to visit you, to see how you are doing?" he said somewhat shyly.

"*Por supuesto, padre*, of course."

"Once you have the operation, what will you do?"

"Go back to work at the mine …"

He nodded. He picked up his hat.

With money from the silver in his pocket, he rode down to the city of Durango where there was a famous *casino* called El Matador in a hotel next door to the cathedral on the city square. He knew that there is no better place to learn the truth than a high-stakes card table.

A two-story building of smooth cut stone, built around a courtyard accented with rows of stone archways and polished wood bannisters atop wrought iron railings, the Hostal de la Monja was a favorite of the upper classes and its bar and casino, the liveliest in the city.

Weary and dirty, he checked into the hotel, bathed, and brushed the dust from his clothes then climbed into the clean soft bed and slept for almost a day. He had to look fresh and be alert for a night of poker. Fatigue had defeated many a man.

He awoke to the warm afternoon sun shining through a light cloud cover outside the hotel window. The day was nothing like the cold snowy days he'd spent in a Washington hotel room with Princess Alexis and yet the room seemed full of memories of her. Perhaps it was the fireplace, cold now, or perhaps the silver tea service on a table by the window. She was like a lovely phantom who traipsed through his dreams then disappeared into the noisy sounds of the city outside. He barely touched her, only lightly, and then she drifted out of his consciousness.

The real Princess Alexis was somewhere, thousands of miles away, in the bed of another man. There was nothing he could do about it at the moment. He tried not to picture it because if he did, it would drive him mad.

He finished the cup of tea, took the last bite of mutton, and wiped his mouth with a white starched napkin. He put on the clean clothes and combed back his hair. The hat, the vest buttoned over the pistol, the wad of money in his pocket. Maybe an evening of cards would obliterate the gnawing hunger in his loins, or maybe it would make it worse.

He began the evening in a low-key fashion at one of the tables in the corner of the courtyard. He won enough to call attention to himself and several hours later, he was at a table with some very high rollers, most of them professional card players. One of them, however, was a man called General Reynaldo who seemed not to have a first name. He was a corpulent short man with a bald head and an annoying habit of wiping his runny nose on his sleeve. But it was quite evident that he had money and he had influence.

When the deal came around to him, Juan Miguel picked up the cards and blew on them then he smiled. "For luck, *amigos*, just for luck." He put the deck on the

ANNA K. SARGENT

table and spread the cards fan-like, picked up the middle of the deck, and put it on top.

"What is this all about?" one of the professional players asked. "Are you stacking the deck, *Señor*?"

"If you think I am cheating, why do you not say so?" Juan Miguel said, the deck in his left hand and a drink in his right.

The man grabbed his left wrist and wrenched the deck out of his hand to inspect it.

"Give him back the deck. Let him deal," General Reynaldo said.

The professional looked dubious but he handed him the deck. Juan Miguel took it and began to deal but the man took offense again. "At this table, we cut the cards, *Señor*. It is my turn to cut."

Juan Miguel took another drink, put the glass on the table, and commenced to deal. The man stood, knocking his chair to the side, and grabbed Juan Miguel by the arm "You *have* stacked the deck ... you son of the devil. You are a cheat ... a card cheat," he yelled.

Juan Miguel paid him no attention and this enraged the man even more. He pulled Juan Miguel up by the lapels and pushed him, up against the nearby wall, his face red and his hands up at Juan Miguel's throat.

Juan Miguel put his hands on the man's arms and in a calm voice said, "You have insulted me the last time, *Señor*. The last time."

"Do you wish to fight?" the man asked. "Or do you wish

to duel?"

Juan Miguel said simply, "Duel."

"Then duel it shall be."

"I wish to know a man's name before I kill him. What is your name, *Señor*?"

"Guillermo Marco. And yours, *Señor*?"

"Juan Miguel."

The room was still. General Reynaldo walked up to the two men and put Juan Miguel's hat on his head and his winnings in his hand. "You've had enough, son," he said. "Come with me ... forget this. Come with me."

"But he has insulted me ... I am not a cheat."

"And you will live to prove that another day. Come with me, Juan Miguel. Let's go have a drink."

He liked General Reynaldo much more than he had planned to. He was a man with a soft heart who preferred to please rather than offend. They walked the streets of Durango talking for an hour or two. General Reynaldo talked about his days in the army and his rancho in southern Mexico. Juan Miguel found himself confessing facts about his own life—his rancho, his daughter, his trip to Washington.

"Come to my house and have a late night meal," the general said.

"*Gracias Señor*, that is kind but ..."

"You need a friend like me, Juan Miguel. Come and meet my wife and have a good meal."

"I am too tired, general, but *gracias*."

"Tomorrow night then. On Consuela Street just past the market with the blue sign. We will expect you." The general started to walk away but he turned around and said, "Don't go back to the casino, *amigo*."

He walked up to Juan Miguel and faced him and, in almost a whisper, he said, "I know you made a fuss at the card table in order to draw attention to yourself. Your reasons are your own, my son, but I fear you have drawn attention from the wrong people."

Juan Miguel started to speak but General Reynaldo put up his hand and stopped him. "Speak no more and ... my advice is to stay in your room ... stay away ... from everyone. I will see you tomorrow evening."

Juan Miguel walked back to the hotel in the light of a full moon. He hadn't heard anything useful at the gaming table but General Reynaldo could be a good source of information if he played the right cards. He rounded a corner and saw the cathedral in the distance. Just as he walked past a back street near the hotel, he felt a rush at his back then hands grabbed him from behind, covered his mouth, and pulled him into the shadows. He saw someone raise a club and everything went black.

Pedro found the Fonda San Saba in Guanacevi just as any traveler would. It was the only authentic hotel for miles around. He asked the old woman at the desk if she'd seen a man fitting Juan Miguel's description. She shook her head no. The man had helped her friend, Anna Maria, so she was not inclined to betray him.

"I am his friend," Pedro pleaded. "He is not in his right mind. He thinks he's a priest but he's not ... and well he's a bit *loco*."

The old woman considered what he said and she knew the words rang true. The man was lovely to look at and beautiful in spirit but troubled. That was obvious.

"*Por favor, Señora*," Pedro said. "I need to find him before something terrible happens to him."

"He left town dressed as a *bandido*," she said. "With a gang ... *insurrectos*, I think."

When Pedro heard the way Juan Miguel was dressed in his latest persona, he felt the color drain from his face. It was the same clothing that Primo would have worn.

He asked around some more and found out that a man fitting Juan Miguel's description rode north toward Durango several days earlier. He felt he was closing in on him and it was probably just in time. The persona of Primo was too dangerous—and too exposed. He nudged his horse with his boot heels and galloped up the road to find him.

CHAPTER FOUR

The day before Charlotte left with Annabelle, she had a horrendous argument with her husband, Lyle. It was a repeat of past arguments except this time, he was adamant about forbidding her to go. As the argument progressed, it became a test of her commitment to him and their marriage. Evidently, she failed the test because he told her if she left, the marriage would be finished, that he would be gone for good when she returned.

He stormed out of the house and rode away. That night he didn't come home. She left on the trip knowing her marriage was at an end.

Riding along in the vast expanse of the northern Mexico landscape had given her plenty of time to contemplate what she'd done and why. After several days of thinking, she understood the fault had been hers. She had never wanted the marriage. She married Lyle for convenience and because she was scared of running the ranch on her own.

By the time she and the other searchers arrived in Durango, Charlotte's thoughts about Lyle and the ranch were far away. She hadn't thought about him in days and she relished the adventure she was on, even if it was brought on by the disappearance of someone she cared for. She felt alive for the first time in more than a year.

Charlotte felt instantly at-home when she walked into the courtyard of the Hostal de la Manjo. It reminded her of the gracious hotels in the south of France or in Spain. She looked up at the wide balconies encircling the second floor and the carved wooden hotel room doors. Potted plants hung here and there from hooks and the sun shone down through the opening in the roof onto rows of dining tables below. At one end were the gaming tables and a bar.

She and Annabelle walked through the café and approached the bartender, who was preparing for the evening's rush. "*Señor*, may I ask you something, *por favor*?" she said.

He nodded his head but continued his work.

"Have you seen a man with curly brown hair and a handsome face ... perhaps dressed as a priest ... or perhaps dressed more worldly ... like a card shark?"

"His name?"

"Juan Lopez ... or Juan Miguel."

The bartender put down the bottles he had extracted

from the straw inside a wooden crate and put his hands on the bar. *"Oh, si ... Señora* ... he got into a fight here in the bar last night. Proclaimed his name very loudly ... for all to hear."

"Which name?"

"Juan Miguel. Anyway, he left with General Reynaldo and hasn't been back. The hotel clerk came around this morning looking for him."

"Where can I find this General Reynaldo?"

"Consuela Street ... on the other side of the market with the blue sign."

Juan Miguel awoke in a puddle of discarded dishwater behind a restaurant. The sun had been up for hours and was beating down on him full force. He had a lump on the top of his head the size of a lime and his head was splitting. He raised up and looked around. He saw no one except a mangy brown dog across the street pulling at a bone with its teeth.

"Ah, Madre de Dios," he said, touching the lump and flexing his neck muscles. He sat up, reached inside his pocket, and felt that his money was gone. Somehow he managed to stumble onto his feet and pick up his hat, which was underneath a pile of thrown-out garbage. He swayed from one side of the dirty back street to the other, walking toward the main street up ahead. Once more, he was overcome with the pain in his head and he had to stop

and lean his back against a brick wall.

He was lost. He recognized nothing. Everything was a blur to him, nothing but the back streets of a strange town. A cathedral bell ringing in the distance. A group of women carrying baskets filled with kumquats and oranges on their heads. A man sweeping the stoop of an adobe building and whistling a song to himself.

The afternoon sun was finding its way behind the palm trees. It must be getting late, he told himself, but what day is it? He tried to remember the previous day but he couldn't. He tried to remember anything, but he couldn't.

He lurched from one wall to the next then to the nearby fence. "*Señor,*" he said, "could you tell me where I am ... *Señor.*" But the man stopped sweeping, looked at him with alarm, and went inside.

He put his finger to the side of his head and felt the clots and some fresh blood still oozing through his hair. He could picture a man standing over him and raising the club to strike but that is all. Nothing else.

Then he saw the specter of a man far down the street hiding behind a building and peeking out at him. He reached underneath the vest and felt for the pistol but it wasn't there, so he took off his hat and found the small gun tucked inside the lining where it should be. He ducked behind a wooden barrel near the corner and shot at him. The bullet ricocheted off of the building. The man disappeared.

He began to run as best he could. He could see a busy street up ahead so he went that way. The man had not shot back at him however he could feel his presence behind him, following at a safe distance, gaining ground on him. He staggered into the main street, ducked behind a family walking home from something, hid amongst a crowd in front of a market, and went inside the tiny church next door.

It was dark inside but he could see that the nun standing at the back of the church quickly darted into the knave and closed a set of double doors when she saw him. He opened the church's front door a slit and looked out into the daylight. The man was gone.

He waited. He closed the door and turned. It was quiet and he could hear the floorboards squeaking on the other side of the inside doors. The nun was still standing there.

"Sister ... I will not hurt you," he said. "Sister, please, I am not dangerous. Please believe me. Sister?"

He didn't hear her walk away. She was still there. "Sister, I need your help. I beg you to believe me. Please ... let me open the door and talk to you."

She said nothing so he slowly opened one of the doors and looked into her face. She was not a young woman but neither was she old. Her face was more stern than frightened. Her hands were clasped in front of her and she was rooted to the spot.

"Do you seek sanctuary?" she said.

"Sanctuary? *Si* ... that and some information ... and I

will be on my way."

"Enter," she said and she stood aside. "Vhat do you vish to know?"

"Where am I?" he said. The small altar and the icons next to it started to spin around him. The whole building whirled as if on an axis. He clutched at his head. "Sister, where am I?"

When Charlotte and Annabelle found the Casa de la Reynaldo just beyond the market on Consuela Street, it looked like a small shop instead of one of Durango's grandest homes. The front was barely there, only wide enough for a doorway and two slim windows. It was painted a pale green trimmed in orange and had a bougainvillea bush growing up and over the roofline.

General Reynaldo was friendly, without an ounce of suspicion when Charlotte and Annabelle appeared at his door. Charlotte explained that they were looking for Juan Miguel and General Reynaldo immediately invited them in.

"*Si* ... a very impressive man," the general said. "I met him last night at cards. After he got into a 'disagreement' ... we left together and then parted. He went back to the hotel for the night."

"With whom did he have a disagreement?" Annabelle asked.

"A man who plays cards there regularly. His name is

Guillermo Marco. But he is a card shark ... a dandy ... a coward."

"You don't think he might have hurt my father?"

"No ... I have known him for years. He is a blowhard ... a puffed up fish ... nothing more."

"May we come in and talk to you about it?"

"My wife and I were about to have a glass of wine. Please join us ... I insist."

Inside, the Casa de la Reynaldo opened up into a grey brick patio that was set back from the street in a garden and surrounded by the rest of the house. Fig trees and palm trees and *abasos* flourished at the back of the yard, fronted by bushes and hedges trimmed into pyramids. It was an opulent sanctuary, hidden among the squalor and poverty and hopelessness apparent everywhere in Durango.

General Reynaldo and his wife were happy people who drank glass after glass of Spanish wine, the supply of which seemed to have no end. They confessed early in the conversation that they had no children and were sometimes lonely. They seemed anxious to chatter on about their own lives, as if they were waiting for a chance to be gregarious.

The night wore on. A wash of stars shone in the clear night sky above them. Candles flickered on tabletops and in every corner of the patio and yard. The heady aroma of bougainvillea blossoms and cigar smoke mingled in the still night air.

Charlotte and Annabelle listened with patience, but at last Charlotte felt the need to interrupt and get down to the reason they were there. "General ... we heard from a young woman we met in Guanacevi that Juan Miguel is looking for the Taxcoco mine. Have you ever heard of it?"

"The Taxcoco mine, hmm?"

"People say it is secret ... but not so secret ... perhaps an ancient mine that was rediscovered?"

"When we were in Guanacevi last year," Señora Reynaldo interjected, her face suddenly animated in the candlelight, "we met a woman who is the granddaughter of one of the Tarahumara slaves who worked the Taxcoco mine for the Jesuits long ago ... in the 18th century. She said that her grandfather was truly a slave ... was paid nothing and treated badly. At some point, the Tarahumaras joined with the Apaches in a revolt and drove the Jesuits away, she said, and then not long after that the Jesuits were expelled entirely from New Spain."

"So the mine was abandoned?"

"*Si* ... abandoned and forgotten except by the Tarahumaras. They handed down tales of the slavery and of the insurrection but they could not remember where the mine was. It was lost out in the wilderness north of Durango."

"So, it truly is lost?"

General Reynaldo started to look uncomfortable, fidgeting and pulling at his shirt collar and trying to catch his wife's eye. But she continued with her story.

"Oh, no, *Señorita* ... not entirely. The Tarahumaras remembered where the entrance was and they remembered a few other landmarks leading to the mine. Several years ago, a group of men spent a lot of money to mount an expedition into the Sierra Madres to look for it. According to the Tarahumara woman, they found it but kept it a secret so that they could spirit away the silver and not pay the heavy government tax on mineral ores."

"So it is being mined again?

"So the woman said ... and I have heard rumors about it. The group of men who found the mine formed a company ... people say that the company is linked to people in high places ... the church, politics, the army ... even people in America."

General Reynaldo took a deep puff of his cigar and stood to pace the bricks of the courtyard. "The whole thing is serious business ... perhaps a little too serious for me. I do not wish to get involved in political intrigue. I have avoided it like the smallpox, but I will keep my eyes and ears open for you. That is all that I can do."

"Were you expecting to see my father again, general? Had you arranged to meet him?" Annabelle asked.

"No ... no. I was not expecting ... no."

"We should go back to check on my father. He may have returned by now."

He ushered them out, closed the door behind them, and looked at his wife.

"Where is he?" she said. "Did you not say you invited

him to dinner?"

"*Si* ... invited but not expected. He made enemies in a very loud manner in a very short time. That is not good."

"But you befriended him. You told me yourself you liked him. You should have told them that you invited him and he didn't come. What is wrong with you ... General Reynaldo?"

"Nothing is wrong with me ... it is you who were foolish. You told them too much, *Señora*. You should have kept your mouth shut. Believe me, it is best to stay out of this. I fear I am already too far into it."

On his way into town, Pedro caught a glimpse of Juan Miguel down a side street, just by chance. At least, it was a man who looked like him. The man shot at him and missed—that was not like Juan Miguel. He ran after him, even called his name, but the man eluded him, waded into a crowd, and vanished.

He walked up and down the street for almost an hour hoping to see him again. It didn't happen. He was gone.

He went into the nearest bar and ordered a drink and sat down to think. Where in the city of Durango would Juan Miguel be most likely to stay? He signaled for another drink and motioned to the bartender to come closer. "Where would a man of means want to stay in this city?" he asked him.

"A hotel downtown, *Señor* ... the Hostal de la Monja or

the El Capitan."

"Downtown?"

"*Si* ... near the cathedral."

When Juan Miguel's eyes opened, he saw that he was tucked into a narrow bed set back in a cove and he was covered with a gray wool blanket. Beside the bed were a straight chair and a small cabinet with a wash basin on it. He saw a window and a crucifix hanging on the wall next to the door. Outside the door, he heard voices, the voices of women speaking in hushed tones. Nuns, it had to be nuns.

He swung his legs over the side and sat up. Everything started to move again, like the ground giving way in an earthquake, unsteady, unsure, rolling around like a ship on the swelling sea. He put his head down between his knees and took a deep breath.

The door opened and in walked the nun he had met earlier and behind her an older nun with whiskers growing on her chin and heavy eyebrows over beady eyes.

"Sisters ... *gracias*," he said then he put his head back down. He felt the nausea welling up, coming to the forefront, into his throat, and ready to spill out onto their shoes.

The younger nun put her hands on his shoulders and pushed him back down onto the pillow. The older one lifted his feet and covered him again. She spoke in English with a German accent. "The doctor vas hier to see you. He told us to keep you in bed for at least *drei* … three … more days. You *habe ein* concussion."

"A concussion?"

"*Ja* … do you remember vas happen to you?"

"No … just that someone hit me over the head and took my money."

"It happen all too often *hier*, I'm afraid. Vas *ist* your nam?"

"I don't know … I don't remember."

"The doctor warned us that your head vill be *unscharf* … 'fuzzy' … for avhile, but he said you will get your brain back soon." Then she chuckled and patted him on the arm and pulled the blanket up under his chin. "Ve vill bring you some soup. Do you like potato soup?"

"*Si* … but I am not hungry, sister."

"I am Mother Veronica. Das *ist* Sister Dagmar. You vill eat potato soup to make you vell … strong … *ist* good?"

He nodded and tried with everything in his power to keep the vomit in his throat from spewing out his mouth.

After he forced a few spoonsful of soup down and drank several glasses of German beer, he did feel better. He was able to sit up in bed even though the world still felt unsteady beneath him. In the afternoon, Mother Veronica came in to check whether he had eaten.

She walked up to him and put her hand on his forehead and smiled down. She smelled like disinfectant and garlic.

"I vant you to see Father Albert. He is one of the Jesuits at the cathedral, a man of much education. He studied the mind in Germany, in the university there. I think he could help you regain your memories," she said. "As soon as you are vell enough, of course."

He felt helpless in the hands of so formidable a force as Mother Veronica. "You remind me of Sister Michael, a sister in Galveston who became one of my best friends," he said.

"Ah, so you do remember some things after all?"

"*Si*, sister," he said, "I suppose I do."

His memories came back like random patches on a quilt, catching his attention for a few moments and then blending into the pattern, melding with it before he could discern the meaning. He struggled to see the whole and not just the pieces, still for days the facts were jumbled in his head.

"My name is Primo," he told Father Albert. "I am an *insurrecto* who feels the oppression of my fellow countrymen, who wants to free those who are bound and assist those who are suffering."

Father Albert looked skeptical. "I find that hard to believe ..."

"But I am also Juan Lopez, the rancher and father ... and I am Martin Zamora, the worldly traveler and connoisseur of the arts ... and sometimes Father Ramirez.

They are all me."

"You mean you pretend to be them?"

"No, I mean I am all of them. I am split into parts. That is something I am only beginning to understand."

"The mind does this sometimes to defend itself."

"From what."

"Bad memories ... painful things in the past. Which one of these people do you prefer to be?"

He looked out the window over Father Albert's shoulder. For days, he'd seen nothing but the inside of this room, the two nuns, and the Jesuit. He'd come to like Father Albert but he also had grown tired of explaining himself.

"I think I prefer Primo right now ... at this moment."

"Why?"

"Because I have something to do ... a mission ... it's linked to St. Michael as I told you, and my feelings of purpose ... and I think Primo is the one who is most likely to succeed."

Father Albert sat back in the straight chair and cupped his chin with his hand. "There is someone I want you to meet when you are well enough. It requires riding north into the mountains but I think he could give you some answers. Are you willing?"

"*Si* ... father ... who is he?"

"He is called Arango. He is a *bandido* ... an *insurrecto* ... a serious one, one who has a plan. He reminds me of you, not just because he is similar to your Primo, but because he also has a number of identities. His real name is Doroteo and they have started to call him Pancho ... Pancho Villa."

Pedro found the Hostal de la Monja and when he entered, he knew it was a place that Juan Miguel would choose. He asked at the front desk and the clerk showed him Juan Miguel del Valle's signature on the register. "But he has been gone for several days, *Señor*," he said. "Two women are also here to find him. Do you wish to speak to them?"

"Two women? What are their names?"

When Pedro heard Annabelle Palmer's name, his knees buckled. He had been under the impression she was safe in Madrid with The Infanta. The moment of panic was followed by a feeling of relief. He had lost her and found her, all in a matter of seconds.

He sat down on a leather chair facing the front door and waited for them.

Next to her father, Pedro was the person who made Annabelle feel most secure. As soon as she saw him, she ran into his arms, something she'd never done before. He held her close to him, not with emotion but with reassurance and strength.

After the three of them gave their explanations and accounts of what they'd seen and heard, they compared notes. They still had no idea why he was here, what he was up to, and which identity to look for. But Pedro was adamant about one thing. Annabelle must return to Texas, by train, as soon as possible, and Cinco and Manny were to accompany her. Pedro would not even entertain an argument for her staying.

"I will stay for you," Charlotte said, holding Annabelle's hand in both of hers. "I will be your proxy. We will find him ... I promise."

"Will you do a favor for me, then?"

"Of course, what is it?"

She handed her a sealed note with the name Carlos Cordova on it. "Will you make sure that he gets this? I saw a bullfighting poster with his picture on it. He is in Monterrey now, that is all I know."

"I will try ... but I cannot promise."

"Hurry up with your excuses," General Reynaldo said to the card shark. "I want you out of here before my wife comes home."

"May I have a drink?"

"This early? All right ... *si*, pour yourself a whiskey but not the good one ... the other."

Marco Guillermo had dreaded this moment for days. He knew sooner or later he would be summoned to the general's home to offer an explanation for why he lost the man he'd been instructed to get information from and then kill.

He sat across from the general and sipped the caustic tasting whiskey and prepared to talk, but the general spoke first, "It is just as General Cordova said, the man is dangerous and slippery and much too curious. And for what purpose? All because a couple of worthless *paisanos* were taken off a train and shot. Since that day, he's been sticking his nose into everybody's business. Sooner or later he will find the mine and that will be an end to the flow of silver across the border."

Guillermo nodded his head and took another sip.

"On top of that, my wife said too much to the daughter and her friend when they came looking for him. And I let her talk so much, *amigo*, because I thought he was dead. I thought you had done as you were told. Performed your duty. Have you forgotten how to take orders since you got out of the army?"

"No, general ... it was an unusual circumstance."

"Go on, let's hear it."

"We hit him over the head and dragged him into a side street but he was out cold. We couldn't wake him up. So ... we waited and waited but nothing. He would not wake up. By morning, we had almost given up but he was still breathing. Then a funeral procession ... a long one ... coming from the cathedral turned onto the street."

"A funeral procession turned into a side street?"

"*Si* ... it is a short cut, I think, to the cemetery. Anyway, the two *paisanos* I hired saw the casket, and they got scared. They are superstitious and to them the casket is bad luck. So, they took off running and I never saw them again."

The general sneered at him as if he was having a hard time digesting such a fantastical tale.

"The procession is coming toward me and I am standing over a man who is knocked out. I left, too. I came back a short time later and he was gone. It was as if he'd never been there at all. I asked everyone around there but no one had seen him."

"This is the second time you have lost him. That is two too many."

"*Si* ... but the first time, it was because he was in the costume of a priest and then he suddenly changed into someone else. He is very good at disguises, general, believe me."

"I will give you one more chance to find him and kill him. If you lose him again, I will lock you up in the bowels of the mine and leave you there to be eaten by rats the size of Chihuahuas."

"The problem is, general, he has disappeared again. He didn't go back to the hotel. No one, not even his friends, can find him."

"You will find him ... before his friends ... and kill him. *Comprende?*"

"*Si* ... but ..."

"Now go, do what it takes. He is too close. He is reaching the point of finding the mine and frankly, both of us will be dead if he finds it. One way or another, our lives will be over. Now, go, *¡Vámonos!*."

Just before Annabelle was to leave on the train, Pedro sat down with Charlotte and told her the truth he'd been withholding, that he was almost sure he'd seen Juan Miguel the day he rode into town, ran after him, and called his name.

"He didn't recognize me or his name," Pedro said. "He shot at me and ran away. I lost him on the crowded street."

"Why didn't you tell us this yesterday?"

"I fear he is not in his right mind, that he is confused. He would not want Annabelle here worrying about him and searching for him. That is the last thing that he would want."

"That is probably true. You know him best."

"And you, *Señora*? What are you doing here so far from your home? I know you are his friend but ... well, it surprises me."

"Yes, it surprises me, too."

"Maybe you, too, should return to El Paso. I cannot tell you what to do however there is nothing you can do here."

Charlotte looked out the hotel window across the city square. Smog had rolled in from the mountains like the smoke settling after a cannon volley. Through it she could see a few people sitting on benches here and there. She had no desire to return to El Paso, none at all.

"I have never felt so lonely but I want to stay," she said,

"for my own reasons."

"Do as you please, *Señora*." He stood to leave. He had his hat in his hand.

"Sometimes a woman needs to run away as much as a man."

"*Si* ... that is true. What are you running from?"

She looked up at the tall, lanky *vaquero* and smiled at him. "My life," she said. "Perhaps I need a new one."

He put the hat on his head and fastened the leather strap under his chin. He scuffed one of his boots on the rug.

She stood and faced him. He put out his hand and touched her arm. Then he withdrew his hand, turned, and left.

Her arm was still warm from his touch even after the door closed behind him. The warmth went through her. There was something about the mysterious Pedro. He seemed rooted to the earth, not easily swayed. Constant— a mountain of a man. When she was in his presence, she felt she was really with someone. She liked that.

In the cool evening, Father Albert and Juan Miguel rode north toward the mountains on mules. "Tell me about being Father Ramirez," the priest said to Juan Miguel. "How did you invent that name?"

"Oh, I did not invent it, father. Father Ramirez was an old priest who died at my rancho one morning. Someone shot him ... the person who is out to kill me, I think."

"There is a Father Ramirez in northern Mexico who helps the *insurrectos*, a true believer, a well-respected man who has saved many from the brutal *rurales* in that area."

"*Si* ... it is the same man, I fear."

Father Albert pulled the reins and halted his mule. "There is a good chance the bullet was intended for Father Ramirez and not for you. Diaz and his men have been out to kill him for a long time."

Juan Miguel stopped, too, and sat thinking about what Father Albert had said. "That is something I didn't consider. The other time I was shot at, a priest was nearby. It was on an El Paso street ... Father Romo, another rebel priest, was walking behind me. That bullet may have been for him. I just never thought of it in that way."

"Father Romo ... yes, I know the name. He is in the thick of it. He is an *insurrecto*."

"How do you know all of this, father?"

"I am also a sympathizer. I believe there is only one thing that will bring relief to the suffering poor of this country ... getting rid of Diaz and his henchmen."

"And yet ... the church may be involved in that suffering."

"Only the most powerful in the church. There are many fathers and sisters who want to see Diaz ousted, believe me."

"Do you know a man called General Reynaldo?"

"Yes, I have heard of him. Why?"

"He befriended me on the night I was attacked."

"General Reynaldo is one of the President's closest advisers. He is Diaz's *compadre* ... an evil man."

A look of comprehension came over Juan Miguel's face. "So, he is the one who set me up. He and the so-called card shark, Marco Guillermo."

"Very likely, my friend. Very likely."

Chapter Five

By the beginning of May, Princess Alexis's gowns were starting to stretch tight in certain places. Her face was fuller and looked sallow, like she'd been bled. She and the Prince arrived back in Madrid just as the war got under way. At long last, after months of back and forth and tit for tat, the nations of Spain and the United States began hostilities, mostly at sea between opposing navies.

The Infanta saw the princess for the first time since her wedding one morning as she walked in a small garden near The Infanta's apartment. She approached her with an entourage of courtesans and hangers-on trailing behind. She turned and shooed them away.

"Pregnant so soon?" she asked, looking down at Princess Alexis's burgeoning belly.

"It happens when one is married, Pilar."

"*Si* ... but usually not quite so quickly. So ... it is the American's baby. Am I right?"

"No, you are not right."

"Of course I am. You are about four or five months pregnant, I would say. That means it happened in December and you were in America in December, romping around a Washington hotel room with the lovely Juan Lopez. You told me about it yourself."

The princess looked smug, not outraged, at the accusation.

"Let us sit down, Princess," The Infanta said. "You look tired."

Princess Alexis sat down next to the woman who once was her friend. Now, she felt she had no friends, not even Pilar. She had no one, only the baby growing inside of her.

"Does he know?" Pilar asked.

"No, and I don't want him to know because there's nothing he can do. We are worlds apart. What happened between us was long ago. Besides, he left me and I haven't heard a word from him in months. I think I hate him." She clutched at her stomach and looked as if she were near tears.

"It is true ... there is nothing he can do. But he should know. A man deserves to know when he's going to be a father."

"And how shall I tell him?" Princess Alexis asked, her eyes burning with anger. "Write it in a letter ... from some other man's wife? No, the book is closed. Nothing can be done now."

"I don't agree. Yes, you are another man's wife. It's only a formality. A royal marriage is only a formality. The book is not closed, my child."

"I want it this way ..."

The Infanta put her hand on the princess's hand and patted her. "You love him. You know you do."

"No ... I may feel his presence. I may even feel like I am with him sometimes. He is that close. But no, I hate him. If he were here, I would tear at that beautiful face."

The Infanta stood and crossed her arms. "This silly war will not last long. Spain will lose and give up its possessions within the year. Then the two of you can see each other again." Pilar said with her usual conviction, "Mark my words, princess, it is not over between you." Then she walked away.

"Pilar," the princess called after her. "Pilar ... don't meddle in this ... Pilar."

Charlotte packed her bags, boarded the train with Annabelle, and rode north through the emptiness she had traversed on horseback for what seemed like endless days and nights looking for Juan Lopez. She had decided to leave Durango. It was not her cup of tea. Instead of returning to El Paso, though, she would say goodbye to Annabelle at the town of Torreon and board another train to the ranch country north of Monterrey.

In the foothills of the Eastern Sierra Madres was a cattle ranch called Los Baños, a place her father had taken her often when she was growing up. It was from the ranch's owner, Hector Hernandez, that her father purchased the bull who sired a whole line of *toros* for the bullfighting arenas of northern Mexico and Texas. Hector and his sister, Deliah, were down-to-earth people, solid *mestizos*, Spanish in strength and resolve and Indian in discernment. She longed to ride the outer boundaries of their remote rancho and feast on the beauty of the mountains and Deliah's good food.

They were at the train station to meet her. About ten miles west of Monterrey in the arid savannahs where few people bothered to get off of the train and leave the beaten path, she hugged each of them like long-lost relatives, mounted the fine pony they brought for her to ride, and rode the forty more miles to their rancho hacienda.

When she'd been there for three days, she got up the courage to ask Hector and Deliah to take her to Monterrey where Carlito Intrepido, the bullfighter extraordinaire, was scheduled to appear. After the bullfight, she waited for him behind the arena and handed him the note from Annabelle. "Go to her ... go to her," she said. "Love is much too precious to waste."

He opened the note and read it. "And you, *Señora*, have you heeded your own advice?"

The next day she boarded the train and went east again, hoping by the time she reached Torreon she would know what to do, either go north to her old life in El Paso or go south to Durango where a man she could truly love might still be waiting for her.

There were not many landmarks between Monterrey and Torreon but she remembered the house on the south side of the tracks painted a bright blue, the color of a turquoise stone. When she saw it go by, she knew she would be in Torreon in a short while.

She was thinking about one evening after dinner when she and Deliah had sat on the rancho's porch looking down the slope to the dry creek bed.

"It will start to rain soon," Deliah had said. "It is either drought or monsoon here, nothing in between."

"So it is in El Paso, too," Charlotte said.

"So it is with love ... feast or famine ... all or nothing."

"I believe you are right, Deliah. May I ask you ... do you believe one can love someone after knowing them only a few days?"

"Of course ... one can love someone under any circumstances. It's what's in the heart that matters."

"Have you ever loved someone?"

"Me? No, just this land. I am in love with this land. And you? Do you still love your husband?"

"No ... I do not, however I recently met someone who moves me. In a way, he reminds me of this land you love so much. One might say he's uncharted but full of riches."

Deliah laughed at her. "Well then ... perhaps you should go explore, my dear."

"How do you know where to find this Arango ... or Pancho Villa ... whatever you call him?" Juan Miguel asked the priest.

"I don't ... but the cave dwellers know. He's been hiding out among them all winter."

"The cave dwellers?"

"The Tarahumara. They winter in their caves. It's about time for them to leave the caves and go up to their summer homes on the high plateaus."

Juan Miguel and Father Albert followed a well-worn path that zig-zagged up a slope to a sharp ridge. Down below was a wide *barranca*, the Indian word for canyon.

"This is why I insisted we ride mules," Father Albert said, laughing at himself as he stretched his cramped legs. "We will need their sure-footedness on the way down."

The floor of the *barranca* was obscured by smoke drifting up in waves from various spots.

"So this is where the Durango smog comes from?" Juan Miguel said.

"Yes, they burn the grasses this time of year. They think it brings on the rainy season. And who knows? Maybe it does."

The mules seemed to know their way down the side of the *barranca*. They knew where to step and were slow and sure. At the bottom, the western breeze blowing up the *barranca* like a wind tunnel had cleared the smoke.

Juan Miguel could see the built-out entrances to cave dwellings dotting the canyon walls, spaced well apart one from another, each one with its round hump-like storage bin for corn and its pen for animals.

Father Albert dismounted so Juan Miguel followed suit. They tied the mules to a nearby tree and walked up the canyon wall to the entrance to one of the most prominent caves. Father Albert sat on a rock wall away from the cave dwelling and motioned for Juan Miguel to do the same. They turned their backs to the entrance and waited.

"They consider it bad manners to 'knock on the door,'" the priest said. "We will wait until they notice us and make themselves ready. Then, they will invite us in ... maybe ... if they feel like it."

After a long wait, a woman came out of the cave, walked up to them, and stood waiting for them to turn around. When they did, she motioned them inside. It was warm and close inside the cave but roomier than Juan Miguel imagined and it was obvious that the Indians took pride in keeping it clean. Everything was in order and a meal was spread out on the cave floor.

The woman's husband appeared with a young man who was probably their son. They sat down and offered their food—corn cakes, beans, cured meat, and cooked squash. After the meal, Father Albert asked where he could find the man called Arango. In Spanish, the Indian man said, "Wait here and I will get him."

Once again, they sat on the rock outside of the cave. In

the evening, just before sunset, the Indian man walked up from deeper in the canyon. Behind him was a young *mestizo* who already had a bit of a paunch, grinning wide and carrying a rifle.

"Father Albert," he yelled. "It's so good to see you. What brings you to the *madres*?"

They spent the evening around an outside fire passing a bottle of tequila that Father Albert had brought for the occasion, although the man called Arango did not drink. Instead, he milked the priest for information—about the revolutionary movement, about Diaz and his activities, about the Concordium company's latest outrages. When he'd had his fill of news from the civilized world, he sat back and lit a cheap foul-smelling cigar.

"This is my last one," Arango said. "Or I would offer you one. Please tell me, father, what brings you here?"

"To introduce you to this man," he said pointing at Juan Miguel. "He also is sometimes a *bandido*. They call him Primo."

"I have heard of you," Arango said. "You are the one who killed Mateo and escaped from his men by offering to blow them up."

Juan Miguel said nothing. He put his hands on his knees to signify that he did not take offense and would not reach for a weapon.

"And ... you robbed the San Vicente silver mine. See? I too, know a thing or two about what goes on."

"*Si* ... this is all true," Juan Miguel said.

"Where is the silver now?"

"High up in the Sierra Madres. High enough to be inaccessible."

"And what do you plan to do with it?"

"To fund the revolutionary movement ... when the time comes and I am confident of who I should give it to."

"Oh, *Señor* ... give it to me," Arango said, then his belly shook as he laughed.

"Perhaps I will ... if I can be sure it would be well spent."

"The revolution will come ... Primo. It will not come tomorrow or even the next day but in ten or twelve years. We must lay the groundwork first. Politics ... as much as I hate politics ... we have to play that game."

"Meaning?"

"Meaning, we have to have the intelligentsia, the smart people, on our side. And that will take some time. But already we are making progress. They write articles. They issue manifestos. They stand for office here and there. When the time is ripe, we will strike, and we will be successful because the people in power are corrupt. They have nothing but their own self-interest in their hearts."

"And what do you have in your heart?"

"Truth ... justice ... passion," he said, again roaring with delight.

"What do you know about the Taxcoco mine? Do you know where it is?"

"*Si* ... but that place is the pit of evil, *Señor*. The men who work the mine are enslaved in every sense. They are not free to leave. They make no money at all and they are worked until they die. The mine is guarded by Diaz's men. A whole army unit surrounds it."

"So there is nothing that can be done?"

"Maybe ... someday with enough men and enough money ... but for now, no. It is a lost cause."

"Suppose you supply the men and I supply the money?"

"That is a big undertaking ... you see, the worst part is the bridge, the only way in and out of the mine. A suspension bridge ... they call it *Puente de Taxcoco* ... crosses a deep, deep gorge, so deep that one can hardly see the bottom, they say. I will think about it. There may be a way if we have enough men."

"If you have a good plan and the men to carry it out, I will give you the money on one condition, that you kill General Cordova."

"General Cordova? He is Diaz's right hand man ... his friend. What do you have against him? Why him?"

"I have personal reasons. I want him dead. Think about it overnight and give me your answer by morning. We leave tomorrow after the noon meal."

"You have given me much to think about," Arango said. He stood up and walked back down the *barranca* in the moonlight.

The next day, Arango said, "I will make a deal with you ... Primo. If you give me the money and we are successful,

I will kill General Cordova myself. But you will have to give me some time. It can't be done overnight."

"I will tell you the location of the silver when General Cordova is dead."

"*Ai, ai, ai ... Señor*, you are too difficult to bargain with. It is a deal but as I said, it will take time. Impatience, *Señor*, will be the end of us."

Juan Miguel nodded. "Send word to Father Albert when the deed is done," he said before mounting his mule for the trek up the canyon wall.

"What have you done in my absence?" Charlotte said to Pedro, surprising him from behind.

He turned and saw her standing there with a valise in her hand. She came straight from the train station to the hotel where she found out where to find him—a saloon down the street that was less opulent than the Hostal de la Monja.

He stood up and took off his hat. He looked surprised and befuddled. "*Señora*, I thought you had gone north ... gone back to El Paso."

"Are you going to offer me a drink?"

"*Por supuesto, Señora*. Please sit down."

She sat down next to him, untied the ribbon under her chin, and removed her hat. "Well, please order me a drink ... tequila ... and tell me what you've done in my absence. Have you found out anything more about where he is?"

"I have been watching the house of General Reynaldo, as you suggested, *Señora* ..."

"Please call me Charlotte. I may not be *Señora* much longer."

"*Bueno* ... Charlotte. I have seen a parade of officials coming and going but no one connected to Juan Miguel. Perhaps General Reynaldo really is innocent."

"I think it's about time for me to return to the Casa de la Reynaldo for a visit. Don't you agree?" She picked up the glass of tequila and downed it all at once then she wiped the corners of her mouth with her fingers.

Pedro watched all of this with interest. When she was through, he smiled at her and ordered her another drink.

"You didn't ask me why I may not be *Señora* much longer," she said.

"That is your business, Charlotte. But I admit, it is not bad news."

Pedro had spent the morning giving Charlotte instructions on what to say and what not to say once she was in the Reynaldo home. "Don't argue. Don't contradict. Don't ask too many questions. Keep smiling. Try to relax. Be sympathetic."

The two of them waited across the street until they saw General Reynaldo leave the house. Then Charlotte crossed, lifting her skirts out of the dust in the street. Señora Reynaldo answered the door, peeking out with a timid look on her face.

"*Señora*," Charlotte said, "I wonder if I could speak with you a moment?"

Señora Reynaldo opened the door wide and stepped aside. Charlotte walked in and followed her out onto the patio where she had been watering the plants in the garden. Señora Reynaldo picked up the watering can and continued to pour small amounts of water here and there at the base of the shrubs and flowers.

Charlotte watched for a moment and decided to proceed. "*Señora* ... I still have not found my friend ... the one we were looking for when we came here before. I thought you might have heard something more about him."

Señora Reynaldo didn't look at her. She walked over to the sideboard and ladled more water into her can from a bucket. When it was full, she turned and said, "I should have told you this when you were here. We were expecting him that evening. Don't ask me why he didn't come because I don't know the answer to that. But perhaps knowing that small bit of information will help you. I hope so. Now, will you excuse me while I do my morning work? And please, Señora Peterson, show yourself out."

Señora Reynaldo turned her back to Charlotte once again and started to pour water from the can onto the new plants at the front of the garden. Charlotte did as Pedro had suggested. She didn't ask more questions. She found her way out of the front door.

When she told Pedro what Señora Reynaldo said, he

nodded. "*Si* ... her husband is in on it. Otherwise he would have told you that when you were there. He kept it from you for a reason. My guess is that his hands are dirtier than we first thought."

"Do you think he set him up for something?"

"*Si* ... but what? What has happened to him?"

The small town of Guanacevi, nestled at the base of the mountains north of Durango, was established in 1569 by the Spanish conquistadors who built a base camp on the site that they used while exploring the area for minerals—gold or silver. In the 1700s, the Spanish crown sent priests to pacify the local population of Tarahumaras and Tepehuans. They built a colonial style stone church with two belfries, a mission, and several adobe homes. Although pacification took place, the Indians clung to their old ways and their religion and staged a number of revolts against the invaders.

The town of Guanacevi didn't become the hub of New Spain that the Spanish had hoped, but because of its location near a number of large mines, it hung on and grew at a slow pace. It was a quiet little village surrounded by beautiful scenery with a few stores and the original church still standing.

Juan Miguel and Father Albert rode into town on a Sunday, the 8th of May in 1898, the feast of St. Michael the Archangel. They stopped in front of a run-down looking saloon and café down the street from the Fonda San Saba, and tied their mules to a signpost.

"Something does not look right," Father Albert said. "It is the feast of St. Michael. They should be out celebrating. The church bell should be ringing."

"Shall we go inside and ask someone. Perhaps someone has died."

At that moment, Juan Miguel saw a young boy, not more than six or seven years old, peek out from behind a building then vanish. Juan Miguel put his hand on his pistol and looked up and down the street both ways. He had an uneasy feeling.

"Where is everyone?" Father Albert said. "The silence is eerie."

A rifle shot shattered the unnatural peace, hitting the sign close to Juan Miguel's head. He ducked then fell onto the ground with his pistol drawn. "Get down, father, get down," he yelled. "It is an ambush."

Before Father Albert could react, another rifle shot rang out. The priest clutched his shoulder, and he fell backward into the dirt. Juan Miguel took him by the arm and pulled him up and into the café. An old man and woman scrambled to the back room and closed the door.

"Is it bad, father?" he asked while looking out the only window. "Are you badly hurt?"

"Yes ... the blood is gushing."

"Find something to tie it off ... stop the bleeding."

"It is too far up ... there is nothing I can do."

"Use your hand to put pressure on it ... don't give up on me, father."

Then he saw the young boy again, walking out from the back of a building. Behind him, pointing a gun at the boy's head, was a man he recognized from the poker game, the man who accused him of cheating, Guillermo Marco.

"Come out, Juan Miguel, and drop your gun or I will shoot the boy," Marco yelled. The boy's face was ghostly and he trembled with terror. He was too much in shock to cry and his eyes were closed as if he couldn't bear to see what would happen to him next.

The horror of hurting a child was too much for Juan Miguel. He walked out the door with his hands up and tossed the pistol on the dirt in front of the man and boy. "Pick it up," Marco said to the boy. He shoved him and the boy bent down and picked up the gun by the barrel and held it out from his body like a lit bomb. "Hand it to me," he said and the boy did, then he shoved him hard out of the way.

"What type of man uses a small boy to hide behind?" Juan Miguel asked. "A coward? Someone without *cajones*?"

"Shut up or I will kill you right here ... and the boy, too. You are far more useful to me alive, Juan Miguel. Get back on the mule."

"There is a rich ransom to be had for you ... whether it

is from someone who hates you or from someone who likes you, I don't care. You are worth more to me alive than dead," Marco Guillermo said. He rode behind him on a horse while Juan Miguel rode his mule through the wilds of the lower Sierra Madres. "But don't think I would hesitate to kill you. You are worth more to me dead than lost again. If I lose you again, they'll kill me."

Juan Miguel didn't reply. He'd been virtually silent since Guillermo finished off Father Albert with another bullet and urged Juan Miguel onto his mule before they rode out of the small town. At least the little boy had been saved, although probably terrified for years to come.

"Have you nothing to say ... Juan Miguel?"

"No ... nothing."

"Don't you want to know where we're going?"

"*Si* ... where are we going?"

"The Taxcoco mine. That infamous place you've been looking for. Once we are there, you can forget about an escape. There is only one entrance, across a deep gorge and ..."

"You can spare me the long explanation. I know about the bridge."

They rode down the back slope of some foothills and started out across a wide playa where only a few cacti and yucca plants spotted the landscape. The west wind picked up the sand and blew it in their faces. Juan Miguel's mouth was as dry as the parched earth. "Can we stop for a drink of water?" he called back to his captor.

"No ... not now. We should get there before sunset."

The Indian slave workers of the Taxcoco mine watched him with pity on their faces as he rode across the suspension bridge on a mule, at gunpoint, his hat gone and his long curly brown hair blowing in the dry wind. They watched out of the corners of their eyes as he was put into an outdoor cage near the mine offices, then stripped of most of his clothing, and left there without water or food.

The night was cold and he huddled in the corner near the office building wall to get as much warmth from it as he could. He shivered and his mouth was dry and his lips cracking. His stomach ached from hunger.

The next morning, one of those Indian workers brought him a bowl of corn and bean mash and a small cup of water. The man opened the door, motioned for him to back away, and put down the bowl. The same Indian repeated that again in the evening. After he set down the bowl, Juan Miguel attempted to look him in the eye. "Do you speak Spanish?" he asked. The man looked uncomprehending and closed and locked the door.

That night a thunderstorm rolled over the valley and dumped rain on the gorge, the stream down below, and the mining operation up top. Lightning struck the mine rigging, thunder boomed down through the canyon and echoed against the steep walls. The rain drenched the cage in which he had been imprisoned. He shivered even more in the wet cold.

He watched as rain filled a sewage ditch that ran between two nearby buildings. The ditch overflowed, widened, and ran like a small stream into the back of the cage. Within a few minutes, the water began to wash away the dirt underneath its back wall. A small opening appeared. He knelt down in the water and dug and dug in the mud until there was an opening just deep enough for a man to crawl through.

By morning, he was weaker than ever from exposure. He sat against the back wall of the cage, his body shaking and his wet hair matted to his face. When the man put down the bowl and cup, he scooted sideways to show him the hole he'd dug. Quietly, he made the undulating noise that Panchito taught him to summon help from the Tarahumaras. The man looked at him and nodded, only once, but it gave him hope.

Close to sunset, the workers came marching out of the mine to be fed. They were gathered in a circle, guarded from behind by the mining officials. From one side of the circle came an eerie, throaty keening noise. Then another, then another. Soon, all of them were making the noise. The guards pointed their rifles and walked among them, trying to figure out why they were making the strange noise.

While the guards' backs were turned, he slipped through the opening. They were so stupefied by the strange noise coming from the Tarahumaras and so busy threatening them if they did not stop that they didn't notice him at all as he walked away quietly. He found a horse tied to a rail by the office, mounted it and walked it slowly to the side of the gorge and then to the bridge. When he reached the bridge, he took off galloping.

The guards fired at him. Bullets struck the bridge suspension, the sides of the gorge, and whizzed past him. But he galloped on, the bridge lurching on its structure high above the deep gorge.

St. Michael guided him, through the bullets' paths, across the precarious bridge, through the fading light, between the startled soldiers guarding the entrance to the bridge. He galloped on and didn't look back. Across the playa, now covered in shallow water, into the low foothills beyond. He dared not stop. He rode on through the night, with barely enough strength to stay in the saddle. He could see the ambient light of dawn over the far mountains as he rode into Guanacevi.

He rode into the middle of the town, got off of the horse, and stood looking around him. Slowly they came out. From the nearby church, from the small houses, from the stores. The people of Guanacevi walked out and surrounded him. A priest walked up to him and put out his hand to steady him. "My son ... we beg your forgiveness for delivering you into the hands of an evil one. And we thank you for saving the life of Raulito."

He nodded at them and collapsed onto his knees, his head sagging. "Do you have some food?" he asked. They helped him inside and fed and clothed him. After he'd eaten, he explained that he was probably being followed by the soldiers who guarded the mine.

"Come with me," the priest said. "I know the perfect place to hide you. It is loud but effective."

At noon, the soldiers rode into town and asked if anyone had seen him. They said no. The soldiers insisted on searching for him. They said go ahead. The bell of the church rang out the twelve strokes of the 12 o'clock hour. The father had been right. The bell was extremely loud, especially if you were sitting right next to it in the belfry.

They searched everywhere but didn't find him so they rode on. His hearing did not come back until the next day and by that time he was almost back in Durango.

"We just have to wait for him. There is nothing else we can do," Pedro said to Charlotte. "He has an uncanny way of getting himself out of any situation. Believe me, it is true. He gets out of things as easily as he gets into them."

She sat back against the pillow and put her hand on his. "I know," she said. She looked over at the man next to her in bed. She knew that he was right, but waiting was difficult.

Pedro had lost no time after she visited Señora Reynaldo. He breached the garden wall in the back of the house and hid in the garden. That evening General Reynaldo received a visitor—General Cordova. They sat in the cool twilight and smoked their cigars. It was dusk but Pedro could see that General Cordova was not the Monterrey warden. Listening to the two of them talk convinced him to stay and hear the whole conversation.

They talked about the coming revolution and what it would do to the mining operations of Concordium, of which they were both owners.

"If Diaz goes, so goes the subsoil ownership of mineral rights," General Cordova said. "He was the one who pushed through the reforms that have made it possible for big companies to come back into Mexico."

"True, general," General Reynaldo said. "If we hadn't found the Taxcoco mine and started mining it again, we would never have discovered the vein of gold running alongside the silver. We'd both be a lot poorer."

They both laughed and picked up their glasses of wine and drank.

"So, we must do everything to prevent another revolution. Anyone who threatens to stir up the people is an enemy of the mining industry. We know that."

"*Si* ... but we have our friends ... in Mexico City ... in Washington. When the war between Spain and America is over, we can renew our efforts to get the reforms in Washington we want. We have enough friends there to do it once they are not so preoccupied with war."

Pedro stepped out of the shadows of the garden with his rifle pointed at the two men. They jumped and General Cordova clutched at his chest. "What do you want?" General Reynaldo said. "If it is money, then take it." They both reached in their pockets.

"I am not here to rob," Pedro said. "I am here to ask questions ... about Juan Miguel del Valle. Sit down, *señores*."

They sat and looked at one another with frightened looks.

"What is Juan Miguel doing here? What is he looking for?"

Once more, they glanced at each other. "We're not sure," General Reynaldo said. "He snoops around looking for information about mining operations ... perfectly legal mining operations, mind you."

"What ... *señores* ... is he looking for?" Pedro walked up to General Reynaldo and put the rifle butt next to his temple. "Either tell me or your brains will be blown all over your *amigo's* fine suit."

"He asks questions about the Concordium company ... that is the extent of our knowledge."

"Where is he?"

"Believe me, *Señor*, we know as little about that as you do. He was expected here for dinner and he never came."

"If you are lying to me, I will return and finish this," Pedro said.

Pedro heard General Reynaldo's wife talking inside. He backed away from the two men and exited the courtyard the same way he came in. He left with not much more information than he had when he went in but he knew enough to wait until Juan Miguel appeared again. He knew that Juan Miguel would let him find him whenever he was ready.

"Are you sure that he knows it's you who's following him?" Charlotte asked him.

"I am sure ... if he is in his right mind, he knows. If he is not in his right mind, well, there is not much I can do."

"But the waiting is so difficult."

"*Si* ... difficult," he said and squeezed her hand.

"Mining? Why is he interested in mining?"

"It has something to do with General Cordova. Other than that, I don't know."

He appeared at the Hostal de la Monja desk wearing the dirty, baggy clothes of a *paisano*, his face unshaven and gaunt, his eyes sunken and his stomach in an uproar.

"Can I help you?" the clerk said.

"It is I, Juan Miguel del Valle ... do you not recognize me?"

He took off the straw hat and brushed back his hair. The clerk looked him up and down.

"*Si* ... Señor Juan Miguel, please forgive me. What has happened to you?"

"I was attacked and ... well it is a long story. But I am here to retrieve the money I deposited in your safe several weeks ago, and my other belongings.

"I will get the hotel manager ... wait here."

It took some fast talk on his part but the clerk verified that it was him, that he was the same man who checked into the hotel and deposited a large sum of cash. Once it was done, he climbed the stairs to a room. Each step felt as tall as a canyon wall. He opened the door, threw the hat on the floor, stepped out of the clothes, and fell on to the bed. He slept for that day, the next night, and the next day—without eating, drinking only the water provided in a pitcher by the bed. When he was rested, he arranged for a bath, dressed in decent clothes, and went to get a meal.

He reached the top of the stairway just as Charlotte and Pedro walked into the hotel lobby to once more ask questions about him. Pedro saw him, walked to the foot of the stairway, and looked up at him as if he were seeing a ghost. When he caught sight of Pedro, tears of joy came into his eyes. He walked down slowly and stepped into Pedro's embrace.

"*Amigo* ... my old friend," he said trembling. Pedro held him tight and said nothing.

He stepped back and looked Pedro in the eyes. "You are the most beautiful sight I have ever seen ... ever."

Pedro looked a little bit embarrassed. "And you, my friend ... and you," he said.

He saw Charlotte standing there behind Pedro. He looked from her to him and back to her. "*Señora*, what are you doing here?" he said. He put out his hand to take hers.

"I came looking for you. It seems everyone is looking for you."

"But it appears you found someone else," he said grinning wide.

Pedro's ears turned a bright scarlet. The color went down his neck into his shirt collar.

"And Annabelle ... she is still in Madrid?"

"No, she is back home. We sent her home."

"Sent her? Was she here?"

"We will explain ..."

"The first thing I want to tell you is that General Cordova is not the Monterrey warden, as you had feared," Pedro told him when they sat down to talk alone. "I've been to Monterrey and seen his grave. I saw General Cordova here in Durango. They look somewhat alike ... perhaps they are related, but they are not the same person."

Juan Miguel looked embarrassed. "You are sure?"

"I am."

"Ah ... I have done the man an injustice, arranged for his killing."

"Can you call it off?"

"I will try but first I have to visit the sisters who helped me so that I can tell them about Father Albert's murder."

"Who is responsible for his death?"

"General Reynaldo ..."

"But they are *compadres*, those two generals. I myself heard them conspiring to prevent the revolution."

"So General Cordova is less innocent than we thought? He killed the priest and he has other blood on his hands as well. The blood of thousands perhaps ... workers in mines whose lives are stolen from them ... and for what? So that he can live comfortably in a big mansion in Mexico City."

"What will you do?"

"I will consider what to do on my way to the church. I can delay telling them about Father Albert no longer."

In a small orange grove in back of the nunnery, they sat on wooden chairs in a circle in the warm spring afternoon. The sisters had served him tea, marmalade, and a pastry they called strudel that reminded him of the apple and cinnamon enchiladas Celita sometimes made for him. He picked up a bite of each and put them in his mouth. The sisters stared as if they seldom got to gaze on a comely male face.

A cat walked in between the chairs then jumped up into Mother Veronica's lap. "This is Chica ... she goes vhere she vants and does vhat she vants. I envy that," the nun said.

"As do I, mother. As do I." Once again he said, "I am sorry, sisters, about Father Albert's death. Please forgive me."

"There is nothing to forgive," Mother Veronica said. "It is not your fault. Now, vill you excuse us vhile we go inside for afternoon prayers? But please remain and talk to me some more. Vill you do that?"

"*Por supuesto*, mother, whatever you ask."

She put down the cat before they walked inside and immediately, the cat jumped into his lap. "You are a little whore, Chica," he said. "You go from one to another without compunction."

Chica sat in his lap and looked up at him. He put his hand on her head and rubbed and she started to purr. One of her paws rested lightly on his arm. Chica's fur was pale orange, the color of blonde hair. It reminded him of the hair of the woman he loved.

"Where is she, Chica? Is she someplace enjoying the spring sunshine? Has she thought of me at all or has she forgotten me?"

The cat blinked and purred. He smiled. "More rubbing? You are shameless … shameless."

He had shed his own fur. He was without the clothing, the mannerisms, the accents, the disguises. He was stripped down to the essentials … bare … defenseless. What would God do with him now? Would he thrust him into the pits of hell again or would he take pity on him?

He put his head back in the sunshine and felt it go through his body. He was at peace for the first time in months. At peace at last but also quite alone. He was surrounded by friends but quite alone.

Mother Veronica disturbed his dozing when she returned. She sat down next to him and poured fresh tea into his cup. "May I ask you a question, *mein fruend*?" she said.

"Ask me, mother."

"Vhat are you doing here? Vhy are you not at home in America vith vife and *kuchen*, children ... as you should be?"

"God keeps kicking me in the backside ... kicking me down the road."

"Ja ... God. He is relentless. Vhy don't you just ignore him for avhile? Vhy don't you go home and rest for avhile?"

"I have one last stop to make, mother, and it's someplace you probably know."

"Vhere is that?"

"Mexico City ... There is someone there with whom I have a score to settle. And I also want to have a word with the Archbishop of Mexico."

"Be careful, *mein freund* ... I hear that he is not one to trifle vith."

"Well, truth be told, mother, neither am I."

"You don't look like such a hard one."

"Looks can be deceiving ... no one knows that better than I. Speaking of looks, mother, may I borrow one of Father Albert's robes? I know it's an unorthodox request but I'm sure he would lend it to me if he were here."

"To bury him?"

"No, I fear the good people of Guanacevi have already done that. However, you could call it a way for Father Albert to live beyond the grave ... a resurrection you might say."

"I do not understand. But you can take the robe ... if

that is vhat he vould vant. I vill request it."

He was a simple, mendicant monk with the robe of a Jesuit but the face of a Franciscan. He raised the hood over his head and shielded his face and walked in to the grand *Catedral Metropolitana Ciudad de México*, one of the largest and most magnificent cathedrals in the world. It had taken more than 250 years to construct and was situated right atop the same ground where the Aztecs' most sacred temple stood—an act of triumph of the Spanish over the Indians, of Christianity over the pagan religion.

The grandiosity was more than he could comprehend. Soaring arches, beautiful frescoes, metal work that was the very best in the world. An altar of gold taken from the rich mines of Mexico and created by skilled artisans, many of them indigenous people. He knelt on one of the benches and folded his hands in prayer. "God, I would not expect to encounter you in such a place," he whispered. "But if you are here, well then, I beseech you to deliver your people from suffering. *Si* ... suffering produces beauty, the beauty I see around me ..." he glanced up at the statues—lovely, graceful, lifelike. "But surely you can ease the people's suffering ... give them hope."

An old priest in bishop's robes fussed with the Eucharist table at the main altar. When he saw the monk kneeling at prayer, he approached him. "Brother, the cathedral is not open ... come back tomorrow."

He stood and looked at the old priest. "You would close God's house to his people?"

"We have hours just as anyplace does. We close to make preparations for the next day's masses. You can come back tomorrow morning."

"I would like to see the archbishop about the murder of one of his priests, Father Albert Herman. I was with him when he died."

"Who are you?" the old priest asked.

"You can call me Miguel ... that is what I have been called."

"Miguel? Brother Miguel?"

"Simply Miguel ..."

"Do you know who committed the murder?"

"*Si* ... as I said, I was there."

"Where are you from, Miguel?"

"Durango."

"I will see if he can talk to you ... wait here."

He waited and waited. The day wore. He wondered if he'd been forgotten. Several hours after midday, the bishop came back. Behind him was another man dressed in bishop's vestments.

"I am the archbishop, brother. What did you wish to tell me?" the man said.

"Father Albert was murdered by a hired assassin several days ago in the small town of Guanacevi."

"We have heard ..."

"The man who pulled the trigger does not matter. The

man who hired him does. He is one of the shareholders in a mining company named Concordium. Have you heard of it, archbishop?"

"I have heard the name."

"This company ... Concordium ... enslaves the Indians and presses them into working the mine. They are held there and not paid for their work. The men who own the mine take all of the profits. I also have evidence that some of those shareholders are priests, men in the hierarchy of the church, and others are government officials close to the president himself. It is an illegal operation, done in the shadows, to avoid paying taxes."

"That is a sad story, Miguel, but what do you expect me to do about it?"

The monk reached up and removed the hood from his head and smiled. He walked over to an apse beside the cathedral's main knave and looked at an altar off to the side, close to the entrance. Set into it, surrounded by gold filigree, was a statue of St. Michael with a raised sword and his boot on the dragon's neck—the devil's neck.

"Saint Michael slays dragons, does he not, archbishop? The question is this ... who are the dragons and who are the saints?"

"You are wasting our time, Miguel. Leave or I will call the guards," the older bishop said.

"*I* am wasting your time? *Si* ... your time is precious ... and running out, I would wager.

"Let him speak, bishop," the archbishop said.

"My message is this," the monk said, "someday soon, you will be held to account, unless you do something to root out this corruption."

The archbishop sneered at him. "Who are you, brother? One of the rebel priests? The pope has warned against rebellion."

"San Miguel is real, archbishop. He is not just a statue. He will take his revenge."

He put the hood back on his head and walked out slowly.

Toward the end of the day, he found the Mexico City home of General Cordova and his wife. It was a grand estate in the rich part of town, set back from the road, surrounded by a park, and fenced and gated. He stood outside the ornate wrought iron fence and waited. A few minutes later, a delivery wagon rolled down the road from the main house. The deliveryman stopped, got out to open the gate, and went through. When he started to jump down to close the gate, a monk standing close by said, "I will close it for you ... go on, *Señor.*" He slipped through the gate and walked up to the house.

He found an open door and crept through the first floor of the house until he found General Cordova sitting behind his desk in the study, his face red and bloated and his neck muscles bulging above his shirt collar. He went in and locked the door behind him.

He pulled a pistol from underneath Father Albert's robe and pointed it at the general. "Don't speak or move, general."

"The safe is upstairs," the general said.

"I am not here for money." He took off the hood and smiled at General Cordova. "You know who I am."

"*Si* ... I see now. Juan Miguel del Valle."

"At least you are honest about that."

"What do you want?"

"You are responsible for the death of Father Albert Herman, *Señor*, and for the deaths of many, many innocent people," he said.

General Cordova put his hand on the desk and fiddled with a writing pen. His face became even redder.

"I know this is true," the monk said, "but I will leave your punishment to God."

He leaned to within inches of the general's face and put his hands flat on the desktop. "From this day forward, you are my sworn enemy. Stay away from my rancho and my family or I will do everything to defeat you. As for the matter of your son and my daughter ... well, that too is unthinkable."

General Cordova cowered in his chair. He looked as if his head might explode but still he said nothing.

"I wish to know one thing and then I will leave you to your own fate," the monk said. "Where is the French woman, the one who was taken in Chihuahua and kept by the army?"

"The mine ... the Taxcoco mine," the general said.

"What is her name?"

"Her name is Anna Maria. She is not kept against her will ... she is a whore."

The name Carlito Intrepido had become well known throughout Mexico during the last year. He defeated the bulls in Mexico City, in Durango, in Guadalajara, and in Monterrey. He was fearless, approaching a bull to within inches of his horns and even turning his back on him and walking away, which was considered the ultimate act of bravery.

While he was in Monterrey the previous week, Carlito visited the grave of his father, Manuel Cordova, the general's brother. He knelt before the tombstone and once again pledged revenge for his death. Although his father was murdered in a prison escape before his birth, Carlito had felt his absence all his life. At an early age, fighting bulls in the arena became an outlet for his rage, but he never forgot the debt he owed to his father—the debt of vengeance.

He had returned home the previous day to tell his uncle that he would not continue at the university as he had promised but would persist in the bullfighting career he had come to love. He walked into his uncle's study just as a hooded monk was leaving, breezing past him hurriedly without a word.

"Who was that, uncle?" he asked.

His uncle was still seated behind his desk. He looked like a man who'd been stricken across the face. He was pale and his eyes were sullen. "That was Juan Miguel del Valle ... in another one of his disguises."

"But he is dead. You told me he died as the outlaw Primo, that only his friend who did the beating was still alive."

"I have not had an opportunity to tell you the whole story. He lives and that was him. He has been living as Juan Lopez all these years."

"Annabelle's father?" Carlos sat down and stared out the window in disbelief.

"Once again he has eluded me," the general said. "I have done everything to lure him out of his lair and yet each time, he slips from my grasp."

He walked around the desk and took Carlos by the shoulders. "Carlito, do your bullfighting if you must, but we must not forget this man and what he has done to our family. And if that were not enough, he comes to our country and dares to stir the pot of things that are none of his business."

"No ... he is the father of the woman I love. He is Annabelle's father. That changes everything." He left the room, a perplexed look on his face. His uncle called after him, "Carlito ... your father's honor ... Carlito ..."

When Juan Miguel arrived back in Durango, Pedro met him with the news that Marco Guillermo was dead. He had stepped into the path of a streetcar in Durango and died instantly.

"Was it you?" Juan Miguel asked.

"Someone pushed him."

"Someone?"

"*Si* ... "

"But they don't know who?"

"An aggrieved card player, perhaps? A *bandido*? An *insurrecto*?" Pedro had the faintest hint of a smile underneath his stoic demeanor.

"Well, the deed is done, however it happened."

"And General Reynaldo ... and the others? What shall we do about them?"

"We must leave this country and let the rivalries play out as they will. But I do wish to tip the balance a bit in favor of the *insurrectos*. So I must ride into the mountains and pay a debt. I have decided to give a large cache of silver to a wild-eyed *insurrecto* called Arango and absolve him of his duty ... the murder of General Cordova. Will you go with me or are you too occupied here with your new friend?"

Pedro was unaccustomed to being teased about women. He raised a cup of coffee to his lips and drank it down and looked at the grinning Juan Miguel. "I will go with you. Charlotte leaves tomorrow to settle things in El Paso."

"Settle things?"

"*Si* ... divorce."

"Do you have something to tell me, my friend?"

"Tell you? No, what do you expect to hear?"

Juan Miguel put his hand on Pedro's shoulder and grinned even wider. "That you are in love with Charlotte ... that you want to marry her."

"She was your friend first ..."

"*Si* ... my friend only. You know that I love someone else."

"Have you heard from her?"

"No ... and I don't expect to. She has married a Russian prince and lives in Madrid. I read about it in a newspaper."

Pedro's eyes met Juan Miguel's for just a moment, as if he wanted a glimpse into his soul, before he looked away.

"I am fine, *amigo*," Juan Miguel assured him. "Fine."

"There is another matter ..."

"*Si?*"

"General Cordova is brother to the Monterrey prison warden from your past. Charlotte has told me. She knows the general's wife."

"There is bad blood between our families ... and that will not go away."

"And what about Annabelle's feelings for the son?"

"She will have to get over them. She could never marry into the Cordova family ... never."

On their way through Guanacevi, they stopped at the

Fonda San Saba to see Anna Maria. Juan Miguel was anxious to tell her about her son, Michelito, that he had lived and was safe at the rancho.

"She did not survive the operation," the old woman behind the hotel desk told him. "She bled to death. She is buried outside of town in a pauper's grave if you wish to visit her."

CHAPTER SIX

By mid August the Kingdom of Spain had capitulated. Naval battles in both the Atlantic and the Pacific and the invasion of Cuba and the Philippines by American forces proved to be too much for Spain. The Spanish national legislature agreed to a peace treaty and the war on both fronts wound down. In effect, Spain was about to lose most of its empire and the United States would become a world power to reckon with.

Although the Spanish legislature agreed to sue for peace, the capital of Madrid was in turmoil because many wanted to continue fighting and still hoped for a victory. Spain had appealed to other European monarchies for support during the war, but in spite of strategic alliances and marriages among members of royalty, no other country came to Spain's aid. The outcome caused bitterness in the minds of some supporters of the monarchy, particularly Prince Sergey himself.

Once it was apparent that Spain would no longer be a dominant world power, the Russian prince saw no need for his marriage to a Spanish princess. He maneuvered to rid himself of her and her bastard child in hopes of marrying someone with more influence and more power.

On the last day of August, only weeks before Princess Alexis was to give birth, Prince Sergey moved out of their apartments in Madrid. He left a letter informing the princess that he was on his way to St. Petersburg for a vacation. The next day, when he was well away from the capital, a contingent of Russian bodyguards invaded her rooms, packed up her belongings, and put her on a train bound for the Sierra Moreno Mountains of Andalusia.In the middle of the night, Princess Alexis arrived in the small town of Jerez de la Frontera. The bodyguards who accompanied her rushed her off of the train and into a waiting carriage. She was driven out of town, up a winding road that led to a remote nunnery named the Convento de San Pedro, and dumped on its doorstep. The Benedictine sisters were ill equipped to deal with a woman who was about to give birth but they did their best to make her comfortable while they decided what to do with her.

Princess Alexis's husband, her Spanish relatives, and her Russian relatives had all abandoned her. When she realized this, she appealed to the sisters to let her stay at the convent and work for them to earn her keep. The sisters let her stay in a room off of the kitchen and work as a kitchen maid.

The Infanta was one Spanish relative who still wanted to help Princess Alexis. But she had to do it carefully without drawing attention to what she was doing. She had acquiesced to the princess's wishes about interfering in her relationship with the American long enough. She sat down and wrote Juan Lopez a letter about the princess, telling him about the pregnancy, the forced marriage, her husband's selfishness and abandonment, and that she had been sent to a convent. It arrived several months after Juan Miguel returned from Mexico, at a time when he was only beginning to settle back into his old life.

When he read the letter, Juan Miguel was overcome with regret. The woman he loved was about to give birth to his child and she was halfway around the world. He read the letter over again, hung his head, and sobbed.

Beatriz heard him crying in the parlor. She went to the door and peeked at him. She put her hand on her bosom and stepped back with tears in her eyes. Rarely had she seen someone so stricken with sadness. She went out to find Pedro.

Pedro walked into the parlor quietly, a large lump in his throat and his hands shaking. Juan Miguel, still overcome with grief, gazed out the window at the evening sky. The deep sobs that had convulsed from his chest had calmed. His face was red and tears still rolled down his face.

"*Amigo*?" Pedro said in a quiet voice.

"The princess ..." The words barely escaped his mouth and he began to sob again.

Pedro knelt on one knee in front of his chair and put his hand on Juan Miguel's arm. "Has she died?" he asked.

"No ... she is having my baby ..."

"And you know this because?"

"The Infanta writes it ... and ... the princess has been abandoned by her husband and banished to a convent in the mountains of Spain. She is destitute ... disowned. My God, how frightened she must be ..."

"Well, my friend, don't just sit there. Go get her."

He put his hand to his face and rubbed his palm over it. "You are right. I will leave tonight."

"Go ... and I will take care of the rancho ... go."

One morning in early September, the princess Alexis went into labor. She suffered terribly. The sisters summoned the only doctor in the small town. At last, more than 48 hours later, using forceps, the doctor delivered a baby boy. The infant was small and weak, only clinging to life, and the princess was so exhausted from hours of labor that she could barely raise her head.

Fearing they were near death, the prioress of the convent brought the local priest to visit them both, in case last rites were needed. Father Giuseppe Roja was a simple, uneducated, strict priest who was more concerned with keeping the church calendar than saving souls. He walked into the princess's room with the sensitivity of a bull.

"Mother tells me your child is illegitimate," he said, passing right over the niceties. "Is that true?"

"Yes, father," she whispered. Her face was drained of color and her lips were flaky and white and her eyes were sunken.

"You must consider how to repent and how to atone for this great sin. Otherwise, the baby will die. His illness is God's punishment."

Tears rolled down her cheeks. "What do you suggest, father?" she whispered.

"Repent completely, renounce Satan and his lustful ways, and give your baby over for adoption. Then, enter the convent as a novitiate and pray every day for God to forgive you."

"Give my baby away?"

"Do you wish him to live or are you so selfish that you keep him for your own even though it might mean death or serious illness?"

"I want him to live, of course, but ..."

"Do you consent or not? The child's life hangs in the balance."

She closed her eyes and whispered, "I consent ... so that he may live."

The priest took the infant with him that night and gave him to a family who had been praying for a baby. The princess recovered and when she was strong enough, she entered the order of the Benedictine Sisters as a novitiate named Sister Mark. She went through the motions and did what was expected of her, hoping God would someday forgive her and not punish her son further.

After the prioress told the princess that her baby was thriving in the care of an adopted family, she became convinced that only her constant atonement would keep him safe. Every floor tile she scrubbed, every dish she washed, every garden row she hoed was another brick in the wall of her child's well being. And the prioress and the other sisters took full advantage of her willingness to work. They were jealous of her beauty and the life she had led as a princess before her misfortunes began.

The princess did hard manual labor from sunup until sundown, and beyond, every day. Her body became thin and wiry. Her face became gaunt and parched from the sun. Her nails broke and one of them fell off. Her feet bled.

There was one sister, however, who didn't feel jealousy for Sister Mark. Sister Magdalene, a young woman who had taken her vows less than a year earlier, loved Sister Mark and felt compassion for her. She often volunteered to help her with her duties because she feared that Sister Mark wouldn't last long at the pace she was going, that her body was reaching its limit.

Juan Miguel reached Jerez de la Frontera after traveling for almost two weeks. He hired a horse from the local inn and stable and rode the twenty miles through Spanish countryside to the convent, arriving at dinnertime. The sisters were seated in the dining hall waiting for their meal.

The evening was dreary. The sky was overcast and a storm cloud hung over the mountains in the distance. A fine mist was in the air. He knocked on the convent door. An older nun opened the door, looked at him without smiling, and said, "*Si?*"

"I am here to see Princess Alexis," he said.

"There is no one here by that name." She started to close the door.

He put up his hand and stopped her. "Please, sister. I have traveled thousands of miles to see her. If she is here, please tell me."

"Wait here," she said.

She returned with the prioress, who asked him to come in, escorted him into a small reception room, and told him to sit. She told him that Princess Alexis was now Sister Mark, that she had taken vows of solitude and would not be able to see him.

Thunder rumbled in the distance and rain started to pound on the convent's tile roof. Lightning struck nearby and thunder roared.

"Sister, please let me see her briefly. I will only take a minute of her time."

"It is impossible."

Lightning struck a tree in the convent garden. A ball of light exploded through the sheets of rain falling outside the window.

"Please, sister."

"You must leave, sir," she said as she stood.

Again, lightning flashed through the darkening skies and claps of thunder boomed one after another.

"I have ridden here on horseback, sister. Do you expect me to go out in this storm?"

The prioress stood thinking for several seconds. Lightning flashed outside the window again. "We will allow you to sleep in the convent barn and a sister will bring you some food. Do I have your word that you will not leave the stable until morning?"

"*Si* ... you have my word, sister."

The prioress asked Sister Magdalene to take a bowl of soup to a traveler taking shelter in the barn. "But don't talk to him," she said. "Under pain of punishment, sister, do you understand?"

Sister Magdalene entered the dark barn with a bowl in one of her hands and holding an umbrella in the other. She looked at the stranger with obvious wariness. "Your dinner, sir," she said.

He stepped into the light and smiled at her. "Good evening, sister, *gracias*. You are called?"

"Sister Magdalene."

"Sister Magdalene. Do you know Sister Mark?"

"*Si* ... I do."

"Forgive me for being blunt, Sister Magdalene, but I am the father of her baby. I have come to get her, to take her home. But I need your help. Please, sister, if God is in your heart, please help us."

"What is your name?"

"Juan Miguel del Valle, sister. Please tell her I am here and bring her to me. Please, sister. I love her very much."

Sister Magdalene turned and walked out. She sat in her small room for almost an hour, wondering what to do. When the rain stopped, she went to the kitchen where Sister Mark was still working. "Come with me, sister," she said. "Come," she repeated and pulled her by the arm.

When she saw him in the barn, a tiny wave of emotion passed across her face. But she retreated into herself. She closed the door of her heart and bolted it quickly.

"Don't ..." she said when he put out his hand to take hers.

"Princess ..."

"My name is Sister Mark now. And that is how it must be."

He nodded and put his hands to his sides. "Tell me why ... sister."

She told him about the baby's illness, Father Roja's intervention, and her decision to give her child for adoption.

He nodded and looked at her with love shining from his eyes. "Sister Mark, the demon ... the devil ... is clever.

He wears many disguises just as God does. Sometimes the demon is clothed in the vestments of an archbishop, sometimes in the robe of a parish priest."

"Perhaps ..." she said.

They had stood facing each other in the dim light of the barn, she shaking under her nun's habit and he using every ounce of restraint he could muster not to touch her. He had been in this argument for much too long. She refused to see anything but her own sin and her commitment to keeping her baby alive by atoning for that sin.

"The devil lies to you," he said. "He wants you to feel that you are not God's beautiful creation ... that you are ugly ... and tainted ... and sinful. But you are not, sister. It is a lie."

"But I sinned ... we sinned."

"You are beautiful. You are everything to me."

She took a step forward and he pulled her into his arms. He had worn her down. He held her and pushed back the nun's habit to expose part of her hair. It was gone. Only tufts of the light color stuck out here and there. He smoothed them down and kissed her head. He could feel her shivering from the cold and dampness. She had grown slight, frail, almost nonexistent.

He picked her up and carried her to the other side of the building where his horse had been stabled. "Come on, Sister Mark, we're going for a midnight ride."

He lifted her onto the horse. She weighed almost nothing. "Now, make no noise, sister, please, or I will muzzle you myself. *Comprende?"*

She nodded.

They were a strange sight, riding down a back road of Spain in the light of a moon that had just peeked out over the storm cloud receding in the distance. A nun and her madman of a captor sliding in and out of the shadows cast by the trees along the road. He held her across the chest with his hand on her shoulder. It was like holding a young boy.

Once they reached the train station and got their tickets, she balked. "I cannot leave. My baby is here," she said in a low voice.

"Remember when I told you about the Great Horned Owl, sister? How he lies in wait until the right moment and then strikes. That is what we must do. We must gather our forces to fight this battle."

"I will go on one condition, that you call me Sister Mark and recognize that I am a Benedictine Sister."

"I will call you 'Mary, Mother of God,' if it satisfies you. Now get on the train, madam, or I will lift you on myself."

On the way to Europe, he had traveled on a merchant steamer because it was the quickest way to get there. He slept below decks with the crew and ate their meager meals. On the way back, he and Sister Mark traveled from a French port on the *SS La Bretagna*. He knew she wasn't ready for anything more than friendship so they slept in separate staterooms.

She sat on her bed most of the time, dressed in her nun's habit, looking scared. One warm fall evening, he sat down next to her and put his hand on her hand. She looked at him and he saw something that might be described as a smile on her face.

"I know it is easier sometimes to hide behind a costume," he said. "It can be scary to take off the costume, but at some point we all have to be ourselves. Just shed one small part of it and see how it heels ... just the veil." He took hold of the front part of the veil and started to lift it.

"No," she said and she pulled away.

"Just try it ... for just a moment. Please, sister."

He lifted off the veil and put it on the table. Her hair had grown out a bit but it was still ugly. "Now the shoes," and he picked up her foot and took off one shoe and then he removed the other one. "And now the lovely stockings," he said smiling. He reached up and pulled down the thick woolen socks. Her skin was red and scaly and tiny pustules dotted her ankles.

"And now sit up, sister." He pulled her forward by the shoulders and lifted the nun's habit off. Only her undergarment, a white muslin shift, remained. She crossed her arms and looked self-conscious. The bones of her shoulders stuck out like angel's wings.

He took her in his arms and held her to him, stroking the stiff, dry stubble on her head. "Look out there," he said pointing out the portal. "You are on your way to America,

Alexis, to be free. You can be whoever you want to be, anything or anyone. If you want to be Sister Mark ... and Alexis, you can do that. Anything ... anyone."

She put her legs up and looked out at the azure sea.

"Tell me, Alexis ... what would you like?"

"I would like some chocolate ... and maybe roast beef and potatoes."

"Are you hungry?"

"Starving ..."

Later in the middle of the night, she crept into his cabin and got in bed with him and snuggled close. He put his arm around her.

"Where have you been and what have you been doing?" she asked.

"Oh, Alexis, that is a long, long story. It will take the rest of the night to tell you."

But he did tell her. He told her the whole story.

During the day, they were Juan Lopez and his friend, Sister Mark. They ate in the dining hall, strolled the decks, and lingered in the lounge. At night, they were Juan Miguel and Alexis, sleeping together and becoming acquainted again. He knew that he should keep his distance. He knew that she was too frail and too weak of spirit to be a lover. But his love for Princess Alexis was so strong that he couldn't keep his hands from touching Sister Mark. His fingers would migrate to caress her breasts, her stomach, her long legs. And he kissed the short stubble behind her ear.

The first argument occurred when he mentioned that they would be living at his rancho. "Then you can eat all the roast beef you please," he joked.

But she scowled at him and shook her head. "No, I will find a suitable convent once we are there. I intend to be a sister ... Juan Miguel. I have not given that up."

"But surely you don't think you still need to atone?"

"I made a commitment to God and to my child. I will keep that commitment as long as he is out of my sight."

"Alexis ... this is foolish. God does not expect ..."

"How do you know what God expects? No, my son is still in the arms of someone else. As long as that is true ..."

"You are only now starting to recover from it. Don't cast yourself back into the hell you were in."

The final argument occurred several days after they arrived at the rancho after a long, tiring trip. He found her sitting in the parlor, her hands folded and her eyes vacant. He handed her a bouquet of Maximilian daisies from the profusion of bushes blooming all over the prairie.

She took them and laid them on her lap. "You loved Princess Alexis," she said, "not the person I am now with the skin disease and chopped hair, the parched lips and sunken eyes. I may never be that person you loved again."

He knelt in front of her and put his hand on hers. "Have faith in me, Alexis. Desire will return. Give it time." He attempted to catch her eyes with his.

"No, our love died the night they stole my baby ... your baby ... from me."

Her words went through his heart like a lance. "I can resurrect you, Alexis. Let me try."

She shook her head. "No ... no," she said.

He stood. His heart was as soft and squishy as a compost heap, a mass of discarded chances and missed cues. "I have failed you ... in so many ways." He put out his hand and helped her stand. "But I can only argue for so long and then it is futile. If you are to return to a convent, I would prefer it were someplace with kinder souls. Someplace in the sun, someplace you can thrive, not wilt."

He wrote to the Sisters of Loretto in El Paso and explained her situation. They accepted her into their small enclave and several weeks later, he put her on a train to deliver her there. She disappeared inside a coach car and left him standing, hat in hand, alone.

Juan Miguel got up early and walked out into the bright sun of an already warm morning in late October. Jose was awake as well and was preparing to ride off. "Where are you going?" Juan Miguel called to him.

"Hunting, *Señor*. A predator got into Celita's chicken coop again last night. It killed a number of them."

"What was it?"

"Either a coyote or a bobcat."

"Ah, the canine or the feline. I will go with you. I would

like to get out in the countryside for a while."

They saddled their horses and rode across the prairie, walking at a slow pace, looking for signs.

"Have you heard the Indians tell stories about the coyote and the bobcat?" Jose said.

"No, what are these stories?"

"They are called the evil twins, two killers, balanced in skills and craftiness, but each using its own method."

"Meaning what?"

"Meaning that when pursuing one's goals, it is well to remember that there are others who pursue theirs with just as much passion."

"Are you trying to tell me something, *amigo*?"

"*Si* ... to be careful, I suppose. To watch your back."

"Wise words, indeed. Let's break up. You go east and I will go west."

They nudged their horses with their heels and parted.

Juan Miguel rode across flat, grassy pastures with only an occasional scraggly mesquite to break the monotony until he came to a shallow arroyo where water had worn away the dark red soil and exposed layers of limestone, jutting out in craggy orange formations, blistering in the hot sun.

He took off his hat and wiped his brow with his hand. The day would be a hot one for October, but that was not unusual in south Texas.

On the other side of the arroyo a stand of prickly pears under a young post oak bloomed with scarlet red flowers.

He walked his horse down into the arroyo and up the other side to get a better look.

Stepping amongst the weeds and wild grasses was a tiny sparrow with a black and white striped head. "The white crowned sparrows already?" he said. "An early winter, I guess." The little bird flitted up into the tree and then took off, soaring away into the blue sky, its goal a stand of live oaks on the horizon.

He watched to see where the bird would land. In between the branches, farther across the prairie, beside an old wooden log cabin wall that still stood, he saw something move. But it could be another bird. Or it could be the bobcat they were looking for. Or it could be something else.

He pulled the reins and stepped back into the arroyo for some protection. Feeling for his pistol underneath his jacket, he stared at the point where he'd seen movement but saw nothing. Then he heard a sound—something different than the soft, rustling of animals and birds and wind through leaves. Something sharp and distinct like a horse hoof on hard ground.

He took out the pistol and rested it on the saddle horn. He waited.

He saw movement again but this time it was farther away, beyond a low rise past the live oaks. He could swear he saw a man's hat, a light brown one, large like the *vaqueros* wear, with a flat brim. But was it his imagination or was it really a rock or even a cloud? He walked his horse slowly up out of the arroyo and put his pistol back in the holster and galloped forward for a better look. Again, he saw nothing there.

It occurred to him that he was too exposed, standing out in the middle of flat ground, surrounded by hiding places. He walked his horse to the row of mesquites up ahead and waited.

The sun beat down through the branches and the tiny, reedy mesquite leaves wafted in the breeze. His horse stepped forward. He reined it back. The mosquitoes buzzed around his face. He grew impatient. Only a few more minutes and then he would chalk it up to his imagination.

He took off his hat and ran his fingers through his hair. He shifted in his saddle. A light brown, wide-brimmed hat. Where had he seen one?

He sat up, a cold chill went throughout his body, and his limbs felt weak. The man he rode out with, Jose. The man who did every odd job around his rancho that no one else would do. The man who was once a *bandido* and cattle rustler, years ago before he returned to Texas and came to live on the rancho with his wife, Beatriz. That man had a light brown, wide-brimmed hat.

But why? Why would he hide from him? What could be his grievance? It was too outlandish. He had trusted Jose for years. Since the day he and Beatriz agreed to bury their own son under the tombstone of the notorious outlaw, Primo, so that he could live again.

Then he saw him hiding behind a tree and he knew the truth immediately. In his heart, in his loins, in his soul. Every man has his price and loyalty can be eroded, worn away like the soil in the arroyo. Every day, a little less loyalty. Then the right incentive and it is gone. Washed down the arroyo with the rainwater.

Jose appeared in the open, sitting on his black horse, on his head the light brown hat, looking straight at him.

"Jose, *que paso, amigo*?" Juan Miguel yelled. "Did you see the coyote ... or the bobcat?"

"No ... and you, *Señor*?"

"No."

"Why don't you come this way? We can ride up that hill and take a look together?" Jose yelled.

"*Si* ... I will."

The wind picked up and blew the dust ahead of him as he rode. He squinted to see whether Jose was still there.

A pistol shot rang out and sliced through the sound of wind in trees. He jumped from his horse and caught the reins. He ducked behind a tree trunk. The shot had come from beyond the hill. He looked up and saw the rifle butt protruding from a rock.

"Jose ... *amigo* ... what has gotten into you?" he yelled.

"Things have changed, my friend."

"What things? What has changed?"

"Pesos ... I need them. And ..."

"And what?"

"I grow tired of your pretenses ... your characters.

They cost me my son and now you no longer care who knows who you are. My son's death was for nothing."

He opened his mouth to argue and decided against it. You cannot argue with a man who is intent on killing you. But he could buy some time with some conversation.

"Who is the one who is paying you?"

"Not one ... many."

"The Concordium company?"

Jose's silence answered the question.

"So, it was General Cordova who hired you?"

"He is one of them ..."

The last couple of answers came from a different direction, closer and more to the left. He looked intently for any movement. He saw nothing.

The waiting was getting to him. It was not a good strategy. He pulled on the horse's reins, stepped into the stirrup, hoisted himself onto the saddle, and took off, back across the meadow, the arroyo, and then down the dirt road that led to it. A few paces behind him, he could hear Jose's horse catching up. He turned and stepped his horse down the bank of a shallow creek.

He jumped off and swatted Jícama on the rump. "¡Vámonos!," he said. Jícama had heard the command before. The horse found the floor of the dry creek bed and ran around a bend. When Jícama was out of sight, he squatted just below the creek wall and as Jose galloped by, he jumped up, grabbed the rider's leg and pulled him off. Jose was soft in the belly and no match for Juan Miguel. He was overpowered within minutes.

Juan Miguel stood and pointed the rifle at the man he'd known and trusted for years. "What am I to do with you now, *amigo*?"

Jose grabbed at the rifle butt and the rifle discharged. His old friend lay shot and bleeding from his neck, blood gushing from the wound. He lay in a pool of blood looking up at him. Juan Miguel knelt and put his hand on Jose's arm. "I am sorry we have come to the end of the journey in this way," Juan Miguel whispered. Jose's eyes rolled back and his head sank to the side. He was dead.

Jose was not the first man that Juan Miguel del Valle had killed. He killed *bandidos* when he defended the Barone Ranch from raiders many years ago. Only a few months before, he'd shot a man called Mateo who was about to kill him. But this time was different. He had killed a friend. A friend who'd lost his way, perhaps, and betrayed him, but a friend, nonetheless. He sat down in the dirt next to the body and wept.

The sheriff of Atascosa County accepted his version of what happened that day. A search of the small house Juan Miguel had given to Jose and Beatriz yielded a satchel of cash stuffed inside a wooden box and hidden underneath one of the porch's floor boards. Beatriz said a strange man had visited her husband the week before.

Juan Miguel bought a train ticket for El Paso so that he

could visit Annabelle, who was concluding her schooling at the St. Joseph's Academy. He had a sad but necessary tale to tell her about Carlito Cordova's uncle.

The headline in the *El Paso Herald* on the morning he returned read "Insurrecto Band in Guanacevi." It was the reporter's first-hand account of Mexican rebels who had moved their base of operations to the small town to harass Diaz's army. The article included quotes from the man who was now called "Pancho Villa" in which he talked about his ability to arm the rebel army. "We have received support from an unexpected source," the quote said.

It was a windy, cool day in early November. The dust of El Paso streets hung in the air. The blue sky overhead blended into a dusty pink near the horizon and tufts of dirt blew up from the carriages and wagons and horses along El Paso Street. Juan Miguel stood looking out the window at the Rio Grande in the distance, the bustling city of Juarez, and the bridge that connected it to El Paso. He was waiting for Annabelle. He was anxious to see her, as always, and yet he dreaded it also. He found himself wringing his hands with nervousness.

Their greeting was warm. They talked about her new crimson hat. She smiled and held his hand as he sat next to her on the small settee next to the window. But when they got into the subject of Carlos Cordova and his uncle, the room turned chilly and a great distance opened up between them. She looked at him with an expression he'd never seen before—disdain, hatred almost.

"I do not believe you," she shouted as she stood and grabbed for her bag. "You sent me away to separate us and now you make up lies to separate us."

He stood and attempted to take her by the shoulders but she wrenched herself away. "You are jealous of Carlito," she said. "You are jealous of his youth and his bravery. I never thought you would make up lies to keep me for yourself."

The words sounded like words coming from someone else, not Annabelle. She walked to the door, opened it, and looked back at him. "Carlito and I are in love, *Papá*. That is something you will have to accept, or we will be estranged forever." She walked out and closed the door behind her.

The grief he felt was almost as overwhelming as the grief he felt when Annabelle's mother died. It blotted out everything good in his life, surrounded him with darkness. He could barely see his way forward.

He sat looking out the window at the dusty day without moving and then sat looking at the black moonless night without moving. When he finally did rise, he found it almost impossible to put one foot in front of the other. Without Annabelle, his life would be nothing, without purpose. Everything in his past would be for naught.

And yet he couldn't erase the truth. He couldn't ignore

the facts. Carlos Cordova's uncle had paid someone to kill him.

He gathered his belongings, put on his coat and hat, and left the hotel room. He handed the hotel clerk an envelope and asked him to mail it for him. It was a letter to Annabelle in which he tried once more to explain everything.

He faced what every parent must face eventually. He couldn't control her. He couldn't force her to believe it. She herself would have to come to the realization and that may take time. Years perhaps. But there was one person he could control—Carlito Intrepido—the matador.

On his way into town, he had seen the posters everywhere, inside the train station, on lampposts, plastered on brick walls of side streets. "Plaza de Tores Juarez, Carlito Intrepido Matador, Dia de Muertos, Wednesday, Nov. 2, 1898," they screamed. Carlos Cordova was the featured torero, the star, the main attraction, at the Day of the Dead celebration. A drawing of Carlito in the classic pose of a matador adorned the posters. His brown hair fell over his eyes and his handsome face looked resolute.

Juan Miguel carried his bag across the bridge and found his way to the arena, following the crowds who were streaming in that direction. Once inside, though, he went to the back rooms where the matadors prepared themselves and knocked on one of the doors. An older man in a suit answered.

"I wish to speak to Carlos Cordova. Tell him it is Juan Miguel del Valle," he said.

"I will see ... he is busy."

The man returned and showed him in to one of the rooms. It was small and dirty, not glamorous. Carlos sat on a chair next to an altar to Our Lady surrounded by flickering votives. His attire was unchanged from the day last year when they watched him in the arena.

"What is it?" Carlos asked without rising. "It is about time for me to go."

"I have much to explain to you ... about your father's death."

"I know all there is to know," Carlos said, standing and picking up his cape. "You are responsible for his murder. I know that much."

"Responsible ... *si* ... but believe me there is much you don't know. Give me a chance to tell you. There should be no bad blood between us ... for Annabelle's sake."

"For Annabelle's sake ... I will listen, but not now ... later." Carlito Intrepido walked out of the room and down the hallway and took his place in the parade of toreros. Juan Miguel went upstairs to watch the bullfight.

Across the arena, on the other side where there was no afternoon sun to warm the spectators, he saw the crimson hat, the one Annabelle showed him the day before, and the long lush auburn hair underneath it. She sat alone, the chilly wind blowing her curls and her arms crossed for warmth.

His heart sank and he was overwhelmed with sympathy. Tears came into his eyes and he wiped at them, embarrassed. He couldn't bear to see her alone. He had the instinct to go to her and put his arms around her, to protect her and make her warm. But of course, he could no longer do that.

The crowd was anxious, suffering through the lesser *toreros* and their inferior skills with little patience. A few boos could be heard when one of the older matadors could not complete a clean kill. After the crowd voted for the bull to live and the *banderillas* coaxed the lucky *toro* out of the arena to fight another day, the poor matador raised his hand in a desultory manner and walked off.

Carlito Intrepido entered the arena to shouts of *ole,* the people jumping to their feet in anticipation of a good bullfight. He flashed a grin, something rare for a matador then got serious again. He looked across the arena at the bull he was to fight. It was large and black and solid looking. No more was Carlito given the advantage of "baby bulls." Now he was required to fight the fiercest, most blood thirsty ones, the ones bred to be violent.

He unfurled his cape and stepped forward to begin the soothing, cooing noises he often used to lure the bull into a pass. "Hoo … hoo …," he said. Then he clicked his tongue against his lips. The bull stared and took a few steps. "Hey

... *toro* ... hey, hey," he said, walking forward a little more.

The bull charged and passed through the bright pink cape. Carlito turned and began again. The bull charged again, this time closer. Carlito seemed off-kilter, off balance. The bull's foot clipped his own foot and he limped away. Two of the other matadors rushed out to distract the bull until Carlito could recover.

Once more, he faced the bull but he seemed flustered. He favored the injured foot. He coaxed, the bull rushed, his horn dangerously close to Carlito's arm. Carlito stumbled out of the way and almost fell into the dirt.

One of the other matadors came into the arena to ask him a question but he waved him away. He raised the cape, the afternoon sun shone directly into his eyes, and he squinted to see his opponent. The crowd was quiet, their lively support for the famous matador all but gone. The only noise that could be heard was the sound of Carlito's voice. "Yah, yah, yah," he shouted. The bull seemed to lean back on its haunches and then rushed forward, this time with fury. It passed too close. The matador cape ripped out of Carlito's hands and stuck on the bull's horns. Infuriated, the bull slashed his head back and forth. His anger grew. Finally, with the cape dislodged from his horns, he ran straight at Carlito. Carlito turned to run away. The bull caught him on the side of the hip with his horn and Carlito went hurtling into the air and landed on his back with his feet up. The bull turned and lunged straight at him. The horn went through his back as Carlito attempted to stand.

The *banderillas* rushed out and within seconds, the bull was dead from their lances. But it was too late for Carlito Intrepido. Men can survive being gored by a bull once. Almost no one can survive being gored twice. They carried him away. The arena sand was stained red from his blood.

Juan Miguel rushed to find his daughter. He could think of nothing except her. He was desperate to find her as he looked through the crowd of people in the back hallways. At last, he found the room where he'd visited Carlito only a few hours earlier. He pushed on the door and there was Carlito, wrapped in white bandages soaked in red blood, his face covered by the pink matador's cape. Annabelle stood next to him sobbing. When she saw her father, she slumped to the floor.

He carried her out of the arena and across the bridge. So anxious was he to get her away from the gruesome scene that he left behind his hat and bag.

For days, she wouldn't eat and couldn't sleep. He sat by the bed and held her when she cried. The El Paso hotel room became a sanctuary for both of them. Against a world that was too much for them. Once again, they only had each other.

CHAPTER SEVEN

D uring the previous year, Francisco Diablo's Santa Clara Winery had contracted to buy spring water from several landowners in the foothills of the Franklin Mountains. His workers built small reservoirs to collect the water that trickled out of the rock outcroppings and ridges. It was then transported by barrels to the winery and bottled for sale, especially to train travelers but also to bars and restaurants as chasers and mixers. The dark blue bottles with yellow labels and the words, "Santa Clara Mineral Water," could be seen everywhere.

Occasionally Señor Diablo himself rode on the wagons back and forth up into the mountains. He enjoyed the trips and the bawdy conversation with the driver, an old man named Hernando who had driven transport wagons forever, seemingly since the beginning of time.

314

They had eaten and drunk wine all day, up through the mountain passes, down the trails that twisted, a steep, sheer wall rising upward on one side and another one falling downward on the other, then out onto the sand before reaching the water collection places. The fine sand stuck to their sweaty arms and necks and floated in the tin cups of Vin Santo and felt like boulders on their eyeballs.

The horses pulling the wagons back down from the mountains slowed their gait, falling under the spell of the drunken men driving them. All of heaven and earth ground down to a leisurely pace. Señor Diablo had reached the point where his tongue and cheeks no longer worked well enough to speak so he merely looked at the darkening landscape all around him, his head nodding onto his chest.

Both men were shocked almost sober when they saw up ahead a silhouette back-lit from the setting sun. Right in the middle of the trail, a hooded monk stood facing them holding a rope tied to a burro. Hernando pulled on the reins and halted the team of horses. "Hoa … hoa …" he shouted. "What is that son of a whore doin'? Why don't he get outta the way?"

When the team and the wagons were stopped, Hernando looked at Señor Diablo then looked back at the monk then leaned over to Señor Diablo. "I heard tell of the ghostly monk, but I never seed him afore," he whispered.

"Tell him to move," Señor Diablo said. "Yell at him …

scare him a bit."

"You there," he yelled, "get off the trail ... stand aside. Did ya hear me?"

But the monk said nothing and he didn't move. He was dressed in a white robe instead of the usual black or brown and the hood hid his face and even the burro was a pale tan, almost white.

If he had been less drunk, Señor Diablo would never have done what he did. But he was drunk, so he jumped down from the wagon and staggered to within feet of the ghostly apparition. He held out his hand with a silly grin on his face. "Pleased to meet you, *Señor*," he said. "Need some help?"

The monk took his hand and shook it. "My burro has gone lame. I would appreciate a ride into town."

"You are more than welcome, father ... or is it brother?"

"It is neither."

"What shall we call you then?"

"I am whoever you wish me to be, *Señor*."

They tied the burro to the wagon and, with the monk sitting between them, they started out.

"Can you at least tell us where you are from, *padre*?" Diablo said.

"I am from the mountain town of Guanacevi in Mexico."

"The town where the *insurrectos* have taken over?"

"*Si* ... they are planning to launch an great offensive

from there."

Diablo looked at the monk but he was unable to see any of his features, only the tip of his chin sticking out from the pale wool. "An offensive against what?"

"The Taxcoco mine … they intend to overtake it and claim it as their own. Use the mine's riches to widen their offensive to other mines. Not a bad plan, eh?"

Diablo felt himself grow cold from the chilly fall night air. His eyes began to blink almost uncontrollably and his heart felt as if it beat only every third time. He never imagined that the *insurrectos* would be bold enough to try to take a mine, especially *his* mine. "Why do they start with Taxcoco? Why that one?"

The monk's maniacal laugh stopped suddenly and he said, "It is an illegal mine. There's nothing that can be done without exposing a good many important people … is that not right, Señor Diablo?"

Diablo lifted his hand and started to pull back the monk's hood but the monk took hold of his hand with his own. Then with his other hand he reached inside the folds of the cassock and pulled out a watch—the watch that by this time was very familiar to Señor Diablo.

"*Madre de Dios* … look at the time," the monk said. "I must be on my way and leave you to your drinking." He leapt over Diablo in one bound, grabbed the burro's rope, and walked off into the night. Diablo looked back for any sign of him but he had vanished.

"What was that all about?" Hernando asked.

"A warning ... a deadly one," Señor Diablo said, his face as pale as the ghostly monk's cassock.

"A warning against what?"

"Opening my mouth ..."

Somehow, Annabelle found the strength to finish her term at the academy and graduated the week before Christmas. Soon after, she told her father that she had gotten a job working for the *El Paso Times* as a writer. In the days that followed, she could often be seen bicycling to work or strolling in the plaza with Cinco, whose friendship she had come to rely on.

She asked her father to stay in El Paso for a while. Because he could refuse her nothing, he stayed. Revenge against General Cordova was not as important to him as his love for his daughter. Every day that the sun went down behind the stark, solid Franklin Mountains, his hatred for the man dissolved a little more. He spent his time walking the downtown streets, playing cards in the hotel bar, and reading in the library. Early the next year, he picked up a newspaper with the headline, "Insurrectos Storm Taxcoco Mine." It was only the opening volley in a revolution that would take years.

"When winter is over, *mi amor*, I must return to the rancho," he told her one night at dinner. "I am useless here and the rancho cannot run itself when Pedro is gone."

She smiled and he smiled back at her. The thought that

their old friend was about to be married was a source of great glee to them.

"But we will all be living here ... I will ... and Pedro and Charlotte ... why not stay, too?"

"As I said, I am useless."

"*Papá*, that is not true."

"I do find the climate and water here salubrious. Charlotte has been bringing me spring water from her ranch to drink. She is convinced it has healing powers."

"She takes water to the sisters at the academy as well. I hear that Princess Alexis is a teacher there."

"Ah, you mean Sister Mark? Well, that is a sore subject and I'd rather not talk about it."

"I hear that she, too, is recovering."

"Annabelle ... you have not been meddling again?"

"I spoke to her ... just to tell her you are here, that's all."

He picked up his wine glass, a disapproving look on his face.

After dinner, they walked down El Paso Street to the Myar Opera House to watch a performance of Sarah Bernhardt in *Camille*. He was in white tie and tails and Annabelle in a light blue column dress with black gloves. More than a few people stared at them or craned their necks to get a peek. It reminded them both of the days they spent in Europe as she was growing up. Even the performance was first-rate. Miss Bernhardt was lovely even though she was now middle aged. She still had a sharp nose and clear eyes and long graceful fingers.

He walked Annabelle back to her room. Snowflakes landed on the shoulders of his black tuxedo like feathers. She tip-toed up to kiss his cheek and whispered, "Good night, *Papá*."

He had moved back to the St. Charles so he could have a clear view of the Franklin Mountains he had come to appreciate. This night they seemed incongruous, white instead of brown, and even the cacti on the desert floor wore a thin veil of powder.

He took off the coat and tie and sat down to watch the snow falling through the cones of light along the city streets. He was awake, much too awake to go to bed. He closed his eyes and replayed the night in his head. His time with Annabelle was precious to him.

Someone knocked on his door. He rose and opened it slowly. Standing in the hallway was Sister Mark, her hands clasped in front of her and her expression set and determined.

"Sister ... what are you doing here?" he asked, clutching at her arm and pulling her inside.

"I want ..." But she couldn't get it out. She couldn't say it.

He put his hands under her elbow and helped her to sit. "Sister? What is the matter?" he asked. He reached out and touched her hand without thinking.

The look in her eyes was supplicating before she

looked away. She put her fingers on the top of her veil and lifted it off her head and put it on the armrest next to her. Her golden hair was thick again, flowing around her face in short waves. He touched it lightly. She moved her cheek to feel his touch.

She stood and took hold of the nun's habit and lifted it slowly over her head. Her body was beautiful again. Whole, supple, curvaceous. He put his hands on her waist and pulled her toward him.

"What do you want, sister?" he asked.

She leaned forward and fell into his arms.

Sometime during the night, he whispered, "I will find your child if it costs me my last breath."

ABOUT THE AUTHOR

This is the third book in my Juan Miguel series. The first book, *The Legend of Juan Miguel,* was a bestseller on Amazon.com and was followed by *The Passion of Juan Miguel* and *The Return of Juan Miguel.* Although these books are romantic historical fiction set in Texas's colorful past, they are really about who we are and how we know who we are.

Some people discover their authentic selves through therapy, others through art and music. A fortunate few know who they are from the moment they take their first breath. I found myself through writing and studying the place where I live. Lucky for me, Texas has an amazing history, full of characters and adventure and extremes of weather and landscape. How people dealt with this place—and how they still deal with it—that's the interesting part. I am Texan through and through and part of every person, battle, tall tale, and twist of history that led us to where we are.

I grew up on the great high plains of Texas, far up on heaven's tableland, a place so flat and empty, you can see the curvature of the earth. For reasons only God knows, it's also a place that fosters an independent mindset and a creative spirit. Many great artists, writers, and musicians come from there. I aspire to be one of them. Sadly, few of them stayed. It's just too hard. Most of us drifted south to softer, more lush climes. For me, it was Austin and that's where I've been.

I worked as a journalist for years. Then one day, life "threw a craving on me," as we say in Texas. I wanted to write fiction. I was done with reporting and editing and page layout. I had acquired useful skills, but my spirit wanted to do what my spirit wanted to do. I wanted to write historical fiction because I love history and I love stories and I love Texas.

— **Anna K. Sargent**

THE AUTHOR'S SOCIAL MEDIA

ANNAKSARGENTAUTHOR ON FACEBOOK
@ANNAKSARGENT ON TWITTER
BLOG/'WOMAN OF WORDS' ON BLOGGER

THE JUAN MIGUEL SERIES

THE LEGEND
OF JUAN MIGUEL

In the first book in the series, the Hispanic hero uses a mix of guises and cunning to recapture his good name, fortune, and lost love after powerful Anglo ranchers swindle him.

THE PASSION
OF JUAN MIGUEL

Juan Miguel returns to Galveston a grief-stricken widower only to be roped into the dangerous mission of helping striking dockworkers by spying on corrupt shippers, in this sequel to *Legend*.

www.ingramcontent.com/pod-product-compliance
Lightning Source LLC
Chambersburg PA
CBHW022134170626
46807CB00005B/1939